POPULAR PUBLICATIONS   FACSIMILE EDITIONS

Dime Detective Magazine #4 (February 1932)

Dime Detective magazine was the flagship detective pulp in the Popular Publications stable, running for almost 300 issues over twenty years. The fourth issue contains stories by T.T. Flynn, Frederick Nebel, Carroll John Daly, Edward Parrish Ware, and J. Allan Dunn, and includes an additional appearance by Nebel's character, Cardigan as well as by Carroll John Daly's Vee "Crime Machine" Brown.

Authors:

T.T. Flynn, Carroll John Daly, Edward Parrish Ware,
Frederick Nebel J. Allan Dunn

Illustrators:

William Reusswig, Amos Sewell, John Fleming Gould

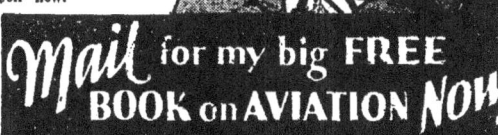

10¢ DIME DETECTIVE MAGAZINE

Every Story Complete   *Every Story New*

Vol. 1   CONTENTS for FEBRUARY, 1932   No. 4

COMPLETE MYSTERY-ACTION NOVEL

THRILLING DETECTIVE NOVELETTES

GRIPPING SHORT STORY OF CRIMELAND

Watch for the March Issue   On the Newsstands Feb. 20th

Published every month by Popular Publications, Inc., North Broadway, Albany, New York. Editorial and executive offices
205 East 42nd Street, New York City. Harry Steeger, President and Secretary, Harold S. Goldsmith, Vice President and
Treasurer. Entered as second-class matter September 30, 1931, at the post office at Albany, under the Act of March 3, 1879.
Title registration pending at U. S. Patent Office. Copyrighted 1931 by Popular Publications, Inc. Single copy price 10c.
Yearly subscriptions in U. S. A. $1.00. For advertising rates address H. D. Cushing, 67 West 44th Street, New York, N. Y.
When submitting manuscripts, kindly enclose sufficient postage for their return if found unavailable. The publishers cannot
accept responsibility for return of unsolicited manuscripts, although all care will be exercised in handling them.

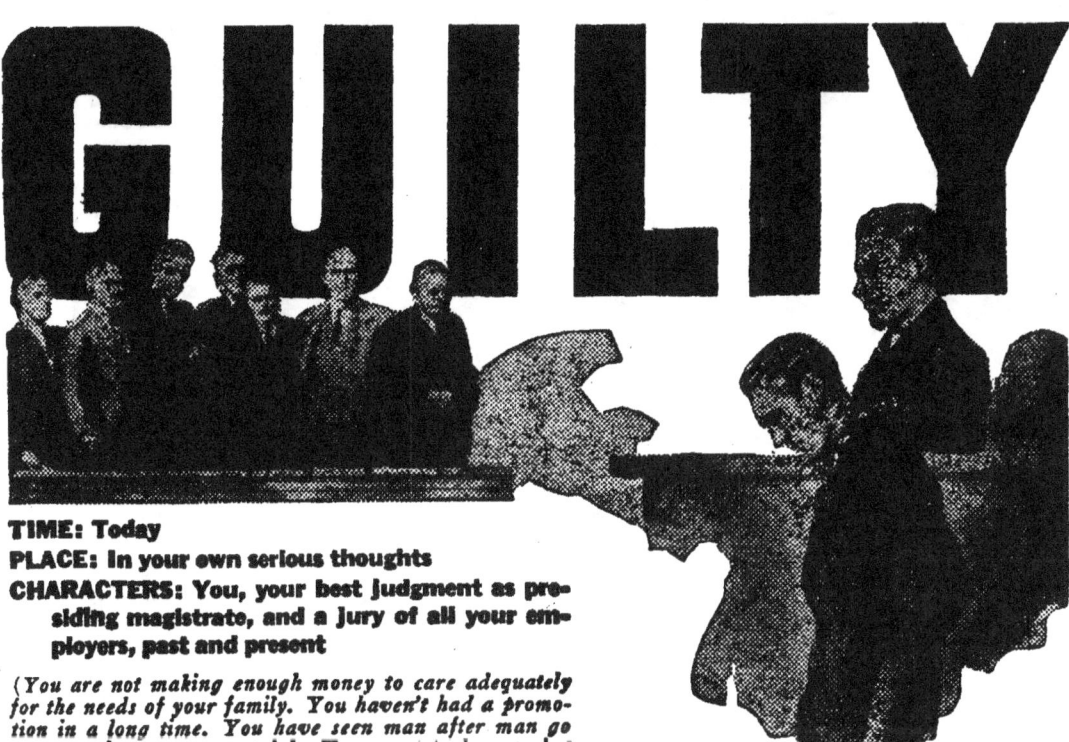

GUILTY

TIME: Today

PLACE: In your own serious thoughts

CHARACTERS: You, your best judgment as presiding magistrate, and a jury of all your employers, past and present

(You are not making enough money to care adequately for the needs of your family. You haven't had a promotion in a long time. You have seen man after man go past you in your present job. You want to know what is the matter—and what you can do about it. In your own mind, you have placed yourself in the positions of your employers and sought the facts. The jury is returning with the verdict!)

"We, the jury, are unanimous in the opinion you are a good fellow. Furthermore, you are loyal and a hard worker. But you never had enough training to be entrusted with greater responsibilities, and this is the only way of getting ahead today. We find you *guilty* of wasting your spare time! That's when a man like you must acquire the training he needs to get ahead. We sentence you to one hour of hard study each night."

Thousands of men who face the same problem that confronts you have solved it by devoting one hour a day to study of an International Correspondence Schools Course. It has given them the training they needed to get ahead, to earn more money—and employers everywhere commend I. C. S. study to ambitious men. Ask your own employer—then mark and mail the coupon. Do it *today*—don't let this trial go any farther! Mail the coupon!

4

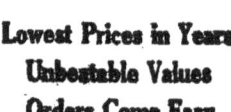

WIN FAME and FORTUNE in RADIO!

Scores of jobs are open to the Trained Man—jobs as Designer, Inspector and Tester—as Radio Salesman and in Service and Installation work—as Operator, Mechanic or Manager of a Broadcasting Station—as Wireless Operator on a Ship or Airplane—jobs with Talking Picture Theatres and Manufacturers of Sound Equipment—with Television Laboratories and Studios—fascinating jobs, offering unlimited opportunities to the Trained Man.

Ten Weeks of Shop Training

Come to Coyne in Chicago and prepare for these jobs the QUICK and PRACTICAL way—BY ACTUAL SHOP WORK ON ACTUAL RADIO EQUIPMENT. Ten weeks' training on actual equipment fits you to go out and take your place in this big pay field. No previous experience is necessary.

TELEVISION and Talking Pictures

In addition to the most modern Radio equipment, we have installed in our shops a complete model Broadcasting Station, with sound-proof Studio and modern Transmitter with 1,000 watt tubes—the Jenkins Television Transmitter with dozens of home-type Television receiving sets—and a complete Talking Picture installation for both "sound on film" and "sound on disk." We have spared no expense in our effort to make your training COMPLETE and PRACTICAL in all branches.

Free Employment
Service to Students

After you have finished the course, we will do all we can to help you find the job you want. We have a real employment department to help our students and graduates. And should you be a little short of funds, we'll gladly help you in finding part-time work while at school. Some of our students pay a large part of their living expenses in this way.

Coyne is 32 Years Old

Coyne has been located right here in Chicago since 1899. Coyne Training is tested—proven by hundreds of successful graduates. You can get all the facts—FREE. JUST MAIL THE COUPON FOR A FREE COPY OF OUR BIG RADIO AND TELEVISION BOOK, telling all about jobs . . . salaries . . . opportunities. This does not obligate you. Just mail the coupon.

H. C. Lewis, Pres.   **Radio Division**   Founded 1899

Coyne Electrical School

500 S. Paulina St.   Dept. 22-5K   Chicago, Ill.

Faces In The Fog

by T. T. Flynn

Author of "The Revel of Death," etc.

Into the night they vanished—these millionaires who controlled the money marts of Wall Street. Now, on the eve of the biggest banking merger in history, Manhattan's fog has swallowed up another victim and sent murder to haunt the murky streets.

CHAPTER ONE

The Vanished Millionaires

IT WAS an arrival such as had been witnessed seldom by even that magnificent hostelry, the Splendide. Out of a sodden, murky night three taxicabs dashed up to the curb and stopped before the lighted marquee. Three hard-boiled hackers leaped out smartly and opened the doors of their cabs. The scarlet-and-gold-braided doorman punched the button that summoned bell-hops and moved hastily began to haul stacks of new, expensive luggage. Gladstones, suitcases, traveling bags and luggage rolls of soft, costly leather. A half dozen....a dozen.... and still more.

The foppishly dressed young man stalked into the magnificent Splendide lobby, ignoring the doorman and the staring pedestrians who fell back before him. The procession across the lobby with a train of heavily laden bell boys staggering behind was like a parade. The supercilious clerk behind the desk straightened and stared. A slight hush fell over the lobby. And the foppish

Water roiled at the stern
as the boat backed into
the foggy night.

forward with his shielding umbrella.

From the first cab popped a broadshouldered, foppishly dressed young man; from the second a massive, beetlebrowed young man plowed deliberately; and from the third cab the driver young man asked the clerk haughtily: "You have a suite reserved for me? Mr. Mortimer Dodwich."

The clerk snapped to life at the name.

"Yes, sir, Mr. Dodwich. The grand suite. We have been holding it for you since yesterday. Nasty weather for traveling. Captain, show Mr. Dodwich and his party to the grand suite." The clerk handed a key to the bell captain who had appeared alertly.

"Is it the best you have?"

"Absolutely the best, Mr. Dodwich."

"Is the suite quiet?"

"Extremely quiet, Mr. Dodwich."

"I insist on that. No unnecessary noises outside in the hall. And I don't want to see any reporters."

The foppish Mr. Dodwich left a blinking clerk at the desk and followed the bell captain to the elevator bank. After them came the mountain of costly luggage.

The party had hardly left the desk when a short, slim, lantern-jawed young man stepped to the desk and asked wearily: "Who was the royal powder puff who just dusted in?"

"He said 'no reporters'," the clerk retorted.

The young man shrugged cynically as if he had heard that many times before. "I know," he agreed. "And when they warble that they're camping by the phone waiting for a reporter to insult 'em. A little publicity won't ruin the old inn. Give me the lowdown and we won't have to bother him. He looks important enough to have a ballyhoo in The Telegram. I saw him slip the hacker outside a twenty-dollar bill."

"His name," the clerk yielded, "is Mortimer Dodwich. He registered from San Francisco."

"Dodwich, eh? I don't place the name. Whose pet is he? Morty never made that dough himself."

"I couldn't tell you. The grand suite was registered for him by wire."

"Ninety-nine berries a day, eh?"

"Yes."

"He must be filthy with coin," yawned the lantern-jawed young reporter. "It's breaking out in a rash all over him. How long is Morty going to be in our midst?"

The clerk shrugged. The cynical young reporter lighted a cigarette and made for the telephone booths at the back of the lobby.

THE bell captain let his charges into the grand suite, superintended the arranging of the numerous pieces of luggage, made sure the windows were right, the heat adjusted, the different rooms in order.

And while he did that Dodwich prowled about, frowning at this and that, as if dissatisfied. Which in itself was enough to command respect; for The Splendide was one of the great hotels of the world. A president had occupied the grand suite and had been more than satisfied with it.

"Is there anything else, sir?" the bell captain finally asked deferentially.

"Yes. Have a Rolls-Royce at the door in an hour. Blithers here will drive me. Here is ten dollars. Tip the boys yourself."

The bell captain touched his cap and retired behind the troupe of bell-hops. And if he could have overheard the remark the deferential and massive Blithers made to his master he might have suspected his own hearing. For Blithers growled: "About one more crack like that and I'll hand you one on the kisser. Get me?"

The door of the grand suite had hardly closed when a remarkable change descended on man and master. The nervous, querulous air fell away from Mortimer Dodwich like an extra skin that could be shed at will.

"Now who will you crack on the kisser, you big ape?" he grinned.

And Blithers grinned back at him. "We took that gang downstairs like

Grant did Richmond," he chuckled. "I seen one guy's chin hangin' clean down in his collar. They know we're here."

Dodwich, who now in repose was an extremely good-looking and rather likable young man, laughed. "We want them to know we're here. What time is it, 'Mopsy'?"

"Say, it's a kick to hear my own name again. If any man'd ever told me I'd be called Blithers in public an' take it, I'd 'a' planted one on his jaw. It's eight-twenty, an' what do we do now? What are you gonna do with that Rolls-Royce you ordered? Let it set out in front to show 'em you can afford the dough?"

That drew a chuckle.

"There's no sense in spending money unless you get return for it, Mopsy. That parade through the lobby cost money, but it was worth it. A hundred pairs of eyes got a good look at us and wondered who we were. This ninety-five-dollar-a-day suite is an investment. It's background, front. That Rolls-Royce I ordered is twelve thousand dollars' worth of front."

"I getcha," Mopsy sighed. "But ain't it gonna be an awful jolt when we get through? It'll be tough to take a caviar an' peacock-tongue appetite back to a pork an' bean life."

Further conversation was cut off as the door opened and a strange man stepped inside without knocking. Mopsy sprang to his feet, shooting an inquiring glance at his companion.

That young man spoke quickly. "I say, explain this intrusion!" he demanded coldly.

The intruder was a short, slight man, dressed in gray, who would never see fifty again. A close-cropped, iron-gray mustache covering a long upper lip gave him a commanding air.

"I am Gerard Breckridge," he answered curtly.

DODWICH instantly became natural once more. "Sit down, Mr. Breckridge," he invited with a slight smile. "I am Larry Lawson. Glad to see you so quickly."

"I happened to be down in the lobby when you made your—er—entrance," Breckridge said curtly. "It was quite open, young man. I overheard many comments about it. And I don't understand it. You were engaged to come here on a very serious secret matter. And you show up with circus publicity. Who is your companion?"

"Mr. Doolin," Larry introduced. "Mopsy to me and Horace to his mother. Mopsy always works with me."

Breckridge nodded reluctantly. "Two of you will doubtless be better than one. You realize, of course, that there is dangerous work ahead?"

"Your long-distance call rather intimated that," Larry smiled.

"Quite right. I usually make myself plain." Breckridge bit off the end of a long thin cigar, lighted the cigar and frowned at the two young men. "I called you in on this matter on the word of one of my business associates out on the coast. I was informed that you have a phenomenal record of solving cases submitted to you."

"I've had a little luck," Larry admitted briefly.

"Whatever you choose to call it. Results are what I am interested in. I want them now. I must have them."

"I'll try to give them to you," Larry said quietly. "Now will you please go over what you told me over long distance, and elaborate?"

"In the last two weeks," Breckridge said with a snap of his jaw, "three of my associates have been kidnaped. One of them we have ransomed for a hundred and fifty thousand dollars. The second was found dead in the bay after the police made a clumsy attempt to catch the kidnapers and failed. The third is still being held. The facts are plain. There is a well-organized and powerful kidnaping ring at work. The police seem powerless to round them up.

"I don't know whether graft is behind it or the ring simply has more brains. Seemingly they can get no clues to work on. The men simply vanish at times and places which show they have been carefully watched and every little detail worked out. And we have reason to believe that many more prominent people who can afford ransom have gone through the same experience."

Gerard Breckridge slapped the arm of his chair smartly.

"This thing must be stopped! For many reasons, among which is the fact that extremely delicate negotiations are in progress leading to the merger of two of our biggest banks. This is confidential, Mr. Lawson, and must not be hinted at outside this room."

Breckridge leaned forward and lowered his voice.

"If, for instance, I or certain of my associates are removed for more than a day or so in the next week, the merger will fail. And the second largest bank will crash, dragging down other banks. It means the crippling of industry throughout this territory and ruin to thousands of innocent people. We are doing everything possible to avert such an event, and while we are doing it we are being hamstrung by this infamous kidnaping ring."

Gerard Breckridge shook his head.

"Sometimes I think," he said bitterly, "that they have wind of what is going on and are deliberately preying on the men who are indispensable to the merger, knowing that they will have to be ransomed quickly. We have employed two detective agencies whose men are doing everything they can. But they seem to be making no progress. That, briefly, is the reason you were summoned so hurriedly and given *carte blanche* with your expense account. Desperate measures are necessary and we are trying to take them. We are counting on you heavily now."

Breckridge frowned.

"And I must say I am rather disappointed at the start," he growled. "You were given *carte blanche* with your expense account, it is true. But I told you we were bringing you in from another part of the country so there would be no chance of anyone here knowing you or suspecting what you are working on. I warned you the utmost secrecy was necessary. And here you come, spending money and attracting attention like a drunken sailor. It looks as if you have blundered at the start, Mr. Lawson. I'm afraid I'll have to ask for some explanation."

The financier looked at Larry Lawson challengingly.

LARRY smiled at him without humor. His eyes had narrowed the slightest bit. "I work in my own way, Mr. Breckridge. I explain my methods to no one and I take orders from no one. Were you intending to direct my methods more or less with your own ideas?"

"What is the matter with my ideas?" Breckridge snapped.

Larry shrugged. "Perhaps nothing. I haven't heard any so far—and I don't intend to. I'll have to insist that you forget about me unless I call on you for assistance. That's final. We might as well understand it now."

Breckridge hesitated, shrugged. "All right. You ought to know your own business. What are you going to do?"

Larry smiled. "Get to work. How

about you. Are you taking any measures to guard yourself?"

"I am!" Breckridge assured him curtly. "Two men are waiting outside for me now. I go no place without them these days."

"Good," said Larry. "Now I don't think I'll go to the police for any information. I don't want them to know I'm interested in the matter. Might be a leak. What leads can you give me?"

"None," said Gerard Breckridge. "And I doubt if you can do any better with the police. The men simply vanished. I have talked with Roger Breene, the man whom we ransomed for a hundred and fifty thousand dollars. He ordered his car to go to the theater one night. It hadn't gone a block from his apartment house when the chauffeur discovered a flat tire. Breene was late already. A passing taxi stopped to see if they wanted any help and Breene engaged it to take him on to the theater, leaving his chauffeur to attend to the tire. Several blocks away the taxi drew in to the curb and stopped. A man opened each door and stepped in. They had drawn guns and Breene was helpless. While the taxi drove on they blindfolded him and held a chloroformed rag under his nose."

Breckridge spread his hands. "Perfectly plain it had all been planned. Tire, taxi and everything."

"How about the chauffeur?" Larry inquired slowly.

"Perfectly all right. Been with Breene for five years. He found that the tire valve had been tampered with so that it leaked. Probably done while the car stood in front of the apartment house and he went in the lobby to let Breene know it was there."

"I see," said Larry. "Then what happened?"

"Breene hasn't any idea where they went or how they drove. When he came to he was in a dark room. He stayed there in the dark. Men came in with flashlights and asked him to write a letter requesting that the money be taken to a certain spot. He refused. They threatened to hold lighted matches under his chin and even went so far as to do it for a moment. Breene saw that it was useless to resist and wrote the letter to me. We needed him badly. The instructions were followed; the money paid over. And a few hours after that Breene woke up beside a country road. He had been chloroformed and left there."

"Didn't he see any faces at all?"

"No. The men who first got in the cab were masked."

"And after him two more?"

"Yes," said Breckridge grimly. "Two more vanished and we received notes demanding money. Notes written under the threat of torture also. The second time I took the matter to the police. They tried to trap the men who were to get the money. No one came. And the next day Kingston was found floating in the bay——dead. That was when I called you. Richards, the third man, disappeared today. I received a note late this afternoon demanding two hundred thousand dollars."

"Have you turned it over to the police?" Larry questioned quickly.

"No. I am afraid it will cost Richards his life. I turned it over to the private detectives working on the case. We have two days to get the money. And it looks as if we'll have to pay it over. There's nothing about the note that can be traced. It was written on a section of brown paper sacking with a soft pencil, and mailed to me in a plain government-stamped envelope with a special-delivery stamp on it from the main post office."

"Is Breene married?"

"No. He is a bachelor."

"The others?"

"Married. Kingston's wife is half dead from grief and Richards' wife is prostrated with fear that he'll be killed also. I haven't informed her of the note I received. I wanted time to think things over. The city's in an uproar; the newspapers are making the most of things and we are getting a lot of attention at a time when we want no publicity. We are afraid that any hour may focus attention on the merger situation and start a run on a weak bank that will be disastrous. You see how things are. We must have results at once."

Mopsy spoke for the first time, entirely unawed by the presence of the great man, and with a trace of sarcasm in his voice. "Sure, we'll step right out an' pick you a result off a bush."

Larry shot him a warning look and diverted Breckridge's angry reaction with a calm remark. "I see your position, Mr. Breckridge. I'll do what I can. But I'm no miracle monger. I have nothing to go on. I'll get to work to-night and call you in the morning."

"What are you going to do?" Breckridge demanded, rising.

Larry shrugged. "I told you I don't discuss my methods."

Breckridge looked disappointed, almost angry. Any confidence he might have displayed in the reputation of Larry Lawson visibly waned. "Very well," he said stiffly. "Call me in the morning." He departed.

When the door closed behind him Mopsy looked at Larry—and Larry looked at Mopsy.

"Can you tie that?" Mopsy breathed disgustedly. "He wants us to go an' chew up a gang of killers just like that! An' then fights the way we work! What are you gonna do, boss?"

Larry grinned broadly. "Go out and chew them up," he said. "Get my dinner clothes, Mopsy."

CHAPTER TWO

The Buccaneer

THE parade of Mortimer Dodwich through the night-life belt that foggy evening was an event remembered for weeks afterward.

A young boy millionaire had come out of the west, plunging high, wide and handsome; pockets full of money, body chocked with synthetic booze, handsome face flushed and movements unsteady.

Before he left the first night-club he had collected two brazen little gold diggers, and as the evening wore on others attached themselves to the party. Girls, and sleek, well-dressed young men, brittle and hard beneath their suave veneer.

As they proceeded others joined them, riding from stop to stop in the large Rolls-Royce driven by the massive, taciturn chauffeur. When the Rolls-Royce could hold no more they added a taxi-cab—and later a second one. Young Mortimer Dodwich's supply of money seemed inexhaustible and his willingness to spend unending.

Someone presently raised the cry: "Let's go to th' Buccaneer!"

"Whatsh 'at?" Mortimer Dodwich queried owlishly.

"Hottest place in town, big boy!" the bleached blonde at his side squealed. "They got *it* at the Buccaneer! An' if there's anyone you wanta see, they'll be there."

Young Dodwich flashed the girl a startled glance, veiled quickly, and demanded querulously: "Who'd I wanna see?"

But the blonde was already on her feet shrieking: "Let's go to the Buccaneer! Come on, people, the Buccaneer for us!"

"Right," young Dodwich mumbled, dragging a handful of bills out of his pocket and beckoning the waiter. "How mush the bill?"

"A hundred and forty-three dollars, sir," the waiter informed him after a moment's figuring.

Dodwich paid without checking the bill; paid with a hundred-dollar bill and three twenties. "Keep change," he said expansively, lurching to his feet and making for the door.

The waiter watched him depart with his satellites, as did everyone else in the big garish room. Two other waiters drifted over. A silent look of understanding passed between them.

"What a sucker!" one of them observed, sotto voce. "What'd you make outa him, Pete?"

"Seventeen-dollar tip an' twenty-dollar overcharge," Pete said, winking. "He's about the hottest proposition that's been in town since that oil millionaire busted loose last year."

The third waiter grinned. "They take him for a cleaning at the Buccaneer," he said wisely. Not one of the three disputed that.

There was no lack of directions as to how to reach the Buccaneer. Mopsy Doolin followed them and the big Rolls-Royce purred into a section of the city they had not visited before. Dark lowering buildings and rough streets marked the fringe of the business district.

And then the water front, deserted, silent at this time of night. The dark, looming pier sheds thrusting out into the bay waters; the bows, masts and stacks of ships barely visible in their slips through the wet blanket of murk which had descended on the city. Now and then a furtive figure could be discerned hurrying along through the milky wraiths of fog. The whole neighborhood had taken on an eery, unreal quality under its sodden mask.

"Thish pretty bad neighborhood, ain't it?" young Mortimer Dodwich questioned thickly.

A shout of amusement answered him. "Get that, folks! Morty wants to know if this is a bad neighborhood!"

"They order murders with their meals," one of the sleek young men stated.

"I don' wan' murder with m' meals. Maybe we better go back."

"Lay off the rough stuff," a voice advised calmly from the back seat. "They don't have murders down here. You'll scare Mr. Dodwich away from a good time if you go on talking that way."

The speaker was a square-faced young man attired in well-tailored dinner clothes, who, with the henna-haired beauty beside him, had joined the party at some point in its perambulations. He was not as drunk as the rest and for the most part had little to say.

"Can't scare me!" Dodwich insisted drunkenly, twisting around in the front seat. "Who saysh I'm afraid?"

"Bill said it!" the blonde shrilled, wrapping an arm around Dodwich's neck as she half sat on his lap in the front seat.

"Who'sh Bill?"

"Just Bill," answered the square-faced young man soothingly. "And I didn't say that, old man. I know you're not afraid. Aren't we going there?"

"Sure, we're going there 'f you say so, Bill," Dodwich yawned, and faced front again.

THE surroundings grew more squalid. Lighted windows, gaudy paper signs, scroll-work architecture and other indications of alien life announced the fringe of Chinatown. The huge dock sheds along the edge of the bay gave way here to smaller ones. And finally to one with a faint blue light, burning dimly through the mist in front of it.

The blonde called to Mopsy Doolin: "Turn in there under the blue light! Blow your horn!"

Mopsy obeyed directions, and brakes shrilled behind them as the two taxis stopped also. Mopsy blew the horn loudly.

The dock shed was closed but a moment after the horn sounded the iron door before them rolled up silently. A strange and bizarre figure stepped out into the headlight glare.

It was a bearded giant of a man, dressed like a buccaneer out of the lurid and dangerous past. He wore leather boots and sash. Cocked hat and golden earrings glittered and huge old-fashioned pistols were thrust in his belt.

The leather boots creaked as he stepped forward and flashed a light in the Rolls-Royce. "Them other two cars with you?" he queried.

And on being vociferously assured that they were, the small cavalcade rolled into the big, dimly lighted shed. It was bare of freight, holding many automobiles, parked in orderly rows. A second pirate showed them where to park.

There was a concerted rush toward a large door at one side, and through a small passage that ended abruptly in the interior of a ship.

But no ship like this had ever sailed the seven seas. Interior partitions had been torn out, a smooth dance floor laid, festoons of lights strung across the ceilings, tables scattered around the walls. An orchestra was playing at one end. Waiters attired as ferocious pirates were hurrying about.

The head waiter who met them at the door quickly ordered several tables put together. He was a short dapper man, clad in the black of his profession,

swarthy-faced, with shining patent-leather hair and a bowing, ingratiating manner. Some of the party greeted him as Raoul, and he smirked and bobbed from the hips in acknowledgment. Drinks were quickly brought, consumed, more ordered. Several couples slipped off to the dance floor. The bleached blonde who had attached herself to Larry snuggled close and pursed her over-rouged lips.

"Wanna dance, nice man?"

Larry pushed her away, shaking his head. His eyes were half closed. But beneath the lids his glance was keen, watchful, and decidedly sober. For ever since Mopsy had driven him away from the Splendide in the big Rolls-Royce, Larry had been acting. Every moment of the time he had watched for the first lucky break. He shoved a twenty-dollar bill in the blonde's hand.

"Go 'way," he told her. "Buy y'se'f a dancin' man."

The blonde left. Her place was immediately taken by the square-faced young man who had lurked in the background since joining the party. "How about a few turns of the wheel?" he suggested.

"Sure," Larry agreed.

As they left the table Larry caught a signaling glance between his companion and the henna-haired beauty who had been with him.

Larry yawned as they cut across the floor. "What's your name?" he asked.

"Tilson."

"Never met you before."

"You have now," said Tilson jovially. "Stranger in town?"

"Yes. From San Francisco."

They went through a door at the end of the room, down a flight of stairs into another large room in the bottom of the ship. A room with paneled walls and thick carpets underfoot, vastly different from the gay scene overhead. For it contained the conventional gambling layouts that one might find anywhere, roulette, craps, blackjack—even stud poker. And the sober-faced housemen wore dark suits and were entirely businesslike.

LARRY and his new friend found places at one of the roulette tables. The poker-faced croupier nodded at Tilson. Larry caught the quick droop of Tilson's eyelid, the slight answering droop of the houseman. Without indication that he had seen, he began to play recklessly.

And he won—consistently. His luck was amazing. The stack of bills before him grew steadily. Tilson followed his bets with smaller ones, talking steadily under his breath. Larry realized he was being pumped skilfully for information about himself—who he was, where he was from, the amount of wealth he possessed. To a smiling comment that he must be pretty well fixed with money, Larry shrugged negligently.

"The pater left me a few millions," he answered in more sober tones. "All alone now. Got plenty to see me through. Gettin' plenty more here too."

"This is your lucky night," Tilson chuckled.

But for some unaccountable reason Larry's luck changed after that. He won and lost, won and lost, staying about even. Finally he crammed the stack of bills in his pocket and turned away from the table. "Got enough," he said.

Tilson touched the pocket where the money was. "You're carrying a lot of cash there, old man," he warned. "Why not come into the office and let Myerson give you a check for it? He likes to see his guests take away checks so there

won't be any chance of a hold-up and a kick-back about some crook spotting their roll here in the club and following them."

"'S'good idea," Larry agreed.

Tilson took him upstairs again, through a door in the back of the fantastic night-club room, down a paneled passage into a small office built into the stern of the boat.

Tilson threw open the door without knocking. They were in the office before it was plain that they should have knocked. A man and a woman were in there, the woman standing before a dark flat-topped desk, and the man standing on the other side facing her.

The woman swung around as the door opened. For an instant Larry caught sight of her white drawn face, saw that she was young, pretty, slender and well dressed. And then with an effort the lines smoothed out of her face and she stared at him fixedly.

The man was short, fat, gross—almost swinish. A roll of fat swelled over his collar; his mouth was large and loose-lipped and his forehead bulged curiously over his eyes. His face was flushed and angry as they came in but that wiped away quickly as he smiled oilily.

"Hello, Tilson," he greeted. "Something I can do for you?"

Tilson seemed in no wise abashed at the intrusion. "Sure," he said. "My friend here has got some money he wants a check for. He's been taking one of your wheels for a cleaning. Good evening, Mrs. Breckridge. How are you tonight?" The last to the girl, with the barest hint of a sneer in his voice.

And as she gave him a glance of disdain and scorn Larry was almost jolted out of the role he was playing. The meeting was so unexpected, so staggering that for a moment his thoughts floundered helplessly.

He knew this woman! She had been a crook. And here she was being called Mrs. Breckridge. Gerard Breckridge . . . . Had he been recognized and led into a trap?

Larry's hand crept up toward the button of his coat. Under his left arm an automatic hung ready.

SHE was staring at him with wide eyes. Larry recalled the tiny scar at the corner of her mouth, almost invisible, but one of the things he always looked for. They didn't change.

She had been called Elise Marrow, had been a decoy for a con gang. He had sent two of the gang to court, where a jury freed them. She had been arrested too, but discharged without trial. They had met once before her arrest, never after. He had been wearing a dark mustache then; and without doubt after her arrest she had known he was a detective. Now he had no mustache—and she was staring at him fixedly.

Tilson noticed it, said mockingly: "May I present Mr. Dodwich, Mrs. Breckridge? Perhaps you two know each other. You're both from San Francisco."

Myerson chuckled down in his throat. "Hey? Is that so? Both from the coast, eh?"

Larry said politely: "How do you do, Mrs. Breckridge?"

His fingers had unbuttoned the front of his coat, clearing the path to his gun. His arm was still rigid and ready for trouble. He was certain now that it was a trap. They were jeering at him before they sprang it.

The girl's eyes went from him to the two other men, and back to him. Larry was certain he saw disgust, dislike—no, worse than that, hate in her glance. It puzzled him.

"How do you do, Mr. Dodwich," she said in a curiously calm and strong voice. He remembered that too—her voice. It hinted at strong reserves of character and power.

A loose-lipped, greasy smile was slashing Myerson's gross face, as if he were getting a great deal of enjoyment out of the moment. Larry felt an almost irresistible impulse to plant a fist in the center of that smile—and promised himself he would do it at the first opportunity. Myerson reminded him of something fat and slimy out of a dark corner—something that needed squashing.

"Good evening," said the girl icily, including them all in a curt nod, and she was gone, leaving behind a breath of perfume.

Tilson and Myerson exchanged veiled grins, as if enjoying a private joke between themselves. Larry was puzzled. He didn't understand it. There seemed cross currents under the surface of things. He was certain Elise Marrow had recognized him. Why hadn't she said something? And why had they called her Mrs. Breckridge? Too much coincidence about that to be healthy. But he said nothing. He waited.

Tilson said briskly to Myerson: "Mr. Dodwich brought a pocketful of money away from one of your games. I told him he'd better trade it to you for a check. Not so much danger carrying that home."

Myerson washed pudgy palms together. "Sure," he said. "How much?"

No menace here, on the surface. Larry's hand dropped down to his pocket and pulled out the batch of currency. It counted to thirty-two hundred dollars. Myerson stacked it neatly, put it in a drawer of the desk and wrote him a check for the amount.

"How about a drink, Myerson?" Tilson suggested, stepping around be-

behind the desk. "Mind if I pour a couple?"

"Make it three," Myerson invited, tearing out the check and handing it to Larry.

A walnut cabinet stood against the wall behind the desk. Tilson opened it, revealing bottles and glasses inside. With his back to them he poured the drinks, and turned, handing one to Larry, one to Myerson, and lifting the third himself.

"More winnings," he toasted Larry, tossing it off.

Myerson and Larry followed suit. The liquor was raw, biting, had an off taste about it. Larry's suspicions flamed. He stepped quickly around the desk to the cabinet.

"I'll have another," he grinned, picking up a clean glass and the bottle as Tilson reached for it. He poured half a drink, drained it slowly. The taste was right this time.

Myerson and Tilson were staring at him fixedly. Inwardly Larry branded himself a careless fool for letting Tilson pour his drink while bottle, glass and hands were shielded by the man's body. There was something wrong about that drink. Larry looked at his watch with drunken gravity.

"'S'late. Hotel for me," he decided, turning toward the door.

"Good night. Had a mighty nice evening," Tilson remarked, making no move to go with him.

Larry wondered about that as he closed the office door on the two men. Why was Tilson letting him go alone? As he approached his table he caught sight of the slender Elise Marrow just leaving the room. Larry lurched over to his waiter and demanded: "How much is my bill?"

"Three hundred and ten dollars, sir."

Larry gave him three hundred and fifty. "I'm going," he said thickly.

"Tell that crowd they're on their own now." And careful to stagger slightly he departed through the boarded tunnel into the cavernous depths of the dock shed. It was dark and there was a penetrating chill there after the stuffy warmth of the Buccaneer. Larry pulled his coat collar up close around his throat.

An automobile engine was just starting. A sleek expensive roadster backed out of the banked cars as he made for the Roll-Royce, still staggering. A woman was driving—the Marrow girl. There was no drunkenness in Larry's voice as he leaped into the Rolls and snapped to Mopsy lounging behind the wheel. "Follow that car! Careful she doesn't see you!"

CHAPTER THREE

The Car Behind

MOPSY went into action without a word. The Rolls glided out into the murky street a few moments after the girl. Larry leaned out the window, thrust a finger down his throat, and after a few painful gasping moments sank back in his seat, wiping his face and panting.

"They musta had rotten booze in there," Mopsy commented with a grin. "You always handled your liquor before."

"Usual stuff," Larry panted. "But I think they slipped me a doped drink. Watch me, Mopsy. I may start to keel over any minute."

"Whadda they want to dope you for?"

Larry shrugged, looked behind. The sleek roadster was leading them out of Chinatown at a smart pace. They turned into a wide traffic artery, liberally sprinkled with cars even at this late hour. And before they had gone a block a pair of headlights swung out of the same street and came after them. As near as Larry could make out, peering back at them through the vaporous night, they were keeping an exact pace with the Rolls. Larry lost sight of them from time to time in the foggy banks which veiled the streets but they always reappeared.

"I think we're being followed," Larry said finally.

"Now ain't that nice," Mopsy grunted. "Did some bright guns make your roll back there an' figger on takin' up a collection?"

"Wish I knew," Larry confessed, and yawned. A lethargic feeling was creeping over him insidiously. It would have taken him by surprise if he had not been looking for it.

Larry slapped his face, shook his head vigorously. "Open the windshield, Mopsy!" he rasped. "They slipped me dope all right! Lead in my eyelids already! Must have absorbed part of the dose before I got rid of it!" Larry yawned again in spite of himself.

The cool damp blast of air through the open windshield cleared his head a little. Larry pinched himself, slapped his face, swung his arms as he fought against the almost irresistible urge to sink back and sleep.

"Maybe I better get you back to the hotel while the gettin's good," Mopsy suggested with a trace of uneasiness in his voice.

"The devil you will!" Larry refused vigorously. "Follow that woman! I want to know where she goes!"

"You're the boss," Mopsy assented, hunching over the wheel. "But I got a hunch we're in for trouble."

"That's what we came here for, isn't it?"

The girl was a fast driver and more than once Mopsy almost lost her. In no time at all they were far out toward the north side of the city where the houses and grounds were much larger. Twice the roadster ahead made dangerously swift turns on the slippery concrete, finally swinging into Orchid Avenue, one of the most exclusive streets. A short distance further on it turned abruptly into a driveway that vanished behind a high hedge and a fringe of big shade trees inside.

"Want to stop?" Mopsy asked out of the corner of his mouth.

"No! Straight on. Want to see what that car behind will do." For the headlights that had been dogging them steadily were still there, gleaming like two great yellow eyes through the wetness.

A curb lamp shed light on dripping stone pillars at each side of the driveway entrance. Large handwrought iron numerals fastened to the stone gave the address of the house back there in the huge grounds.

"Don't forget it, Mopsy! 4716 Orchid Avenue!" Larry muttered, blinking his eyes and slapping his face hard.

That portion of the drugged drink his body had absorbed was still sapping insidiously at him. He was fighting with the last reserves of will power to keep alert for what lay ahead.

Something was on the cards. The headlights came on, drawing closer as vacant stretches of land began to appear and the open country drew near.

Mopsy looked anxiously at Larry, caught him in the midst of a mighty yawn. In a troubled voice Mopsy said hastily: "Maybe we better make a break back to the hotel. That auto back there is followin' us all right. Maybe somebody made us, an' it's a committee to rub us out. They may be packin' a Tommy gun. An' we won't have a chance against a Tommy gun."

LARRY drew the automatic from under his arm and gouged the muzzle behind his ear. The excruciating pain from tortured nerves wiped away the drowsiness. He saw the justice of Mopsy's stand. The drugged drink might have been a prelude to a delegation of killers sent to get him out of the way. For ever since the instant that bitter drink had passed his lips, Larry had been certain that his plan had succeeded.

The rich, lavish young millionaire from out of town had baited the kidnapers into the open. He had been steered to the Buccaneer, had been allowed to win money, had been pumped for information, and drugged. And had been recognized by the girl, perhaps before he had seen her. An execution squad armed with a machine gun or sawed-off shotguns was not too much to expect.

"All right. Try to get back to the hotel," he told Mopsy.

Mopsy was driving fast. A cross street leaped at them, marked only by a single, wan overhead light—the last light. Ahead the road speared black and straight into the country.

Rubber shrilled. The car lurched and skid as Mopsy slammed on the brakes. They careened around the corner off the pavement. The car swayed over a puddly road, none too smooth.

Brief moments later headlights raced into the road after them, coming fast, evidently suspecting they were trying to get away.

"They're going to give us a run for it!" Larry rapped out.

The big Rolls was rocking, bouncing, spraying up muddy water, as Mopsy drove it recklessly along. "They'll get a run!" he promised grimly.

There were trees along the road, a ditch now and then, fields. Orchid

Avenue was evidently one of the main arteries that crept out like tentacles from the teeming torso of the city. Stay on one and you were in the city, leave it and you found open country at once.

Once or twice they passed houses, small crouching bungalows lonesome and forlorn in their solitariness. There were curves in the road. Mopsy skid around them on two wheels, recklessly, masterfully. And then without warning the motor faltered, spit, coughed, missed repeatedly. A few half-hearted backfires gave way to silence.

Mopsy cursed, peered at the instrument board, joggled the accelerator with his foot, tried the ignition—all without success. The speedometer dropped rapidly.

"Plenty of gas!" Mopsy swore angrily. "Spark's all right! Sounds like the carburetor's clogged up."

They rolled around a sharp curve, tires crunching on the wet ground. Bushes grew close to the road on either side, a line of trees behind them.

"Stop here! Get out!" Larry snapped.

They stopped with a jerk. Larry hit the ground running. He dashed around the front, calling to Mopsy: "Over here in the bushes!"

Mopsy dove out of the car and plunged into the bushes, swearing loudly as he plowed down into a hidden ditch behind the leafy screen. He picked himself up, wet but none the worse for the experience. "I almost shoved a shoe in my ear!" he grumbled.

"Back this way!"

The sudden crisis that had come upon them had done what other remedies had failed to do. Larry's head was clearer now, he felt more like himself.

As he led the way back along the ditch a sheen of light cut through the fog silvering the other side of the bushes. The pursuing automobile swung around the curve, running fast. Brakes squealed suddenly, the light wobbled drunkenly as the machine skidded to a stop behind the car. Doors opened, feet struck the road, low voices murmured something. And Larry snaked through the bushes to the road, his automatic gripped in his hand.

THE silhouette of a dark sedan blocked the road a few yards away, its headlights bathing the Rolls brightly. Two dark figures were slipping toward the Rolls, hands in their pockets. A third had stepped out from behind the steering wheel and stood in the shadows beside the car watching the advance of the other two. Larry made out the dim blur of a gun in this man's hand.

One of the two men stopped behind the Rolls and called: "What's the matter? Have an accident?"

Larry eased silently toward the figure waiting beside the sedan.

"Where the hell are they?" came from the man beside the Rolls.

"Nobody here," his companion answered and raising his voice he called: "Who belongs to this car?"

Larry reached his man, jabbed his gun roughly into the fellow's back.

"Don't move or you'll get it!" he husked under his breath.

The man froze.

"Drop your gun!"

The weapon thudded softly at his feet. Larry kicked it under the sedan and crouched invisible behind his prisoner. A swift glance over his shoulder showed Mopsy slipping shadowlike around to the other side of the sedan.

The two men at the Rolls separated, walked around it, met again beside it.

"They've lammed!" said one.

"What for?" asked the other.

"Maybe they've gone for help."

"Where'd they go? They wasn't back along the road, an' they didn't have time to get down the road out of the light."

"Then they beat it off in the bushes. Maybe they're hidin' out there listenin' to us now."

"One of them ought to be in the car."

The man speaking opened a door and peered inside. He slammed it shut and said disgustedly: "No one in there!"

"Hell, there ought to be! You said they slipped him—"

"Shut up, you fool! You don't know who's listenin'."

They stood uncertainly, then turned back toward the sedan. Larry got a good look at them in the headlight beam. Both were strangers, wearing dinner clothes, well tailored, smart. Both were young men, soft hats pulled rakishly down over their foreheads.

One was taller than the other, with a long bony face. The shorter one was more stolid, swarthy. In the night-club they might have seemed scions of respectable families, employes possibly in banks or brokerage houses. Out here in the dark night, hands thrust suggestively in the bulging pockets of their dinner coats, there was a different air about them. Efficient. Deadly.

"Harry!" the bony-faced one called. "Let's look through these bushes. There's something funny about this."

Larry prodded his man with the gun. "Answer them!" he ordered.

"Yeah," said Harry to them, standing rigidly.

"Come on, don't stand there like your dogs are lead! What's the matter with you?"

Larry grabbed his man's coat collar and urged him forward. "He's bashful," he called. "Stick 'em up, boys. I'll save you the trouble of poking around in those bushes!"

The two wheeled, their hands jerking guns from their pockets. Larry's gun was resting on the shoulder of his prisoner, covering them. An oath spat from the lips of the bony-faced one. "What the hell, Harry!"

"It wasn't my fault," Harry defended disconsolately. "He sneaked up on me from behind an' jammed a rod in my back. I didn't have a chance."

"Why didn't you yell?" the shorter one snarled.

"An' get my liver sewed up with lead? What the hell do you think I am, a hero?"

From the other side of the sedan Mopsy barked suddenly: "Pitch them rods in the dirt, suckers! You're on a spot if you don't!"

AFTER a tense sullen interval in which the two obviously weighed the chance of shooting themselves out of it, their two automatics struck the ground. Mopsy walked out into the light and gathered them up in a big paw.

"Didn't your mothers never tell you not to go pokin' around dark roads after night?" he inquired facetiously.

"Go to hell, you big gorilla!" the bony-faced one snarled at him.

"Yeah," agreed Mopsy amiably, pocketing the guns. "But not now, boys. Not now. I got other things to do. Turn around."

Mopsy's big hand gripped the shoulder of the horse-faced one and swung him around roughly. In a few swift seconds Mopsy frisked him expertly. Without ceremony he treated the other to the same attention.

The shorter one blustered: "What's the idea of a hold-up on the road like this?"

"Don't make me laugh!" Mopsy jeered.

"If it ain't a hold-up, what is it?" the speaker insisted. "Here we come down along the road, find a busted car

and stop to help, and we get rods stuck in our faces for our trouble."

Mopsy clenched a big fist and thrust it aggressively under his nose.

"You're lucky this ain't shoved in your snoot hard enough to upset you. If I had my way, I'd run the three of you back to town on your knees. Maybe I'll do it yet. I never did like mugs followin' me around when I'm out takin' the air."

"Not a bad idea," Larry approved soberly. "You may get a chance to do it yet, Mopsy—if they won't talk."

"Talk about what?" the shorter one queried.

"Lots of things. What's the idea of following me?"

"We wasn't following you!"

"Just out taking the air too, I suppose?" Larry inquired mildly.

"Ain't the night free?"

"Not to mugs like you!" Mopsy growled. "What'll we do with 'em, boss?"

Larry had been wondering that himself. He knew the type well. Cunning, close-mouthed, wise, they'd never talk unless forced to. Certainly not in front of each other, where the first man to speak would be branded as a squealer.

Larry seized the collar of the short stocky one, shoved him back toward the shadows behind the sedan.

"Hey, what's the idea?"

"We're taking a walk," Larry answered grimly, and shoved his captive through the bushes into the ditch, where he stumbled and went to his knees. Larry yanked him up again.

"Listen, fellow, what's the matter with you?" the prisoner protested, uneasiness in his voice.

They were out of earshot now. Larry stopped, said ominously: "You're in a tough spot. You get one chance to talk and get a break for yourself. Clam up on me and it'll be too bad for you.

I want the works on these kidnapings."

"You're a dick, ain't you?"

"Bright boy. Going to come clean with me?"

"I don't know anything about any kidnapings," was the sullen answer.

Larry shook him savagely. "Don't stall, you rat! Who's the big fellow on this? Where were you three going to take me tonight?"

"I don't know nothin'. You're wasting your time, flatfoot."

It was useless. A sharp swipe of the gun barrel dropped him there in the darkness. And then very calmly Larry fired a shot into the earth and walked back to the cars alone.

Mopsy gaped at him. The two prisoners stared uneasily.

"What'd you do with him?" Mopsy demanded.

"He wouldn't talk," Larry growled. "Come here, you. We'll take a walk too."

HE marched the man he had surprised first back the same way, prodding him with the muzzle of his gun.

"Say, mister, you didn't croak Sammy, did you?"

"No," said Larry. "I chased him off and threw a slug after him to make him go faster."

That convinced the man that Sammy had been shot down in cold blood. "What kind of a guy are you?" he got out uneasily. "You ain't no sucker from the coast."

"Think of that! And I was just beginning to believe I was," Larry retorted, shoving him down into the ditch also, where he stumbled over the prone body in the bottom. That was the last straw.

"Good God, mister, have a heart! You can't croak us out here like rats!"

"Why not? You're rats to me. I gave your buddy a chance to talk and he wouldn't. Now I'm giving you the same break. Do you talk?"

"H-how do I know you won't croak me anyway?"

"You don't."

Larry felt him shiver at the thought. "What do you want to know?" he whined.

"You birds were going to snatch me, weren't you?"

"Y-yes."

"Working for yourselves?"

"No. Sammy was givin' orders."

"He wasn't the arm behind it."

"No—I guess he wasn't. But he gave orders to us. I don't know who give them to him. Honest to God, mister, that's all I know." And as the man's tongue was unloosened by fear his words tumbled out fast. "Sammy tells me to drive the car while we go out an' snatch a rich sucker from the coast. That's all he said, so help me."

"Just like taking candy from a baby, eh? Well, you never can tell about suckers. They backfire sometimes. Where was this committee on transfer going to take the sucker?"

"Sammy didn't say. Back to the dock, I guess."

"And what then?"

"I dunno. Load him in a boat an' put him on ice until he sprung hisself with sucker money, I guess."

"I think you're lying!" Larry said harshly.

But the fervent protestations of the prisoner refuted that. The prone body at their feet had loosened his tongue as nothing else would have. He talked swiftly, almost incoherently, swearing that he and his companion knew nothing more. They had been together at the Buccaneer when Sammy had cut them in on the job hurriedly. It was their first kidnaping. Before that they had been running liquor for Sammy and Myerson and doing a little hi-jacking now and then.

"Who owns the Buccaneer?" Larry demanded.

"Myerson runs it but he ain't the big fellow. He takes orders, an' I don't know who hands them out. That's God's truth, mister!"

"Where did they hide Breene and Richards and Kingston?"

"Who?"

The puzzled question sounded sincere. And despite further questioning Larry could get nothing out of the fellow about the kidnapings he was trying to solve.

"Pick that body up and put it in the back of your car," he ordered curtly.

That was done with much grunting and stumbling in the dark. In his pocket Larry had a pair of tiny steel thumb cuffs that he always carried. He locked the two men together by their thumbs, herded them in the back seat with their feet on the limp body of their companion.

"We'll leave our car here," Larry said to Mopsy. "Drive back to that house where the girl turned in. I want to talk to her. I've got a hunch she's got some information that will help a lot."

CHAPTER FOUR

The Crimson Stain

THE roadster was standing before the big stone house, gravel behind its rear tires slashed where they had slid to a furious stop. Mopsy stopped the sedan on the circling driveway behind it.

Larry got out, leaving Mopsy to watch the three sullen prisoners in the back. For Sammy, the man he had knocked out, had revived with many groans and curses as they drove; and now Sammy was huddled on the floor with Mopsy draped over the back of the front seat adjuring them in a fatherly manner to make a break so he could do something about it.

The house had several lighted windows looming up eerily through the wisps of curling fog but for the most part seemed dark. Larry walked up on the porch, pressed the bell button beside the front door. It was opened by the girl he had come to see—Elise Marrow.

She caught her breath at sight of him. Larry saw the blood recede from her face.

"Wh-what do you want?" she asked unsteadily.

"A little talk with you," said Larry, looking past her into the large reception hall where evidences of wealth and good taste were apparent.

"I don't want to talk to you."

Larry smiled coldly. "Too bad. But you're going to talk."

He studied her keenly as he spoke, noting the strain on her face. What was she doing here in this big fine home? Was this the hangout of a prosperous gang, using that best of all masks, respectability? With a little surge of excitement he wondered if this could be the place he was searching for —the rendezvous of the kidnapers.

Elise Marrow started to close the door. Larry thrust his shoulder in, crowded through. "Not so quick!" he advised.

"Get out!" she cried furiously "I— I'll call the police!"

"I was thinking of that," Larry agreed. "Call them."

For a moment she stood there rigidly, then relaxed, saying no more about the police. She didn't want them any more than he did. It confirmed his suspicions that something was wrong.

"I suppose you're going to tell me

you're not Elise Marrow," he said, closing the door and putting his back to it.

She flinched, as if a whip had been laid across her spirit. Her eyes did not leave his face. They were blue, deep and stormy. And Larry saw growing anger there. Anger such as he had not seen in a woman's face in years.

"I thought so!" she flared. "You rat! I'll tell you something else. I'm through! Tell Myerson I meant every word I said tonight. And if he ruins things for me, I'll settle with him! And it won't be nice! That goes for you too!"

She was panting when she finished. Admiration swept Larry in spite of himself. She was like a beautiful leopard at bay, unsheathing its claws. Beautiful and mysterious. Her every word and act had mystified him since that first sight of her in Myerson's office.

"I don't know what you're talking about," Larry said as quietly as possible, for he saw she was under a terrific strain of some kind.

"No?" she sneered. "Get out before I have you thrown out!"

"You'd better call the police," Larry suggested, growing angry himself. "You're in bad again, sister. If you won't shoot straight with me, you can go down to headquarters and have a little talk with them!"

Again that had a telling effect on her. Larry saw her hand tremble slightly as she pushed a strand of hair away from her forehead.

"What do you want?" she asked in a tight voice.

Larry did not answer. His eyes had gone past her to a door in the side of a hall, and noted something on the floor. He stared at the spot in fascination. And a prickly surge of warning swept over him. For the light overhead was glinting off a spattering of dark spots just inside the door. Spots that had been wet and were now moist. Spots that lay on the sheen of varnished wood with grisly significance. Larry had seen spots like those before on other floors. Blood!

HIS eyes went back to the girl, standing there in troubled fear. It was fear; he saw that now. And he thought he understood it. It hardened him. He had suspected her—but at no time had there been thought of anything like this. Blood—wet blood—fresh. What gruesome story lay beyond that door?

"Do you live here?" Larry asked mildly, straightening up and hunching his shoulders so the gun under his arm was free.

"Why—yes. What difference does that make? You seem to know anyway."

"Just wanted to be sure," Larry drawled. "Had any trouble here tonight?"

"No."

"Not even a nosebleed or anything like that?"

"No," she denied impatiently. "What are you driving at?"

"That," said Larry—and he pointed.

She gave him a doubtful glance, swung around warily. A little gasp burst from her as her eyes fastened on those grim moist spots.

Larry stepped to her side. "No trouble, eh?" he questioned softly.

"I—I don't know what it is."

"Strange," said Larry. Didn't you ever see blood before?"

"Blood!" She whispered it, fright, horror, fear in the word.

"Blood," Larry agreed. "It looks bad. I don't suppose you have any objection to showing me around?"

His shoulder was touching hers. He felt her shudder. "But—but," she stammered, "everything has been all right since I came in the house. I didn't see that there. It wasn't there when I came in, I am sure."

"Didn't know a thing about it, eh?" Larry asked quizzically.

"No! I came in and went up to my room at once. I've been there ever since."

"Strange," Larry sighed, "how people are never around when there's trouble. You didn't know a thing about that business out on the coast when the police talked to you about it."

Her face, when she looked at him, was tragic. "Isn't it possible for a person to live down unfortunate mistakes they have made?" she pleaded.

"Sometimes," Larry assented. "But —not that kind of mistake." He pointed to the moist spots on the floor. And she shuddered again. "Who's in the house?" he demanded.

"Nobody—that is, except the servants." She added the last hastily.

"Stand there," said Larry, stepping clear of the spots and laying his handkerchief over the door knob. He turned the knob, opened the door. The room beyond was dark, a drawing room of some kind as far as he could see by the light coming in through the door. "Where's the switch?"

"On the wall there."

Larry stepped in and felt on the wall. His fingers were just on the switch when he became aware of a quick stir in the darkness behind him. He whirled— too late. A smashing blow struck the top of his head.

Larry staggered back and turned, trying to draw his gun. He didn't have a chance. His dazed eyes caught one glimpse of a silent shadowy figure looming there in the half light. A squat, grotesque, horrible-looking apparition. A dead white, ghoulish face with long pronglike glistening teeth showing in

a gaping mouth. And an arm swinging down in a second blow.

One quick moment of thought Larry had before he went down. The girl had put on a wonderful act for his benefit. She had tricked him neatly. And his mounting wall of evidence was now being shattered by his carelessness. Was this the end for him too?

All that in the space of a breath as he tried to dodge the blow. It caught him on the side of the head. He dropped.

LARRY opened his eyes and light struck into them. He blinked painfully and looked again. He was lying in darkness, staring through a rectangle of light into the hall.

He recognized it and remembered. The hall, the girl, the blow on the head —and that dead white staring face in the darkness. There was absolute silence around him.

For a moment Larry wondered if this was death, and then decided it wasn't as he struggled to a sitting posture. His head hurt too badly for that. He got to his feet, swaying dizzily as he lurched to the door. His gun was gone. The hall was empty. There at his feet were the spots that had lured him into this—still moist.

A glance at his wrist watch showed that a matter of fifteen minutes had passed. Not much—and yet a lot. Where was Mopsy? Why hadn't he come in looking for him? And where was Elise Marrow? And that grotesque apparition that had struck him down? Why had he been allowed to lie on the floor that way, neglected, forgotten?

He found the switch a second time and pressed it. The flood of light that filled the room at his back caused him to blink again. It was a drawing room, spacious, richly furnished in period pieces, paintings on the walls.

The room was deserted. Larry was on the point of going out in the hall when his eyes were caught and held by a thin trail of spattered drops leading from the doorway across the room. He followed them in fascination until they disappeared at the end of a couch standing across the far corner of the room, with blank wall behind.

Nothing there. Yes, something. A shoe just visible on the floor there, its toe pointing up in the air. No shoe would stand that way unaided. This one was not doing it. A long step away from the door and a second look showed a trousered leg attached to it. A man was lying behind the couch.

Larry pulled out the piece of furniture, and whistled softly at what he saw. It was a nasty mess. Blood, plenty of it, around the head of a middle-aged, dignified man. He was lying there on his back where he had been dragged and dropped, and the couch moved back in front of him. His eyes were closed, his chalk-white face smeared horribly with blood.

At first Larry thought the whole front of the face had been battered in. But when he stooped and looked more closely he saw no wounds except a badly crushed nose that had all the appearance of having suffered from a tremendous blow.

The flesh was warm. He found a pulse when he felt for it. The man still lived!

Vastly relieved, Larry pulled the couch out still more and examined the victim further. He found a bad gash and a large swelling in the thinning blond hair. By all that he was able to visualize a scene in the hallway.

This man had been struck as he stood near the doorway. Perhaps he had fought back and received a blow on his face. Bleeding copiously he had been subdued, dragged across the room, dumped behind the couch.

And the man who had done it had been lurking inside the door while Larry had been talking to Elise Marrow! He scowled at the thought. What an actress she had been.

The victim's skull seemed to be all right. He would probably come out of it. Larry left him there for the time being and catfooted to the door again. In all his moving about, the house had remained silent as a tomb. An automobile horn sounded faintly out on the street, reminding him that a great city surrounded the spot. That was the only sign that the house was not miles from anywhere.

That silence puzzled Larry. Where was everyone? What were they doing? What was Mopsy doing? Still watching his prisoners? Larry turned to the door.

THE front door of the house was thick and heavy, with small leaded panes shoulder high. One of those panes had been shattered by a bullet since he had stood before the door!

The silence, the marks of violence were beginning to get on Larry's nerves. He opened the door, looked cautiously out into the pall of gray-white murk. The front porch was unlighted. There in front of the house still stood the rakish roadster of Elise Marrow. But beyond it was no sign of the sedan that had brought him.

"Mopsy!" Larry called.

And there was no answer. Only the sough of wind through the moisture-laden trees at the side of the house. Larry was stunned, then apprehensive. Something had happened to Mopsy, who would never have vanished this way of his own accord. They had been in too many tight places together. You could always count on Mopsy. These massive shoulders and the fighting spirit behind them were worth three men in a tight place. And now Mopsy was gone.

A faint groan came eerily out of the house. Larry whirled, his skin prickling. The groan again. And unless he was mistaken it did not come from the drawing room and the unconscious man.

The hall was large, spacious. A sweeping staircase at one side led up to the second floor. Under it at the back was a door, giving access to dead space under the stairs. As Larry looked, that door swung open with a slight creak. A man lurched out, groping blindly in front of him.

His breath was coming in harsh, sobbing gasps. He was stooped, like an old man—only he was not old. He turned to Larry with no sign of recognition. A groan rattled in his throat. One slack-kneed step he took, and then stumbled and pitched forward on his face heavily before Larry could get to him.

"What's the matter?" Larry demanded sharply.

A leg twitched. The fingers of one outstretched hand clawed convulsively at the smooth waxed floor boards, and then curled inward rigidly. The whole body grew stiff. A gasping rattle died in the throat . . . .

It did not need the froth of blood bubbling past set lips to tell Larry that he was looking at a dying man. No —a dead man! For when he dropped to his knees beside the still form he found there was nothing to do. The stranger had died before his eyes.

Larry shivered as he got to his feet and reached for his cigarettes. His hand was shaking as he struck a match and inhaled deeply. He had known tight moments, met strange happenings, but never had he plunged into such a stark

and eery mystery as he was finding in this dead lonesome house.

Who was this young man, not over twenty-eight, with a frank, open, rather worldly face? Where had he come from? What had happened to him—and the others—in that fateful fifteen minutes Larry had lain unconscious in the next room?

That froth of blood was the only sign of violence. But when Larry bent and opened the coat he saw a small hole in the front of the blue shirt. A hole ringed with damp blood. A bullet hole.

Shots had been fired. A bullet had gone into this man's chest. Most of the bleeding must have been internal. Who had fired that shot?

Larry was on his knees by the body when he heard the scrape of steps on the front porch. He leaped to his feet, ready for trouble. He had closed the door again when he stepped back into the hall. It opened briskly. A young woman entered, turning as she came to close the door.

"Hello," said Larry.

She faced him in quick surprise, young, pert, pretty in a cheap way. Her eyes widened at sight of him. Then dropped to the body at his feet. She screamed.

"Here, don't do that!" Larry ordered sharply.

But she paid no attention to him. She turned, clawing at the door knob, scream after scream shrilling from her lips in terrified crescendos.

Larry leaped for her.

CHAPTER FIVE

Wanted For Murder

THE girl fought him, blindly, insanely, clawing at the doorknob, at his face when he pulled her away from it. His reassuring words made no difference. Force was all he could use in keeping her from the door; and force he used. Anything to keep her from dashing wildly out into the night uttering those terrified cries.

He swung her away from the door as gently as he could. The screams choked in her throat. She fainted in his grasp. Larry held her limp body for a moment, finally laying it on the floor.

For a moment he looked down at her helplessly, getting his breath. Fright had given her extraordinary strength. He wondered who she was, where she had come from, for what purpose. Wondered that and many other things.

The house was still silent.

Larry knelt by the girl, started to chafe her wrists.

He was still at his crude first aid several minutes later when the unmistakable sound of an approaching automobile came to his ears. Larry jumped to his feet and looked out the door.

Headlights were sweeping up the drive, turning in front of the house. A small coupe stopped beside the roadster. He saw the shadowy silhouette of a figure getting out, heard the door slam behind it. No secrecy there. He opened the door and stepped out, closing it behind him.

Brisk steps ran lightly up to the wide front porch. Then a form and face materialized through the fog.

"Hello," a voice said.

"Hello," Larry answered.

"I wasn't sure I'd find anyone up this time of the night."

"Indeed," said Larry. "What made you think that? And who are you, by the way?"

"The name," said the other a trifle wearily, "is Ben Evans. I am from The Telegram. I regret the late hour but my paper considers it necessary that I get an interview tonight. The matter is pretty important. We don't want to print anything until we get a comment on it."

"Who do you want to interview?" Larry parried. His pulse was ticking fast as he considered what to do. A reporter was the last person he wanted to see at the moment. He had not forgotten Gerard Breckridge's instructions that things connected with him and his bank must be kept out of the papers at all cost.

"Mr. Breckridge," said the reporter wearily. "And don't tell me I can't see him, please. I have to."

Larry gulped. It was the last thing he had expected to hear. "Breckridge," he mumbled. "What made you think you'd see him here?"

"Why not?" Ben Evans retorted. "We have information that he started home an hour ago."

"Then why come here?"

"Please don't kid me," Ben Evans pleaded with a sigh. "I've got a headache."

"Say, who lives here?" Larry blurted out.

There was a moment's silence, in which he saw the reporter peering at him.

"Don't you know?"

"No," Larry confessed.

"Gerard Breckridge does. And what the devil are you doing here on the front porch if you don't know who lives inside?"

Before Larry could answer, the door was suddenly opened behind him. The girl bolted out, stumbled against him, and began to scream again as he caught her. Screams that quickly died into terrified whimpers as Larry begged her to be quiet.

Ben Evans watched the scene fixedly, obviously ready to take a hand if needed. As the girl's cries died down his voice cracked bruskly: "What's going on here?"

"I wish I knew," Larry confessed. "Perhaps this girl can tell us something. Who are you, sister?"

"Myra Johnson," she whimpered. "I work here. This was my night out. W-who is that man in there on the floor?"

Ben Evans stepped to the door and shoved it open. A grunt escaped him at sight of the body on the floor. He swung back and gripped Larry's arm.

"Come in!" he ordered. "We'll see about this!"

AS they went through the doorway Evans got his first good look at Larry's face. "The powder puff from Frisco!" he gasped. "Dodwich! What a break!"

Larry had never seen him before. "Dodwich is the name," he agreed. "But how did you know it?"

"I was in the Splendide lobby when you blew in. Got a line on you for the paper." Ben Evans looked at him appraisingly. "You don't look like the same feather that dusted in there this evening. Some fast worker. Suppose you break down and tell me about it. I'll stick with you to the last day of the trial."

Ben Evans forgot the body for a moment as he talked fast for his paper. "Give us the exclusive and we'll treat you right, Dodwich. While the other sheets are riding you, we'll be pulling for you. What happened here? You had a good reason for croaking him, of course. I guess he's dead all right, isn't he?"

"Yes, he's dead," said Larry shortly. "I don't know who he is, who killed him, or where he came from."

"Now, now," Ben Evans chided. "That isn't the way to go about it. Maybe you don't want to talk in front of the girl here. Step in the other room and tell me about it before I telephone in. You need good advice and I'm the man to slip it to you."

Larry was trapped. Publicity now, with a vengeance. No way out of it. For the first time he realized how he stood in the matter. No witnesses—a dead man—another unconscious. Who would believe the wild story he had to tell? Certainly not this cynical reporter. Swiftly he sized up the short, slim, lantern-jawed Evans. A cynical, hard, sophisticated young man; but a good one underneath.

"Ever see that man on the floor?" Larry asked the housemaid.

"N-no," she stammered.

"Come in here."

Larry led them into the next room, showed them the unconscious figure in the corner. A gasp of fright burst from the girl.

"Thomas! The butler!"

Ben Evans' eyes were glistening. "Fine," he breathed. "Got any more of them around the house?"

"Perhaps," said Larry shortly. "I haven't looked anywhere else."

"Where's a telephone? I want to get a flashlight man out here before the police get on the job."

"No you don't!" Larry snapped. "No cameras and no police right now. You say Breckridge started home?"

"Yes. He was at a board meeting. Left there, got in his car and started home, the office tells me. They had the meeting covered."

Larry was gripped by a premonition of trouble. There certainly had been no sign of Breckridge around the house. He might have been delayed for some good reason, but probably not.

"Sit down," Larry ordered the girl. "Come over here," he said to Evans, taking him out of earshot. Under his breath he asked curtly: "You want a good story, don't you?"

"Atta boy," Evans grinned, patting him on the arm. "I knew you'd see the light. Sure I want a good story. I've got it. But you can make it a lot better. What happened here?"

"I don't know. When it breaks it'll be big. I've got a hunch. Have to follow it down fast. Telephone the police and a doctor. Then come with me. I'll give you a chance to work it out with me and get all the breaks."

Ben Evans grinned cynically. "Nix," he refused. "Do I look like I'm still downy around the ears? It'll take a better yarn than that to get you away from here. I'll just hang on to you until the cops get here. Better come through with me."

Larry had no time to argue. Nor did he dare wait for the police. Their first move would be to lock him up. He couldn't give the whole story out now.

"Better come," he urged in a last effort.

"Nix," Ben Evans refused. "We stay right here until the cops come."

"Right," said Larry briefly. "Sorry."

And his clenched fist chopped hard to the reporter's chin. Evans tottered back on his heels. A glazed look came into his eyes. Then he pitched forward, knocked out. Larry caught him, lowered him to the floor.

The girl cried out and jumped to her feet.

"Be quiet!" Larry told her coldly, nursing his bruised knuckles. "This man will be all right in a few minutes. I'm going to leave. Tell him I'll see him at the hotel some time before morning if I can."

Ben Evans was already beginning to stir on the floor. Larry ran out of the house and jerked open the door of the speedy roadster. The ignition key was in the lock. He slid behind the wheel, stamped on the starter, and jerked the choke. The rear wheels threw gravel as the roadster careened around the circle and rushed down the driveway.

THERE was still life in Chinatown as Larry drove through the district, but it was thinning out for the hour was late. The blue light burned wanly before the dock-shed entrance to the Buccaneer. The corrugated iron door was rolled down as Larry drove slowly by. Faint sounds of music were audible. Dancing, gambling, merriment were still to be found in there.

Parking half a block further on, Larry walked back toward the blue light.

He had no definite plan, little enough to go on. It seemed that every move had taken him deeper into a tangled web. His mind was filled with confusing questions to which he could find no answers. For instance, the Marrow girl who had been introduced to him in the Buccaneer as Mrs. Breckridge. What was behind that? She was not Gerard Breckridge's wife. Yet he had found her in Breckridge's house.

It must have been without Breckridge's knowledge. That meant a cold-blooded piece of business which had culminated in murder!

Larry wouldn't have classed her as a killer. Yet—the spots of blood in the hall, which she had ignored, the lurking figure beyond the door through which she had deliberately let him, were indisputable evidence. In his mind's eye Larry saw again that dead white, ghoulish face materializing out of the darkness, pronglike teeth gleaming in its gaping mouth. And the bloody form of the unconscious butler stuffed out of sight in the corner.

What gruesome acts had been going on in that house before his arrival? Who had been there? And who was that young man who had staggered out of the closet under the stairs and died at his feet? Even the maid had not known him. Larry wondered if Elise Marrow had fired the shot that had killed the stranger.

One thing was certain—he, Larry Lawson, bore the guilt of one killing on his shoulders, perhaps more. Ben Evans, the reporter, would see to that. Even now the police were probably at the Breckridge house, with Evans stirring up the hue and cry after him.

He had no defense that would hold. Breckridge, the only man who knew why he was in town, had vanished. Larry had a premonition that Breckridge too had met foul play. If he went to the police they would only arrest him, hold him until too late. The one chance of doing anything lay in the swift prompt action he was taking.

The iron door rolled up with a dull grating sound; a silver headlight beam stabbed out and an automobile followed, whirling down the street. Larry saw a single couple, man and woman, in the front seat. No one he was interested in. As the iron door started down again he stepped inside.

The bearded giant in the pirate's costume confronted him. "Something you want, mister?" he demanded suspiciously.

"I'm going inside," Larry said coolly.

"Where's your car?"

"I'm walking."

"Where from?"

"All over," Larry told him curtly. "Ask Myerson if you want to know anything more."

"Uh—you know Myerson?"

"What does it sound like?"

"Sorry. My mistake," the big guard apologized. "We gotta be careful here. Never know when a raid is gonna be pulled off."

Larry nodded, strolled on into the cavernous dock shed, examining the parked automobiles. Many had departed, but there were still quite a few left. He was looking for a familiar machine. There was none.

HE was disappointed. He had been hoping that the automobile Mopsy Doolin had been guarding might have returned here. Evidently it had not. One more glance of success gone glimmering.

Larry's hand was in his pocket as he walked through the boarded passage to the bizarre interior of the ship moored at the dock. The head waiter recognized him.

"You have returned, Mr. Dodwich? We are glad to see you. Part of your party is still here."

Larry waved him aside. "Let them stay here. I don't want to see them. I'll go down and have a whirl at the wheel again."

The head waiter nodded understandingly. The dance floor was still comfortably filled as Larry skirted its edge and walked to the door leading to the gambling rooms below. A quick step took him through the adjoining doorway, into the paneled passage ending in the small office at the stern of the boat. He opened the door and stepped inside.

Myerson stood up quickly behind his big flat-topped desk. His swinish face paled slightly as he saw who it was. The large, loose-lipped mouth opened, closed; Myerson said uncertainly: "Hello."

Larry closed the door, slipped the catch that locked it and advanced to the desk. Myerson started to open one of the desk drawers.

"Don't do that!" Larry warned sharply.

His hand was in the side pocket of his coat, and a little bulge in the cloth betrayed the gun he was gripping. Myerson was evidently no stranger to such actions. His eyes stared at that bulge in fascination, then lifted to Larry's face.

"What can I do for you, Mr. Dodwich?" he questioned, forcing a strained smile on his gross face.

Larry smiled too, a thin-lipped, cold, chilling smile. "I'm back," he said.

"Ha-ha—yes, I see. And mighty glad to see you back, Mr. Dodwich. Are you going to try your luck at the wheel again?"

"Not at the wheel," Larry grinned at him mirthlessly. "Come out from behind that desk, Myerson!"

"Huh? Er—I don't get you, Mr. Dodwich. You're talkin' funny. What's wrong?" Myerson steadied as he talked fast. "If anything's wrong, tell me," he urged with smooth cordiality. "We want our patrons to be satisfied, Mr. Dodwich. If there's any mistakes, and dissatisfaction we want to know about it. We'll make it right. The customer's always right at the Buccaneer, Mr. Dodwich."

"And a very good rule in business," Larry agreed. "Always right, except when he's wrong, eh? Well, we'll see about that. I've got a complaint to make my friend. Don't reach for any button under the desk! Keep 'em out in plain sight!"

CHAPTER SIX

Terror On The Wire

MYERSON'S thick fingers had strayed imperceptibly to the desk edge and were reaching underneath. The movement stopped at Larry's crisp warning. Myerson's pudgy hands pressed palms down on the desk top.

"I don't get you, Mr. Dodwich. I don't like the way you're talking.

That's no way to come into a businessman's office and act."

"Bad, isn't it?" Larry agreed, moving slowly around the end of the desk, opening the drawer Myerson had reached for and taking a thirty-eight automatic out of it.

Myerson's eyes followed the advance. A glint of fear became visible back in his swinish eyes. He adjusted his collar under the porcine roll of fat that swelled over it. The fingers trembled slightly.

"I'm not a customer," said Larry, moving close to him. "Not the kind you're used to dealing with, Myerson. First, my complaint. I don't like your liquor. Or rather, I don't like the liquor you served me."

Myerson smiled uneasily. "What's the matter with it, Mr. Dodwich? It's the best we could get. Right off the boat. Not even cut, if I do say it. You'd be surprised at the premium we have to pay to get liquor like that."

Larry's left hand shot out, closed hard about the man's fat gross throat. "And you'd be surprised," he said through his teeth, "how dangerous it is to give doped liquor to some of your customers!" He shook Myerson roughly, hurled him back a brace of steps away from the desk drawer. "Especially customers like me! I don't like to be doped, you rat! I didn't think you'd have the nerve to try it, or I'd have watched what I drank more closely."

Myerson gasped, choked, clawed at his throat which bore the angry red prints of Larry's steel-like grip.

"I don't know what you're talkin' about!" he gulped. "I never doped no liquor for you!" In his excitement Myerson lost the suave smooth speech he affected, reverted to type. "You ain't doped now!" he gasped.

"No fault of yours!" Larry rapped at him. "It almost knocked me out.

If I hadn't got rid of what was in my stomach, got plenty of fresh air and a lot of excitement I'd be out cold. Now listen, you fat hog! Listen carefully! You're in trouble! Anything can happen to you! If you want to save your skin, talk——fast and straight! Get me?"

"Wh-what d'you want to know?" Myerson gasped, backing off a step from the cold menace confronting him.

"Who do you take orders from?"

"No one," Myerson denied quickly.

Larry's hand shot out again to Myerson's throat. He drove Myerson gasping and choking back against the wall. His right fist came out of his pocket and smashed into Myerson's purpling face. It was rough, brutal work, but Larry knew this man's type. Myerson's kind understood only one thing—force. He'd never talk otherwise. And he had to talk!

Myerson moaned, wheezed, cringed as Larry's fist doubled again.

"One yip out of you for help and you're a goner!" Larry snarled at him. He relaxed his grip so Myerson could talk.

"Don't hit me again!" Myerson quavered. "My God, don't! You'll pay for this! Damn you! Who are you, anyway?"

Larry stopped his lips with another blow. "I'm the guy who's beating you up," he grated. "And I'm the guy who's going to make a mess out of you if you don't talk! Get it through your thick head I mean business and save yourself a lot of grief!"

"You're not—not Dodwich, the rich young guy from the coast?"

"That's better," Larry approved. "No, I'm not Dodwich. Who do you take orders from?"

"I can't tell you," Myerson whispered, his face a ghastly livid hue. "You're a dick, ain't you?"

"Well?"

"If I told a dick that, it'd be my finish. They'd find me out in the bay tomorrow."

"Like Kingston, the banker?"

Myerson flinched.

"Do you want to cook in the chair for Kingston's murder?"

"I don't know anything about it!" Myerson whispered hoarsely. "You can't pin that on me! I'll take my chances with the law instead of—of—"

"Instead of the men who murdered Kingston?" Larry finished for him. "All right, take your chances with the law —if there's anything left of you for the law to claim after I'm through with you!"

LARRY drew the gun from his pocket and so savage and menacing was his attitude that Myerson cringed, stark terror and sickly cowardice graying his face.

Larry let him stand that way a moment while he hefted the gun in his hand; let the fear of physical injury and pain do what the threat of the law could not in overcoming Myerson's fear of his accomplices. He wouldn't kill Myerson, of course. But he was willing to do anything else. The urgent need for haste was driving him on. If he failed now Mopsy might be killed; Breckridge himself. It was no time for wishy-washy methods. One clue was all he needed—and that clue had to come from Myerson.

"I can't!" Myerson squealed. "I can't!" He was almost sobbing with fright and terror as he wrenched the words out. "They'd knock me off! They'd torture me! Stop! You don't know what they'd do!"

"I don't care what they do!" Larry snapped. "It's what I'm going to do if you don't talk that matters now."

For a moment it looked as if Myerson was going to dissolve in a jellyfish mass of swinish fear. And in that moment the telephone bell rang sharply.

The sound steadied Myerson. A cunning gleam came into his eyes. He straightened. "I'll—I'll answer it," he said, starting toward the desk.

Larry shoved him back against the wall roughly. "I'm the only one you'll answer right now Stay there!"

He took out the gun, backed toward the desk, watching Myerson closely. Lifting the telephone from its cradle he said: "Hello—Myerson's office."

"That you, Myerson?"

"Yeah," said Larry, mouthing the words as Myerson did his.

And Larry stiffened as the voice at the other end said hurriedly: "This is Sammy!"

Myerson was backed against the wall staring with wide-eyed anguish. Larry's eyes narrowed; a cold grin of satisfaction played around his mouth as he said: "Sammy, eh? What luck did you have?"

Myerson started at that name. And Sammy's voice came sharp, excited, disturbed. "We didn't have no luck. For cripes' sake, did you know who you sent us after?"

"No," said Larry.

"There's gonna be hell to pay! That guy wasn't no more a young millionaire from the coast than I'm a duke! He was a dirty dick! We followed 'im out in the country, an' he an' his driver musta got wise. They stopped their car, got out, an' threw the drop on us when we stopped to get 'em. It wound up in a hell of a mess at Breckridge's house. You better jump in the boat an' come over while we get things straightened out."

"Tell me about it."

"Can't over the telephone! Hurry up! Never mind hangin' around there! There may be trouble yet tonight!"

Then a sudden deep call for help came over the wire. A man's voice—followed by the sharp crack of a shot.

And then the connection was abruptly broken . . . .

LARRY jiggled the telephone until central asked: "Number, please?"

"Get me the number I was just talking to!" Larry demanded harshly.

"The party you were talking to has disconnected, sir."

"I know that! Find out what number was talking and its address!"

"I'll connect you with the chief operator," said central impersonally.

It proved to be impossible to trace the call. Larry hung up disgustedly. Myerson stared at him uneasily.

"That was Sammy," Larry said.

Myerson nodded mutely.

"He wants us to take the boat and come over."

"What boat? Over where?" Myerson whined. It was plain that he was lying.

"Do I have to work on you again?" Larry grated. But before Myerson could answer someone tried the door knob, and then knocked sharply.

Larry tensed, eyeing Myerson closely. Had the fellow managed to get a signal out of the room in some way? Or had someone come to the door and overheard them?

"Myerson! What the devil! Open up here!"

Myerson's jaw dropped. He seemed about to cry out something, and the words died in his mouth as Larry made a threatening motion with the gun. A quick step took Larry to the fellow's side. His hand gripped Myerson's collar, jerked him away from the wall, shoved him toward the door.

"Coming," he mouthed.

And he forced Myerson to the door, unlocked it and hauled Myerson back.

The door swung in—was kicked in, would be a better word—and a stranger strode into the room.

Larry was standing behind Myerson; the newcomer didn't see him for a few seconds as he slammed the door and demanded irritably: "What the devil are you locked in here for? How did things come off tonight? Did the boys get...." And then the newcomer made out Larry behind Myerson. His pudgy jaw bit off the last words with a snap. He swore: "Who's that?"

"I'll bet you're going to be paralyzed when you hear," Larry grinned unpleasantly. "Step right over to the desk and make yourself at home, mister. We're having a little family gathering here, and it looks as if you belong in with the family."

The stranger who had addressed Myerson so bruskly through the door was tall, heavy set, powerful of build. There was fat on his frame, but it was not unhealthy fat like Myerson's. His cheekbones were high, his nose large, his mouth thin-lipped and tight. And a pair of the coldest blue eyes Larry had ever seen glared out from under heavy, scraggly blond eyebrows.

No evening clothes for this man. He wore a dark gray sack suit, and there was about him an air of harsh commanding power.

"Who is this man?" the stranger rapped at Myerson.

Myerson cringed from Larry, gurgled in his throat.

"He's not feeling as well as usual," Larry explained. "Permit me, my dear sir. I am one of those strange creatures called detectives. You may have heard of them?"

"Is this true, Myerson?"

Myerson nodded mutely.

"Then why the devil didn't you sing out when I came in?" And to Larry: "What's your name? Where are you assigned from? What are you doing here? By heavens, you've got your hand on Myerson's collar! What's coming off here?" All that in a harsh domineering voice. "I'll have your shield for this!" the stranger went on bruskly. "Take your hand off Myerson's collar and get out!"

"Tut-tut," Larry reproved. "That's no way to talk. I'll have my hand on your collar if I feel like it."

"Why, you—" The stranger's face reddened with furious anger as he bawled out—and then he suddenly shut up and backed away a step as Larry shoved out the gun that had been concealed behind Myerson's body.

"Exactly," said Larry. "Now keep that loud mouth of yours quiet or the same thing may happen to you that happened to Myerson."

"What's that?" the stranger clipped out. "What happened to you, Myerson?"

MYERSON gulped, obviously ashamed to say. Larry spoke for him icily. "He was tamed, my friend. And I'll probably tame you, too. Get over there near the radiator, and if I see a move out of you I don't like, I won't be responsible for what happens. Git."

And so ferocious was Larry's order, backed by a wave of the gun, that the stranger backed hastily across the room to the radiator.

"I'll have your shield for this!" he choked. "You fool, don't you know who I am?"

"No," said Larry with interest. "I was just wondering."

"I'm Joe Sandford!"

"Hmmmm," said Larry. "Joe Sandford, eh? Glad to meet you, Joe. Very glad. In fact you don't know how glad I am, even if I never saw you before."

"Well? Doesn't that mean anything to you? Put up that gun and get out!"

"I'll bet," said Larry, "that you control a lot of votes. One of the big boys behind the scenes, eh?"

"The mayor does what I tell him," Sandford growled. "Now get out!"

"But I'm not the mayor," Larry explained brightly. "I'm not even a city dick. In fact I don't belong in the city departments at all. I haven't any shield you can get, any job you can take, or any damn thing you can do for me. What does a dirty crook like you do when he meets someone like that? Think fast."

Sandford's face was a study. "Who is this fellow? What does he want?" he shot at Myerson.

And Myerson groaned: "I don't know. He come here earlier in the evening with a crowd of table lice, throwing money around like he owned a printin' press, an' posing as a young millionaire from the west coast. The boys told me he had made history at every night-club in town before he wound up here. I—Sammy—er, some of the boys went out after he left. And after while this fellow come back and pulled a gun on me. He accused me of doping his drink and wanted to know who I took my orders from. When I wouldn't talk he got rough. Sammy called up an' he answered the phone an' talked to Sammy for me. And then you come in. He was threatenin' me about the Kingston killing. Said I would burn for it if I didn't talk."

Sandford's harsh strong features set like granite as Myerson talked. His cold blue eyes narrowed under the shaggy blond brows.

"I see," he said slowly. And then evenly to Larry: "Could you use fifty grand cash money tonight?"

"I had all the money I needed tonight," Larry pointed out.

"A hundred grand then to get out of town and stay out! Who are you working for?"

"My, I thought I was the only curious one here tonight," Larry mocked.

"That's a lot of money! I might even go higher! You're a fool to turn down anything like that!"

"I guess I always was a fool and always will be one," Larry sighed.

"Fools," Sandford snapped, "don't last long in this town."

"Warning me—or telling me?"

"Both."

"Big-hearted Joe," Larry murmured. "Now then, Joe, lie down on the floor before I knock you down with this gun."

An oath answered him. But when Larry herded Myerson close to the big man and made plain his intention of carrying out the threat Sandford lowered himself to the floor, sulphurous oaths dripping from his clenched lips.

FLAT on his stomach, hands behind his back, Larry prodded him, and then ordered Myerson, who seemed about to faint at the idea of Sandford getting such rough treatment, to take down two large oil paintings that hung on the walls.

A few prods with the gun muzzle hurried Myerson in stripping off the picture wire and hogtying Sandford, wrists and ankles, drawn up near each other in back so the man could hardly move. From a small washroom opening off the office Larry got towels to gag the raging politician.

"Pretty rough," he sympathized at the last. "But you've probably done a lot worse, Joe. Now park yourself here in the dust while Myerson and I take a little stroll."

"Where we going?" Myerson faltered.

"Out," said Larry. "And if I catch you making sheep's eyes at any of your payroll as we go through it's going to be a sad, sad story. Come on. Keep close; keep quiet; and keep moving!"

He herded Myerson out of the office, set the spring lock and closed the door. Side by side they walked into the stale cigarette smoke, liquor-tainted, perfumed atmosphere of the big room.

Larry was grinning broadly, chatting amiably under his breath, saying *sotto voce*: "Watch your step. Eyes front. Act like you like it." And his hand was on the gun in his pocket, the muzzle only a few inches from Myerson's body.

An overdressed, over-rouged girl called a greeting to Myerson, received a blank nod. And the next moment Larry's muscles tightened. Rising from a table across the room was Tilson, who had doped Larry's drink.

Tilson's squarish face was a study in amazement, consternation, bafflement. He seemed about to come toward them, but hesitated. It was plain he was stunned at seeing his victim back here in the Buccaneer, walking with Myerson. Stunned, apprehensive, not certain what to do.

And while he hesitated, Larry and Myerson walked past the head waiter, through the tunnel-like passage into the dim cavernous depths of the dock shed. "Now the boat!" Larry gritted at Myerson. "Sandford can't help you; Tilson can't. The first one of your men who comes at me brings trouble for you."

Silently Myerson stumbled to the right, where some twenty feet of end space was partitioned off by a heavy wooden wall. A single door with a stout lock gave access to the other side. Myerson fumbled out a key. His fingers were trembling, the key wobbled all around the keyhole before it slipped in.

And in that moment Larry froze as a triumphant voice rasped from the nearest automobile: "What's the hurry?"

It was Ben Evans, the lantern-jawed reporter.

CHAPTER SEVEN

The Shadow on the Blind

LARRY pushed Myerson through the doorway, stood by him silently as Evans confronted them.

"Two old buddies, eh?" Evans commented sarcastically.

Larry had to grin at that. "We're as close as twins right now," he replied.

Ben Evans felt his jaw tenderly. "That was a dirty slam you gave me," he rebuked.

"Sorry," Larry apologized. "I hated to do it. But I needed a little peace for a few minutes and you wouldn't listen to reason."

"Yeah, I know that kind of reason. I've got a deaf ear on that side. So you're in with Myerson? I often thought he was a little sour, but I never figured he went in for murder."

"How did you get here so quick?" Larry queried curiously.

"A hunch," said Ben Evans curtly. "I was out of Breckridge's house quicker than you thought I'd be. Saw you turn south out of the yard and followed. Couldn't catch up, but you were heading toward this part of town so I cruised along. Recognized the car parked out there at the curb as the one you lammed in. Pretty plain you must be around the Buccaneer, so I eased in and kept my eyes open. Now do we go back?"

"We do—like thunder!" Larry slipped the gun from his pocket. "Step in friend—the water's fine."

"Gun work on me, too, eh? All right, see where it gets you, wise guy.

Before I crashed in here I telephoned the office. Told 'em what happened at Breckridge's, and said I was going to the Buccaneer—after you. And if I didn't phone back in thirty minutes to send a squad of cops around."

Larry chuckled. "Fine. The quicker they get here the better. We'll all three be gone. Myerson is going to take us on a sightseeing tour. I promised you a big story, Evans. You're going to get it. We're calling on the gang that's been doing all this kidnaping lately. Myerson's hooked up with them. But he's small potatoes. I just left his boss inside, tied and gagged. Perhaps you know the gentleman. Joe Sandford."

Ben Evans' eyes widened; he stared incredulously; his cynical air vanished. "Joe Sandford? That's a hot one!"

"It probably will be when it breaks."

"Say, feller, I don't make you out. What's the idea? You're no powder puff from the coast."

"No," said Larry. "Private dick from the coast. Brought here to do a little gumshoe work. Open expense account. Sky the limit. And laddie, we're hitting the sky. I don't know this Sandford, but he sounds like a hot one to me."

"Hot," said Evans reverently. "He's sizzling dynamite. Joe Sandford is the big hush-hush behind this village. The club that smacks the boys who won't stay in line. There'll be a blow-off that'll scatter wise guys from here to forty states. Let's go in and have a look at this trussed turkey. Seeing is believing with me."

"You believe—but you don't see right now," Larry said curtly. "D'you think I'm fool enough to go back in that den of meat eaters when I've got my hands on their fat bone? Nix! We're this far and we keep going. Do you come peaceable, or do I have to get rough again?"

"I always was a sucker," Ben Evans sighed. "Lead on, big dick."

"Good boy," said Larry, punching a light switch inside the door, and closing the door with his foot. "Here, you may need this." He gave the reporter the thirty-eight automatic he had taken out of Myerson's drawer.

"This goes further with me than a dozen affidavits," Ben Evans grinned as he hefted the weapon. "If you're willing to pass me artillery I guess you're shootin' straight. That is . . . ." He slipped out the clip, made sure its was loaded. "Yep, I believe you now." he finished.

THERE was a hinged bar inside the door. Larry dropped it in place— and none too soon. There was rush of feet outside, a hand laid hold of the door violently; an oath ripped out when the door would not open.

"Hey, Meyerson!"

And when there was no answer a voice rasped: "Go find a key to this lock! There's something funny about this!"

Boxes, barrels, chairs, tables and odds and ends crowded in the space. Cringing as Larry threatened him, Myerson stepped over to a trap door, raised it, descended damp slippery steps into blackness.

Little wavelets lapped softly against a forest of creosoted piles down there. Light through the opening overhead glinted against black uneasy water, made visible a long speedy motor boat moored at the foot of the steps.

The boat rocked as Myerson stepped into it and Larry followed him.

"I can't run this," Myerson disclaimed sullenly, but a gun in the side changed his mind.

Larry untied the mooring rope. A starter whirred; a powerful motor housed amidships roared hollowly. Water roiled at the stern and the boat backed slowly out into the open night.

They had been heard, seen. A shout came from the end of the dock, a warning to stop. The long speedy craft swept around in a sharp circle and headed out into the bay, sheeting spray as it gathered speed.

Myerson handled it skillfully enough. He must have been certain of his route and destination or he would never have dared to drive the craft with such speed through the white pall which had settled over the harbor. The fog was so thick it seemed a tangible thing—an entity which might be clutched and held but notwithstanding this they were soon far out in the bay, the ring of lights around the shore fading quickly into the night. And as the cool wind rushed against his face and drops of water spattered on him, Larry wondered what they were going to find ahead.

What had that call over the telephone wire meant? And the following shot? Someone killed? And if there was killing going on might it not have been Mopsy, for instance?

A searchlight on the bow poured a path of silver light into the mist ahead. Myerson was heading for the south shore of the bay, where desolate, lonely South Point formed a barrier to the sweeping waves of the open ocean.

As they drew in closer to the land Myerson slackened speed, peered anxiously ahead as if searching for landmarks. Suddenly he twirled the steering wheel and headed straight into shore. When it seemed as if they must surely run aground the searchlight beam poked into the fog-smoked mouth of a small narrow tidal creek, fringed on both sides by a heavy growth of trees.

They entered this creek slowly, the muffled exhaust of the motor sounding loud and hollow in the narrow lonely forest aisle they were traversing. The creek turned sharply a hundred yards inland. From that point on they were cut off from the bay, isolated, alone.

A last turn and the creek abruptly tripled in width, forming a small tree-girt lagoon. On the right bank a low wooden boat house loomed up out over the water with footboards and docking space on each side of it. Myerson spun the boat around, jockeyed it alongside the landing stage and cut the motor.

"Here we are," he said sullenly.

And from the corner of the boat house a voice called suspiciously: "Who in the hell are we?"

A figure stepped into view there, limned indistinctly by the reflection of the searchlight. A drawn revolver glinted threateningly.

LARRY'S gun jabbed hard into Myerson's side in silent warning.

"It's me, Myerson."

"Who's with you?"

"What's the matter?" Larry called roughly. "Why the devil wouldn't Sammy tell more when he called up? What happened before he hung up? Myerson said he heard a shot."

They had clambered out of the boat as they talked, moved toward the speaker, Myerson walking ahead. The fellow peered at them. There was more light on his face than on theirs. Larry recognized the long thin bony-faced man whom he had left prisoner with Mopsy. And as he stepped in close the other recognized him.

"Say, what the hell! Myerson, where'd this guy come from?"

Larry hurled Myerson into him, driving them both back against the side of the dock shed. His drawn automatic whistled past Myerson's head and smashed the skull of the cursing victim.

"Don't shoot!" Myerson squealed.

There was a moment's tangle of bodies as the bony-faced one fell against Myerson, tripping him. Myerson scrambled free and the body slid down heavily. Larry dropped to a knee and fumbled for the revolver. And as he did that Myerson fled around the corner of the dock shed.

Trees, bushes grew down to the end of the boat house, and a path led through them. They could hear Myerson running up that path, then crashing into the bushes off to one side. Larry followed him in the undergrowth a few moments later, but stopped after a few steps. Myerson had stopped also, was probably creeping away silently. To ferret him out of that maze of undergrowth in the murky darkness would take more time than they had to spare. Larry snapped to Ben Evans, behind him: "Quick! Up the path! See where it leads to!"

The path wound upward, debouching suddenly into a clearing. Panting from the run they stopped there. A huge rambling frame house and several outbuildings sprawled in the clearing, gloomy, sinister, forbidding.

Lights were visible behind shuttered windows. Deep silence gripped everything. A cool wind off the sea rustled eerily through the tree tops behind them.

There were no more challenges. The one guard down at the boat house seemed all that had been posted.

They paused beside an outbuilding. Larry's shoulder brushed against a ladder hanging on cleats there. He touched Evans' arm, whispered: "Grab one end of this."

Evans caught on instantly. They lifted the ladder down, approached the house stealthily. A wide veranda ran around two sides of it.

Quietly they placed the ladder against the porch roof. Larry mounted, Evans at his heels. Weather-warped shingles on the roof creaked softly under their weight. A thin ribbon of light seeped over the shingles from a curtained window. Down on the driveway in front three cars were parked.

A door in the porch beneath them opened. Steps walked out, crunched on gravel. One of the car doors opened, closed. The steps crunched back to the porch, paused a moment as the man stood silent, finally reentering the house. Larry crept to the lighted window.

MUFFLED voices were speaking inside. There were two of them apparently—one a deep growling snarl, the other the lighter tone of a girl's voice, excited, fearful. Then there was the sound of sudden movement behind the blind as though a scuffle were in progress and then deathly silence.

Larry tried the window. It was locked. As they crouched there undecided what to do, the shade suddenly flew up with a bang. At what he saw, the hairs on the back of his neck prickled and he stopped breathing for there limned against the yellow glow of the lamplight, hideous, silent pantomine was being played.

Squat, grotesque, horrible, leering behind a dead white mask of a face, Larry saw the figure of a man. And this bestial creature had his great hands about a woman's throat. Her body was bent backward at a torturous angle and her long hair streamed down nearly to the floor. Through the eery half light Larry could see her fear-crazed eyes roll back in their sockets. As the monster, intent on his murderous task, swung his victim away from the window Larry caught a glimpse of her profile and gave a startled gasp of horror to recognize Elise Marrow.

As Larry raised his revolver to fire

through the pane the creature suddenly turned his head and gave a quick glance through the window. A look of maniacal hatred crossed its features as he spied Larry crouching outside. With a low growl he flung the girl's body between himself and Larry who dared not fire for fear of hitting her. Ben Evans, rushed forward to smash the glass but before he could reach the window the man inside dropped the limp form of the girl and ran quickly from the room.

Evans shattered the glass with the butt of his gun and Larry eeled into the room with the reporter close behind him.

"We'll have the whole pack down on us now," the reporter said as Larry bent over the girl. "That breaking glass made enough noise to wake the dead."

Larry was vigorously chafing Elise Marrow's wrists. Color began to flood back into her pallid cheeks under these ministrations and finally she opened her eyes, was able to sit up.

She gulped uneasily. "Who are you? Where did you come from?" And, peering into his face: "You're Mr. Dodwich, aren't you?"

"I am," said Larry grimly. "Who's in the house here? Hurry. They'll be up on us any minute."

"I d-don't know."

"Don't lie to me! Who was that man who tried to choke you? He's the same one who tried to do for me at the Breckridge house."

"I'm not lying. You f-frightened me. He's one of the mob, I think. Everything is so mixed up—"

"Tell me another one," Larry rasped sarcastically. "You got by with a good piece of acting at Breckridge's house. It won't go here. Understand?"

In the thin moonlight her face shone pale and drawn, like a frozen cameo. "I'm not acting! I wasn't acting! Did it look like I was acting when you came through the window. *Ugh!*"

Ben Evans touched Larry's shoulder. "What's that?" he whispered.

It was a muted groan; followed by a muttered oath, coming through the wall from the adjoining room.

"Who's in there?" Larry asked.

"I don't know. I—I heard him a while ago."

Larry struck a match, saw they were in a bedroom. A connecting door was set in the wall. The match went out. He moved to the door, tried it, found it locked.

"Watch her," said Larry briefly to to Ben Evans, and moved to the door in the adjoining wall. It opened. He looked out into a long lighted hall, empty, silent. He slipped to the next door, tried it, found it locked also. And as he stood undecided what to do he heard someone coming upstairs.

A swift rush on tiptoe carried Larry to the stairs. He waited, flattened against the wall. A sleek young man, spare, hard, sophisticated, mounted into the hall and turned toward him. He saw Larry, stopped abruptly—opened his mouth to cry out. And Larry's fist drove the words back in his throat.

At the same moment a door was wrenched open below. Myerson's shrill frightened voice echoed through the house.

"Sammy! Boys! Quick! Come here! There's a dick upstairs! I saw him use a ladder and get up over the porch roof"

Larry barely got that as he swarmed after the reeling young man, grabbing him by the throat and shoving his gun hard in the victim's stomach. But he had tackled a wildcat this time. The other's hand had slipped in his coat pocket as he staggered back.

A muffled shot exploded close to Larry's body. He felt the hot surge of gases as the bullet just missed him. Dodging aside he struck up with his gun barrel; hard against the side of the stranger's smooth-shaven jaw.

The fellow dropped.

CHAPTER EIGHT

The Fight On the Stairs

IN the sudden silence that fell, a voice shouted downstairs: "Leon, what's wrong up there?"

Myerson stuttered: "I'll bet it's them! Dodwich is a dick! He's here with a reporter! Made me bring them here! I got away down at the boat house! They'l bust everything wide open if you don't get 'em!"

Steps rushed up the stairs. Larry saw the swart compact figure of Sammy through the stair banisters. He threw a shot down at it. Sammy tumbled back out of sight.

"Stay down there where it's healthy!" Larry called.

But he realized the odds against them. They didn't have much ammunition. Even if they could hold the others off for a time, there wasn't any way they could escape.

Ben Evans had rushed out of the bedroom at the shot. Larry dragged his unconscious victim out of the line of fire from below and snapped at Evans: "Shoot the first one who tries to get up here!"

And he dropped to his knees by the limp form and went through the pockets hurriedly. An automatic and an extra clip of cartridges was the first thing he got. They'd come in handy. Money, cigarettes, a pocket lighter and keys.

Larry jumped to the locked door with those keys. He tried the first one that looked as if it might fit the lock—without success. The next one did the trick. The door opened in.

Another bedroom. And bound on the bed was Mopsy. Coat off, shoulder of his shirt red and stiff with blood, hair tousled, face bruised, Mopsy was not a pretty sight. But there was life in him.

"I had a hunch they hadn't croaked you like they told me they had!" Mopsy exploded. "Get me loose an' gimme a gat! I want to start in on that gang of gorillas down there! No lousy crowd of body snatchers can rough me like they did an' get away with it!!"

"Some of them have had a little roughing tonight themselves," Larry told Mopsy as he stripped the cords away and helped him to his feet. "They've got us cornered, Mopsy. Here's a gat I took off that fellow out in the hall. What's the matter with your shoulder?"

"Winged me a while ago," Mopsy snapped. "We was down in the hall when one of them called up a buddy an' told him to get around here. I grabbed the phone from him to yell for help. One of them tried to drop me an' only got my shoulder."

Mopsy was already at the door as he finished speaking. And as he and Larry crowded out into the hall a fusillade of shots roared and barked from the bottom of the stairs.

"Don't shoot back!" Larry yelled at Ben Evans. "Let 'em waste their ammunition! Keep back from the stairs. If they try a rush up, get a man every time you shoot!"

Elise Marrow had stepped out in the hall, was standing stiffly by the door.

"Get back in there!" Larry ordered harshly. "Stay out of this! I'll attend to you later!"

She disappeared in the room.

Larry, Mopsy and Ben Evans flattened themselves against the walls, watching the head of the stairs as the barrage of shots continued.

A door panel down the hall splintered out as blows rained on it from inside. The whole door gave way. A head and shoulders thrust out and glanced cautiously toward them. Larry aimed his gun. Ben Evans took one look and slapped the arm down. "Watch out! That's Richards, the missing banker!" he bawled.

"Holy smoke!" Larry breathed, lowering the gun.

RICHARDS recognized Ben Evans, crawled through the wrecked door, and came toward them. He was a well-fleshed, spare, middle-aged man, haggard and disheveled now.

"I thought those shots meant help of some kind!" he gasped as he staggered upright among them. "Are the police here? Is everything all right?"

"Everything is not all right," Larry told him. "It looks like we're going to be laced up with lead before we're through."

Richards gulped. "Got a gun?" he asked.

Larry had to shake his head at that. There was a window in the end of the hall. Glass splintered from a shot outside. Another shot fanned the air on Larry's head.

"Get down!" he shouted, and jumped for the light bulb overhead. A swipe of his gun, a dull *pop* that was drowned by the roar of a third shot, plunged the hall into blackness. And as Larry dropped to the floor he pumped two shots at the shattered window. No more shots answered him.

"Watch those stairs and the window," Larry cautioned, and scrambled for the door into Elise Marrow's room.

A piercing scream inside met him as he got to the door. Larry shouldered in—and caught his breath at what he saw. A silent shadowy figure was just coming in through the open window.

For a moment the wan moonlight outlined it plainly; the hideous creature who had tried to choke Elise Marrow once before.

That one scream from Elise Marrow was the only sound she made. The figure at the window sensed or saw Larry almost as soon as Larry saw him. A streak of flame stabbed the blackness. Lead smashed splinters from the door jamb at Larry's shoulder. He dropped, his gun leaping and roaring in his hand.

The target against the moonlight was perfect. The squat, white-faced figure toppled forward and crashed heavily to the floor. Harsh gasping breaths rasped in the throat as Larry sprang toward it. Legs kicked into the floor. He dimly saw an arm trying to raise a gun and aim it. He stepped on the wrist, already growing lax.

He looked out the window. The porch roof was clear. But in the thin moonlight surrounding the house he saw four figures running from the trees.

It looked bad—bad. There wasn't much chance that any of them would ever get away alive. The hall was quiet. The firing had stopped below.

"What d'you think they're up to now?" Ben Evans whispered loudly.

"Trying out something new," Larry guessed. "Watch out for it, boys."

They didn't have long to wait. Another fusillade of shots spat and hummed up the stairway. And a moment later shots began to pour through the window at the end of the hall.

A death hail of lead was sweeping the hall; more coming as their assailants closed in from every side. Only the fact that they were flat on the floor saved the four of them from being mowed down at once. The shots on the stairs sounded nearer as the gunmen came up step by step.

Larry crawled nearer the stairs. "Wait till you can see 'em, boys!" he urged quietly. "We might as well do as much damage as possible before they get us."

He set himself, looked down toward the stair landing. The lights had been turned out below. But licking spurts of flame marked the guns that were throwing lead up. Larry aimed carefully, shot once—heard steps stumble down.

In the pitch blackness of the upper hall a gun spoke near the end window. Mopsy's voice rose in a shout of jubilation. "I got 'im!"

Without warning loud shouts sounded outside in the night. Guns barked out there too. A voice bawled hoarsely downstairs: "The cops!"

The blizzard of fire stopped as suddenly as it had started. Feet trampled down the stairs, rushed outside. Shots sounded out there. More shouts.

Larry slipped down warily, fearing a trap. No one disputed his way.

"Come out before we come in and get you!" a gruff voice ordered from the front steps. "The house is surrounded!"

"Who by?" Larry called.

"The police!"

"Walk right in and make yourselves at home!" Larry yelled. "But have on a uniform. No tricks."

IT was five minutes later. The lights had been turned on. The lower hall was crowded with bluecoats and sullen prisoners. Ben Evans was explaining things to the officer in charge, Lieutenant Black.

And Black explained their presence.

"Headquarters got a call from your paper, Evans, to send a squad to the Buccaneer for you. Said it tied up with the trouble at Gerard Breckridge's house. Before they could leave the chief operator at the telephone company called in and said one of their operators had plugged a call from this number to the Buccaneer. The operator heard a call for help, a shot, and then the line went dead at this end. Two squads went out—one to the Buccaneer and one here. It sounded like a battle when we drove up, so we spread out and surrounded the house. There were some fellows up on the roof and some inside. Guess we got 'em all."

"I'll say you did," Ben Evans chortled, staring at the prisoners. For among them were Sandford and Tilson, who had evidently come on the scene near the last.

"Who are you?" Black asked Larry gruffly.

"Private detective from San Francisco," Larry told him. "Gerard Breckridge had me come here to see what I could do about these kidnapings."

Larry explained briefly how he had masqueraded as a rich young man from out of town, how he had been followed, and what had happened to him at the Breckridge home. "I don't know what happened there," he confessed. "The girl must have been mixed up in it some way. Mopsy, what happened to you?"

"I was sittin' there holding a gat on the fellows in the back of the car when some louse popped up an' threw a gat on me," Mopsy grunted. "Don't know where he come from or who he was. They knocked me out, piled me in the back an' brought me here."

"Gerard Breckridge is gone," Ben Evans said sharply.

"I know that," Black retorted.

"Is someone speaking about me?" a voice asked at the top of the stairs.

There had been no time to search up there. Larry gaped as he saw Gerard

Breckridge walking down the stairs with Elise Marrow. Breckridge was disheveled, pale, but his curt manner and commanding air was still with him.

"Where did you come from, Mr. Breckridge?" Ben Evans gasped.

"From the room where I was confined," Breckridge answered curtly. "I was kidnaped and so was Elise. One of her abductors was that horrible-looking creature lying upstairs. He's a half-witted monster who escaped from an asylum and has been living here with the mob. He has the mentality of a child and they used him as a tool because of his immense strength and willingness to do their bidding. Elise has just been telling me some of her horrible experiences with him. She says that she came home from a visit to a night-club where some men were trying to blackmail her over an incident of her past. The servants were out and the house was quiet and deserted. She was coming down to get a book when some-one came to the front door. She answered it, and the visitor saw blood on the floor. When he stepped into the drawing room to investigate the blood stains he was knocked down by a man standing in there. And the same man leaped out and seized her. She fainted, and came to here."

BRECKRIDGE squared his shoulders, said harshly: "It was plainly part of a plot to get me. For when I came home a few minutes later with my two guards we were surprised in the front hall by three men. My guards pulled their guns and there was shooting. One of them was killed, I think. And I was seized and brought here. It is an infamous business, gentlemen. Sandford, what are you doing here?"

"He's one of them," Larry said cooly. "The brains back of everything, I think we'll find. He probably saw a

chance to make easy money and played his cards to the limit."

And suddenly every confused fact became clear to Larry. He saw Sandford's men taking possession of Breckridge's house either before or after the girl got there, knocking out the butler and waiting for Breckridge. Larry and Mopsy had blundered on the scene and suffered for it. That young man who had staggered out into the hall was Breckridge's wounded guard.

Gerard Breckridge looked at Larry levelly. "I seem to have guessed right when I sent for you," he commented, and that was the nearest to praise Larry ever heard from him. Breckridge did add: "I'll see that your work tonight is appreciated."

Myerson suddenly got nerve enough to threaten Breckridge and the girl who stood beside him. "Maybe you'll see a lot of things when you and that girl get in court. The jury will be interested to know about her.'"

"This young woman is the wife of my dead son," Breckridge told him coldly. "I am not a fool. I had her investigated when they were married. I know her past, although she never knew it before. I'll tell her and any black-hearted blackmailers who try to capitalize on her past, that the girl she is today is all I am interested in. And I'll use every resource in my power to fight back at any one who tries to cause her trouble. Do you understand?"

Myerson muttered something and fell silent.

And Larry stepped to Elise Marrow's side as Lieutenant Black's crisp orders sent some of the men upstairs and others to taking prisoners out.

"I'm sorry," Larry apologized to her. "I didn't know, it looked bad."

Elise Marrow gave him her hand— and Larry took it gladly.

The Sixth Bullet

A Vee Brown Story

by

Carrol John Daly

Author of "The Crime Machine," etc.

It should have followed the other five into Aaron Greenburg's back—that mysterious final bullet—but the murderer's hand wavered. Now his own death warrant was written on the wall for Vee Brown to read in letters of flame.

Plainly I saw the tiny hole, then his body lurched slightly and he pitched forward on the desk.

IN answer to the telephone call from the district attorney's office I reached the dilapidated warehouse before the body was removed.

By the litter of cans, between the broken sections of wooden fence, and through the police cordon that completely surrounded the block I entered the building and stood at the foot of the narrow flight of stairs. Plainclothesmen and uniformed officers formed a semicircle. Some were whispering—an inspector called loudly—a great yellow light illuminated the stairs. A man back of a camera was snapping pictures. And in the center of that group was the sprawled body of a dead man.

He lay on his back, his head and shoulders on the rough, wooden, uncarpeted floor of the hall. One hand was stretched out above his head, the other folded grotesquely beneath him. The lower portion of his body was upon the dirty, smeared and dust-laden steps of the stairs, a leg caught between the uprights in the banister. He had been shot five times in the middle of his back, the gun pressed close against his spine.

"Stand away, buddy." A huge harness bull thrust me roughly back as I pushed between men, seeing for a moment those open, sightless, staring eyes, those twisted, distorted lips.

Then a hand upon my arm, a soft low voice in my ear, and I was dragged away from the gruesome scene by Detective Vee Brown—killer of criminals—whose cases I had been covering for The Morning Globe.

"It's Aaron Greenburg," Vee Brown whispered, as he pulled me down the hall. And in answer to my exclamation, "Certainly. The best, or worst-known figure in the city's night life. Gambler, fixer, friend and buyer of political influence. Super-racketeer, if one had to write an epitaph, Dean, it

would be simply—*Here Lies Aaron Greenburg. He Had It Coming To Him.* But one thing interests me greatly. Aaron Greenburg was shot five times in the back. Now—why five times, when one bullet—or possibly two—would have turned the trick?"

"Wanted to make sure, I suppose."

"Exactly," nodded Vee Brown. "But why not six then? Why not the final bullet that remained in the murderer's gun? I'm quite sure that further investigation will reveal that the bullets were fired from a six-shooter. Now I hazard the guess, Dean, that the murderer intended to empty his gun—and did empty it. Look here." Vee Brown darted the pencil of light from his tiny flash suddenly upon the dirty, plastered wall. "Now, don't tell me that hole looks like the work of a knife—for I took the trouble to dig the bullet out of that wall less than five minutes ago."

"What a break!" I half gasped.

"Yes, there are breaks for the detective of fact as well as for the detective of fiction. But not this time. You see, I was looking for the bullet." He juggled a bit of lead between his fingers a moment, then dropped it back in his pocket. "This, I guess, is the sixth bullet." And turning toward the stairs, "It very easily might have been fired from where the murderer stood and would enter the wall at about this place." He indicated again the hole in the wall.

"But why—why would he fire there?" I wanted to know.

VEE BROWN looked up at the small gas jet; looked over at the arc light above the stairs, then moving slightly, pointed out his shadow.

"The yellow light for the pictures obscures it greatly now, but before—in the semidarkness—a figure passing by this gas jet would throw a shadow about

—maybe, between the back of the murdered Greenburg and the eyes of his murderer. It was at the figure who cast that shadow that the murderer turned and fired. And as the figure was probably small—about my size, and not yours—the sixth bullet in the murderer's gun planted itself above his head in the wall.

"So—the police must find that witness—that shadow."

"Not the police. I work alone."

"Then you alone will be interested in finding that shadow—that witness of the crime."

"Not exactly." Vee Brown showed his teeth in a smile, but his black eyes flashed. "Not me alone. Remember —the murderer will be interested in finding the owner of that shadow, and I will be interested in finding the one interested in that shadow. A little involved in expression, perhaps, Dean, but crystal clear in point of action." His teeth closed with a snap and he dragged me from the building.

Through another narrow alley, and we entered the rear door of the building facing on the next street.

"The Blue Blood Club," Vee Brown explained to me as we pushed through a little knot of frightened waiters and an entertainer or two, who were huddled together in the hallway talking in whispers as the police questioned them.

The piano banged out a few chords; a feminine voice shattered the bushed uncertainty, and Vee Brown and I stood in the doorway to the dining room. It was scarcely nine o'clock and few people occupied the tables.

The singer was pretty, with a cold more than a sinister sort of beauty. But there was a hardness to her lips and a lack of warmth to her eyes which did not fit at all the sentiment of her tune —a soft, crooning melody of mother love.

Vee Brown's sharp eyes studied her. "She can't sing, you think, Dean. Well, maybe not—and certainly not the piece she's tearing the heart out of. I know, because I wrote it myself."

"Are you interested in the girl?" I asked him.

"Not until this moment." Vee Brown twisted his lips into that little crooked smile. "And more in a business than in a—shall we say a vulgar way. Her name is Grace Gay and I think I'd like to talk to her. She doesn't seem sufficiently sad for the occasion. You see Aaron Greenburg was very fond of her."

"She loved him."

"I didn't say that. I said that Aaron Greenburg was very fond of her. There is a vast difference between the two."

"Maybe she doesn't know."

"Doesn't know?" Brown's eyebrows shot up. "She's of the night, Dean. In the racket they always know," and to the owner of The Blue Blood Club, Nick Delanto, who came toward us rubbing moist pudgy hands, "I want to speak to Miss Gay—here in the hall."

A few minutes later, back in the dimly lit hall that led to Delanto's private office we met Grace Gay. Sharp black eyes looked directly at Brown. Red lips were a straight thin line. It wasn't a hard face but decidedly it was not a soft one. There was no weakness in it either—rather a determined, cold, calculating sort of beauty.

"You wanted to speak to me?" she said when Vee Brown made no attempt to speak.

"Yes." Vee Brown jerked up his head suddenly and looked at her. "I thought you should know that Aaron Greenburg is dead."

"Yes," she said slowly. "Why?"

"You did know it then?"

"The waiters are talking about it," she explained without being asked. "Why should you tell me?"

"Because he was very fond of you. And he is dead."

"Lots of men are very fond of me and—and lots of men die."

Brown chuckled audibly but shook his head when she asked in that cold dispassionate voice if he wished to question her further. We watched her slender graceful body turn and pass down the hall.

"Character, ambition and, in a way, something of bitterness that is attractive in her face." Brown nodded after her. Then with a shrug of his narrow shoulders he led me out onto the street, up two blocks, down a third, and into a small side street where an expensive car waited, a Japanese chauffeur behind the wheel.

"I can't take you with me, Dean." Vee Brown pushed me into the rear seat. "But it's the uninteresting usual routine of any detective worth his salt. Aaron Greenburg was quite a lad. It may be hard to find out who shot him, but rather simple to find out one who should have shot him." He gave some quick instruction to his chauffeur, and before closing the door said to me, "Stay at my apartment, Dean. I will want to keep in touch with you and of course you'll keep my secret—" again that crooked smile "—and my shame."

His "secret" and his "shame." Under the single name of Vivian, Vee Brown was a composer of popular song hits, the income from which netted him more in a week than his salary as a first-grade detective assigned to the district attorney's office paid him for a full year. Vee Brown, Killer of Men, he was known to the criminal world.

Vivian, Master of Melody, to tin pan alley.

FIVE days later I was still in Vee Brown's luxurious penthouse atop one of Park Avenue's most pretentious apartments. And all the time the papers used great screaming heads on the Aaron Greenburg murder, and scathing editorials on the inefficiency of the police and the incompetence of the district attorney's office.

Ever since his return that night three days ago, worn and tired, Vee Brown had kept to his studio, paying me an occasional visit in the library and discussing—anything but the sensational murder. Day and night—night and day—at intervals he strummed the piano.

On that fifth day, when he hurried into the library—a sheet of his own composition in his hand, a shine and a sparkle in his eyes as he hummed—I cut in on his enthusiasm. "This dual personality of yours is—"

"No—no, Dean. Perhaps you're right, but I don't like the expression 'dual personality.' It hurts my sense of creative art. If we must have a name for it, then I like to think of my two lives as a 'double emotional identity.' The same thing, you say. But not at all." And when I started in on his promise to the district attorney he ran in on me. "I come and go as I please. It's our agreement. Now—listen to this." And he had me by the arm, pulling me into the music room. He almost leaped upon the stool before the piano and ran his fingers quickly over the keys.

The music was eery, yet with a certain touch of soft, dreamy allurement in it. There was a harshness to the notes, yet a harshness that seemed to hide a rough sort of sentiment. There were words too. Queer, sharp, jerky words that spoke of love and life and passion among the back streets and basements of the city. He got it out with feeling. A low, ominous chant that sent involuntary shivers up and down my spine—to change almost at once to a pitiful appeal to the heart. And then he was up from the stool again, talking rapidly.

"I can write the music, Dean—master the lyric. But I can't play—I never will play. Just make a noise on the damn thing. But don't you see what I'm driving at? The songs today are full of spring and summer, and young love among the flowers in the country. A girl waiting on the farm back home. A moon, low in the Miami sky! But the girls wait in a basement too, and the moon shines down on a back alley. There is love and passion in the underworld—in the heart and soul of crime. What of the gun moll who follows her racketeer, while just around the corner is the shadow of the electric chair? She must have as great an emotion tearing at her heart as the milkmaid who keeps silent, perhaps, while her country lover waters the milk.

"There are the emotions, Dean. Love and hate and greed—and ambition. Does the country girl have a greater love, a greater ambition than the woman of the night? Doesn't ambition draw at the very soul of—"

"Brown," I cut in sharply, "it's five full days since Aaron Greenburg was murdered. You made a promise to the district attorney to deliver the murderer within a week. Now you talk of love and ambition, which have nothing to do with—"

"But they have. Everything to do with it. Your life and mine, Dean, may even rest upon the love of a man and the ambition of a woman."

"You don't think—it was a hired killer!" I wanted to keep Brown on the subject of the murder and away from song writing.

"No!" he said emphatically. "It would take an immense sum to have such a man as Aaron Greenburg put on the spot, and a far greater sum to keep him there. He would have known, as he always knew. The man who killed him was working alone. He was in a position to guard himself against quick and sure retribution the moment Greenburg was dead. He was close enough to Greenburg's activities to take over the leadership in Greenburg's place; close enough to be welcomed as the new super-racketeer by the Greenburg crowd. And he was close enough to Greenburg to meet him alone and shove a gun against his back. He was, therefore, Greenburg's closest friend and associate."

"That would leave only Vincey Maria, Greenburg's right-hand man." I glanced into the other room and at the pile of newspapers I had been reading.

"Exactly," said Vee Brown. "Vincey Maria is our man."

"But he couldn't be. At the time of Greenburg's death Maria had an alibi which—"

"Which I must break down. You have not forgotten the sixth bullet which missed the witness in the hall."

"You have—found the man?"

"It was not a man," he corrected me. "It was a woman."

"And you have arrested her—made her talk?"

Vee Brown smiled. A twisted bit of a crooked grimace. "You don't know life, Dean. Not the life of the underworld. Women of the night don't talk—for threats or abuse. I found the woman by watching Maria. He sought her too."

"Bad business." I shook my head. "While you have been here writing songs the girl's life must have been in constant danger."

"Her life is not in any more danger now than it was the time Vincey Maria missed her in the hall. Maria is a dead shot. Calm and sure of himself in a tight corner—but subject, I am afraid—to his emotions. He could hardly have missed her at that distance, yet he did. He missed, Dean, because he jerked up his gun the moment his finger closed upon the trigger."

"But why?" I gasped.

"Because he recognized the girl—and because he loved her. Love. A peculiar word, as we understand it. Maybe 'desire' is a better word. Maria killed Greenburg because of the girl. Greenburg was in the habit of getting what he wanted. He wanted the girl." Vee Brown shrugged his slender shoulders. "He didn't get her, Dean."

"She loves Maria?"

"Ah! There's the part that human emotions must play in life—and we are back to ambition again. But I have much to do."

And he was gone; back into his studio, slamming the door. And again—the intermittent strum of the piano; the soft humming of his voice; the steady tread of pacing feet.

IN the next two days Brown left me twice for fairly long periods. That last night, when he returned, he threw himself on the couch, waved away my questions and made me read over again the newspaper accounts of the murder, from the very beginning.

He chuckled over the funeral of Greenburg. The twenty-thousand dollar casket, the officials that attended, and the magnificence of the floral piece sent by Vincey Maria. But he seemed most interested in the insignificant item that Vincey Maria, "distressed and saddened by the death of his friend," had left the city for a few days' rest.

"You don't believe that?" I asked him.

"Well—hardly. For, you see, we are to meet Vincey Maria," he glanced toward the clock and suddenly came to his feet, "within the next twenty minutes."

Things were confusion after that, Brown's talk dismissing my eager questions.

"You must carry a gun, of course, and I, too. It must all look natural and aboveboard. A mutual friend arranged the detail of our meeting. Maria does not suspect that I found the witness. And if he did, he would not believe that she would talk. He thinks it guesswork on my part, I suppose. He may suspect a shakedown, or a threat—or perhaps he plans for a one-way ride for us. But he does know that if I do not see him tonight the warrant for his arrest will be issued tomorrow. Not that he's afraid of a warrant, but it would embarrass him greatly at a time when he must keep his fingers on things in the city, if he is to lead the Greenburg outfit. But—come. We must be punctual even in death. By God! Dean, I have no right to take your stake your life, perhaps, on the ambition of a woman."

But just the same I did go along. It was my duty to see Vee Brown in action. As we rode up to Central Park in a taxi he talked incessantly.

"There is something about this girl that is gripping and compelling—and an ambition, Dean, that will make or break her. No love in her cold, sinister, beautiful body? None in her heart or soul now? No room for love, she would tell you. But there is room. She's a woman of ice—but a false, manufactured ice that is simply a barrier to hidden fires. I—" he paused, parted his thin lips. "I have always wanted to talk to someone, Dean, but you must learn to stop me when I become an idiot." He leaned forward suddenly and tapped on the glass. "We get out here. A change of cars."

For perhaps five minutes we stood in the dark on the lonely park road. Then a big sedan drew up, a man stepped out and walked toward us.

"Maria said you wanted to see him." The man spoke to Brown without introduction. "Is this the mug you're bringing along?" He jerked a thumb toward me.

"Yes. If there's any objection he can stay behind."

"No—he can come. It's a 'fix' you want with Maria?"

"I want to talk to Maria," and with that wistful smile that took the sting out of Brown's next words, "not the whole town." But to me he whispered, as we climbed into the car, "He'd rather have you with me, Dean, than have you stay behind and know that I'd gone with him."

THE ride through the park, uptown and over to the Bronx was uneventful. Then the man seated on one of the small seats across from us pulled down all the curtains.

"Maria's got a little private place," he said simply. "No reason for you to remember it."

After the shades came down our speed increased. We must have been well through the Bronx when the car turned down a side street, swerved suddenly to the right, ran a hundred feet or so, and, mounting an abrupt incline, came to a stop.

The driver of the car jumped from the front seat and opened the rear door. The man in the car with us spoke. "I'll have to take your guns," he said, a bit nervously. And in explanation. I thought, "You ain't a man Maria would be likely to over-trust. You've

got a playful way of killing a guy, you know." And when Brown hesitated, he added indifferently—or perhaps in assumed indifference, "There ain't no other way if you want to see Maria."

For a moment longer Brown seemed undecided. Then both his hands flashed beneath his jacket. Our guide jarred erect as Brown held two guns in hands that had been empty only a second before. For a moment there in the darkness I thought I saw fear in the man's face.

"Cripes," he said. "I always heard as how you were death on the draw." And as he took both guns, "The other mug's heeled, of course."

At a word from Brown I handed over my heavy automatic. Then we climbed from the car and stood on the hard, cement floor of a small garage. The driver and our guide searched us, running deft, sure fingers over arms and legs. So thorough was the search that they even found and took a tiny penknife from my vest pocket.

Satisfied, our guide—who was now our guard also—permitted us to drop our hands as he directed us to a flight of steps. At the top he tapped upon a wooden door and called out: "O. K., boss. It's the killer and the other mug."

The door opened. We passed within and the door closed. The single occupant of the room sat behind a flat desk.

"Wait at the foot of the stairs, Tim," he called out. "Don't come up unless I call."

So we faced Vincey Maria, friend and lieutenant of the dead Aaron Greenburg, who aspired to take his place and his girl.

The room was comfortably furnished. A few easy chairs; the long, flat, mahogany desk; a bottle and sev-

those hard set lips—I caught again, as the artist had caught it, the sinister, cold beauty of the girl we had seen in The Blue Blood Club the night of the murder.

Though all this and the other details of that room I took in, it was the man behind the desk who held me from the first. I imagine he wasn't much taller than Vee Brown but he must have weighed a good twenty pounds more. His shoulders were broad and his arms thick. His lips, like Brown's were thin, and now tightly set over a wide mouth. His eyes were steady. Green, beady globes that seemed to look off the end of his sharp, slightly hooked nose. This was Vincey Maria. And the single impression was—that I could very easily believe he would shoot a man in the back. Yes—a friend, five times in the back.

"Sit down." Maria motioned to a couple of chairs across from him and well back from the desk.

AS I passed around the desk I saw the open drawer and the heavy automatic pistol that reposed in it.

"Take the other chair, Dean." eral glasses— and upon the wall a single picture. The portrait of a girl—and with a little gasp, I thought—"The girl." For in that finely chiseled face— Brown moved his chair nearer the wall for me to pass. "There might be a draft from the window and I'm very susceptible to drafts." And in answer to Vincey Maria's invitation, "I only drink for pleasure."

"Good!" Maria poured himself a drink, offered the bottle to me and then drank his liquor raw. He puffed out his chest, blew once, eyed the bottle a moment, then spoke to Brown.

"So this is a business trip, eh? G-o-o-d!" He had a way of drawing that word out. "I'm a man of few

words, in business as well as in pleasure." He showed yellow teeth. "Now —what do you want—and what do I get for giving it to you?"

"I'm afraid," Vee Brown said very slowly, "that you get the electric chair."

"Yeah?" There was the drawl to Maria's voice, but the indifference had gone out of his face and his right hand slipped from the desk and fell to the drawer. "Yeah?" he said again. "What makes you think that?"

"Well—" Brown crossed his legs and edged his chair closer to the wall, "I know that you killed Aaron Greenburg."

"It won't work on that." Vincey Maria smiled. "It would take a fortune to fix every dick who thinks he knows that. You've got to have evidence, you know."

"I can do better than that," Brown said simply. "I've got a witness who saw you kill him. You had two reasons, Maria. You wanted to be the big guy behind the racket—you wanted Aaron Greenburg's job. And you wanted his girl. But that girl doesn't fancy you. She's put the finger on you, Maria. So there'll be no misunderstanding," he jerked a thumb up at the picture, "that's the little sweetheart. Sings under the name of Grace Gay."

"Yeah." Maria grinned and looked at the picture. "That's your story and you're going to stick to it, eh? Well, I know better. You suspected me of course. Every dick on the force did and half the newspapers. You knew I liked the kid and you hounded her and threatened her—and she made the date with you to come here. Because you wanted to talk to me. And I wanted to talk to you too, Vee Brown. I wanted to find out how much you knew and decide if you'd just come—" he leaned forward now "—and not go back."

Vee Brown shrugged his shoulders.

"You won't believe me, Maria, because you don't want to believe me. But you see Grace Gay told me enough to convince even you. I won't go into the details of the shooting of Greenburg. There will be time enough when she goes on the stand. But I'll tell you exactly what you said when you turned on the stairs and sent that sixth bullet crashing into the wall above her head."

"Yeah?" Maria appeared indifferent but there was keen interest in his face.

Brown nodded. "You said 'I knocked him over for you kid—because I wanted you kid. And now I—'"

And that was enough for Maria.

"The lousy, two-timing little tart." He half came to his feet. His lips twisted, quivering above yellow teeth. Then he slipped back in the chair again. "So—she did tell you. She hasn't gone before the district attorney yet?" And before Brown could answer— "No, I'd know if she had." Then he looked toward the phone on the desk.

"No." Brown seemed to eye him indifferently. "She hasn't."

"Then she won't." Maria set his lips grimly. "I should have given her the works there in the hall." He drew the gun from the drawer now and juggled it in his hand. "You've played the fool tonight Vee Brown."

"It's you who're playing the fool now," said Vee Brown calmly. "If you go with me quietly you can get yourself a good lawyer and have a chance to beat the rap. But the girl knows I'm here and the girl's promised to talk if I don't come back."

"The girl won't live to talk." Again Maria's eyes went to the phone. "She told me you just had a hunch and could be fixed. So I decided to fix you in a way you'd stay fixed. I've got a couple of lads in Jersey who'll swear I was with them tonight. Big shots—officials, that a jury will have to listen to—if there is a jury. Tomorrow the district attorney will have the pleasure of finding you in a vacant lot and that punk you brought along will be with you. You didn't think I'd let you cart hardware up here! Or did you? And then to blow the show to me about the girl as if she could protect you!" His gun was out menacingly, swinging from Brown to me. "How long do you think it will take me to silence that dame after—"

"All right." Brown came slowly to his feet but he backed away from the gun—toward the wall. "Call your boys in and do your stuff, if you think—"

"I don't need any boys." Maria shot the words through his teeth. All his false polish of speech and manner was gone. His left hand came up with another gun. "You're not the only one who can do things with rods."

Vee Brown talked quietly on as he stood before the picture.

"So all you got was the portrait of the girl. I knew this was Greenburg's old hide-out as soon as I saw the picture. The story's around that he paid a pile of jack to have that portrait painted. Don't be a fool now, Maria. Put away those guns." And Brown deliberately turned his side to Maria, stretched up a hand and swung the portrait slightly from the wall. "The best you could have hoped for was the portrait. The girl's straight. So the artist caught the thing in her eyes. That's character, Maria—a hidden fire behind that cold face. She feared Greenburg and she feared you, but there's something in her stronger than her fear; something bigger than that fear. It's ambition."

IF Vee Brown didn't see death in Vincey Maria's face I did. And if he didn't believe in Maria's threats, I did. I saw Maria's eyes contract to two sharp points. I saw the finger of his right hand tighten upon the trigger and cried out my warning. But I didn't move then. I couldn't move.

Brown, I think, half turned toward Maria, his hand upon the frame of the picture. There was a spurt of orange-blue flame from Maria's gun; a lurching, twisting jerk to Brown's slender body as he spun around and crashed against the wall. Then another roar and another tongue of flame. But this time the shot had not come from Maria's heavy smoking gun, but from a tiny black snub-nosed automatic that Brown held in his right hand. His left hand hung at his side; there was a small trickle of blood dripping from it.

As for Vincey Maria he still sat in that chair behind the desk, very stiff and very straight. He had been shot almost straight through the center of his forehead. Plainly I saw the tiny hole before his body lurched slightly and he pitched forward on the desk.

Brown lowered his gun, swayed slightly—then walked toward the desk. "He could only give it—not take it. Nerves? Fear? Complex? You can call it what you will. But it's guts. He just didn't have the guts when he faced death himself. It was a surprise to him of course. He didn't know for sure where I got that gun."

"Nor I—nor I."

There was a tap at the door; the anxious voice of the man who had brought us there. "Hey. Everything all right?"

Brown smiled—at least, the corners of his mouth twisted crookedly as he spoke. "Quite right!" he said loudly. "Vincey Maria is dead." Then he raised the gun slowly, aimed it high at the door and pressed the trigger.

There was a sharp intake of breath, hurrying feet on stairs, the roar of a motor, the grind of badly and hurriedly meshed gears—and silence.

"I could have killed Tim too—or perhaps not." Vee Brown looked at the tiny automatic in his hand. "It's not much good unless properly handled." He glanced at the dead body of Vincey Maria. "I wanted him alive, Dean, but I could have only the one shot He was a little more anxious to gun me out than I expected. But things can't always go as we plan them in life—or in death either, for that matter."

But I was across the room, removing his coat, bandaging his arm as best I could with a handkerchief, insisting that he get a doctor—pointing to the phone.

"The phone is useless to us," he said. "We don't know where we are. As for a doctor—that must come later. New business first. We won't be disturbed in leaving and we must reach The Blue Blood Club before twelve o'clock." He consulted his watch.

"The gun—where did you get it?" I asked as we left the garage, turned up a side street and discovered a taxi.

"That, Dean, is our anticlimax. Oh —I know that's a bad line for a writing man. But if drama is holding the mirror up to nature, it must hold it up to all of nature. Anticlimaxes are not of fiction but we must except them in life. Your story should be ended with the death of Vincey Maria. That's our climax. Yes—yes, I'll see a doctor when the last line is written and the curtain falls. Let me rest now!"

HE wouldn't speak to me again as we rode downtown but as we passed beneath the street lamps and the cab was occasionally flashed into a dull light, I could see the pain in his face. But for his paleness and the awkwardness of the way he held his left hand as we entered The Blue Blood Club, there was nothing to tell that he had been wounded. We were hardly in the door when a big man with a shock of gray hair and a grim, hard mouth jumped from a chair and spoke hurriedly to Brown. I knew him of course. It was the district attorney.

"Vincey Maria is dead," I heard Brown start, but the rest was too low for me to catch. Then the head waiter led me to a table in a dark corner.

"The one reserved for you, Mr. Condon," he said.

Two minutes later Vee Brown joined me. "I took the liberty to reserve this in your name, Dean. But hush— we are just on time."

Nick Delanto, owner of The Blue Blood, was standing on the small stage, raising his hand for silence. Then he spoke.

"Boys and girls. The Blue Blood Club is greatly honored. We try to give you the best in entertainment. To-night one of our little singers has been selected by Vivian. Vivian, our unknown song writer, whose hits of the season are too numerous to mention. Vivian has written a song especially for a little girl who has sung to you often. He selected her, of all the city—all the great singers—to present it to his public—and her public, and—" with an exaggerated bow, "my public. I have the honor to present a little lady who will give to you, exclusively, the Master of Melodies' latest composition *Gun Girl's Love.*"

He turned, faced the little side door and clapped his hands enthusiastically. "Grace Gay!" he cried out loudly, as a slim boyish figure ran out on the stage. She was dressed in a pleated gray skirt, gray sweater, and perched on her bobbed jet-black hair— But why go into that? It was the girl we had seen first on the night of the murder. The girl of the portrait in the room above the garage. The girl, because of whom two men had died.

She sang—and the song was the one Vee Brown had given me snatches of those days and nights that he strummed upon the piano. The words were a part of her sinister, beautiful face. The eery music seemed to belong to her lithe young body. There was an abandonment in her wild song of love. But, as Brown had said, it was an anticlimax. As the crowd roared its approval I turned to Brown.

"She was the witness in the hall?"

"Of course!" He nodded, his eyes shining. "We gave Maria quite a break, Dean. Would her ambition be stronger than her fear? Would 'Vivian' be able to put the song over to her. And, lastly, would Vee Brown, the detective, get the tiny gun from behind the portrait—in time?"

"So that's where you got the gun!"

"Exactly," said Vee Brown. "That was the price of the song. The girl put it there." He lifted his arm and winced slightly as he came to his feet. "We'd better see a doctor about this thing. There's a good fellow—just give me your arm."

He staggered a little and I braced him. Yet, despite the pain he was humming softly as we reached the door.

"Anticlimax, did I say?" He paused as the people shouted and clapped, and the girl took bow after bow. "Perhaps not an anticlimax after all, Dean— but a climax. At least, a climax for Vivian, Master of Melodies."

Another *Vee Brown* story coming *Next Month!*

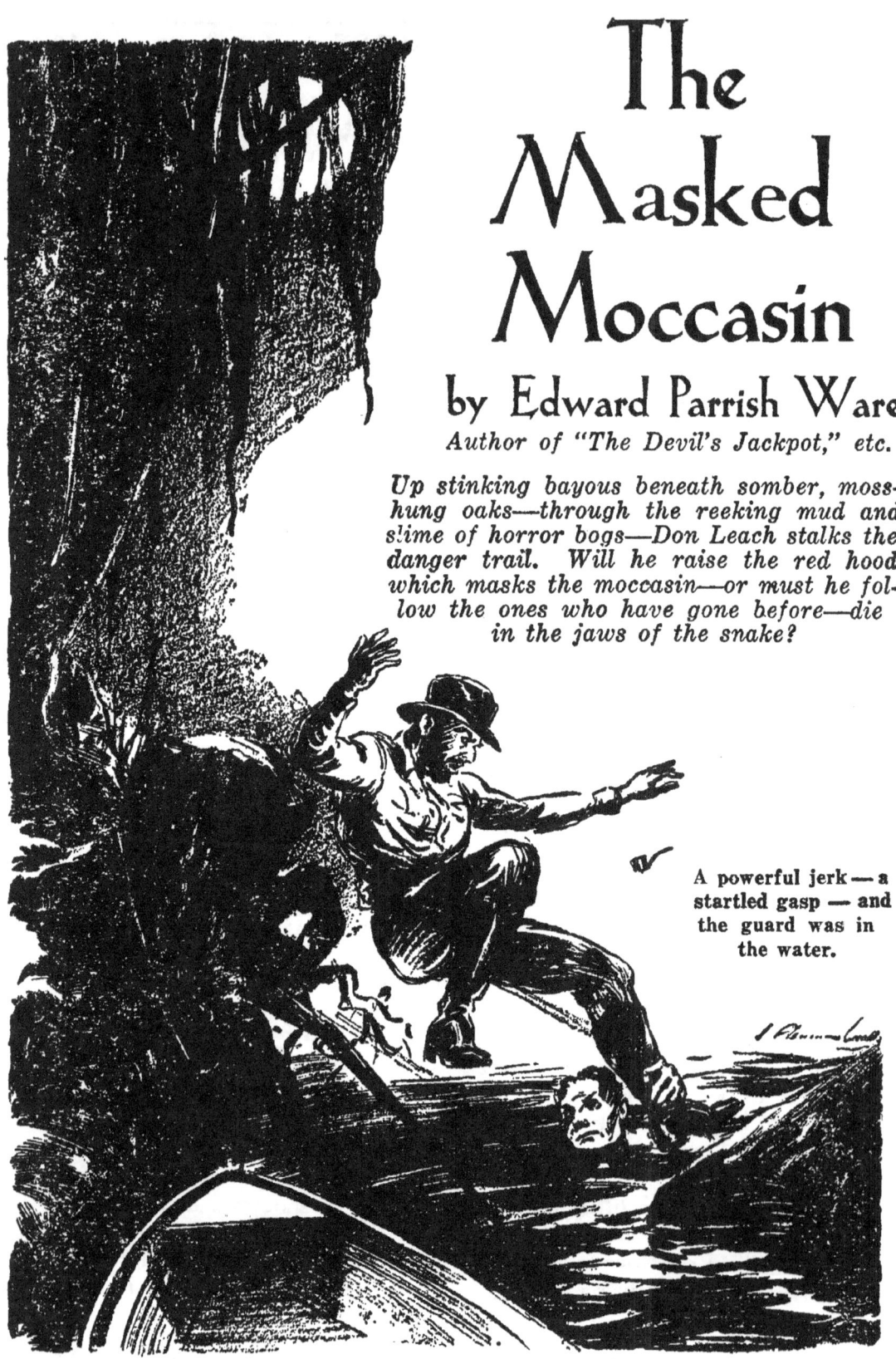

The Masked Moccasin

by Edward Parrish Ware

Author of "The Devil's Jackpot," etc.

Up stinking bayous beneath somber, moss-hung oaks—through the reeking mud and slime of horror bogs—Don Leach stalks the danger trail. Will he raise the red hood which masks the moccasin—or must he follow the ones who have gone before—die in the jaws of the snake?

A powerful jerk — a startled gasp — and the guard was in the water.

CHAPTER ONE

The Snake Wriggles Out

THE judged droned on. "......and there hanged by the neck until you are dead!"

It was a solemn, even ghastly moment. There were only two persons in the crowded Federal court room who did not exhibit some shade of emotional reaction to the dread pronouncement. One was the judge who uttered it. The other was the man whose doom was being sealed.

The look of concern on the swarthy face of Bart Shugrue, condemned outlaw and killer, changed not so much as a shade. The gleam of ironic amusement in his jet eyes, observed and commented upon since the day his trial began, remained the same. His hands did not twitch, nor was there visible movement of a single muscle in his slouchy, powerful body.

Sitting beside him, Cash Hatley presented a vastly different spectacle for the eyes of the morbid among the audience. His lean face was deathly white in spite of his tan, his long fingers intertwined with each other like wriggling worms, and his eyes rolled wildly. His turn came, and the effort required to stand erect at the order seemed to sap the final drop of his strength. He heard only vaguely the sentence of death pronounced upon him, then wilted down into his chair with a hollow groan.

Shugrue turned slowly and gave Hatley, his partner, a look of such contempt that even the trial-hardened judge shuddered with repulsion. Hatley attempted to stiffen his backbone, failed, buried his face in his hands.

"You air a disgrace to Moc'sin Swamp, an' to ever'body thar!" Shugrue spat venomously. "If it had took as much guts fur you to kill as it do fur you to face death, you wouldn't be settin' hyar now. Shame to you, Cash Hatley, fur th' humi'lation you air bringin' on yore folks, yore friends an' neighbors!"

"Gawd, 'Snake'!" Hatley babbled. "They aim to hang us—"

"Silence!" thundered the judge.

Hatley choked, seemed to shrink within himself, and again buried his face from sight. Shugrue turned glittering, defiant eyes toward the bench.

"A jedge kin pernounce, but it takes a hangman to execute," he said with an impudent leer that amazed all those who saw. "When th' hangman gits through with his job, then you kin crow over me—but not ontil!"

"Take them away, Mr. Marshall," the judge, never losing one iota of his dignity, ordered a deputy. "Call the next case!"

Deputy Marshals Spillman and Fellows moved to obey. Spillman snapped handcuffs around the unresisting wrists of Hatley, whose wild eyes seemed unable to focus anywhere except upon the austere face of the judge. As the lock clicked on the cuffs, he started violently, staggering a few steps toward the bench and his voice rose in a shrill screech.

"Don't let 'em hang me, jedge!" he implored. "Tell 'em not to, an' I'll say words in yore years that'll raise th' ha'r on yore haid! I'll tell you th' name of th' man you really oughta hang! Lissen at me, jedge! Will you lissen?"

Shugrue had stood like a man of iron, hands extended in readiness for the bracelets which Fellows thrust toward him. Then, before anything could be done to stop him, the outlaw snatched the heavy cuffs from the deputy, swung them above him and crashed them down upon the head of his fellow murderer. One blow, and he leaped back against the rail, folded his arms, and his face resumed its look of calmness and unconcern.

Cash Hatley slumped to the floor, body quivering convulsively, fingers tearing at the frayed rug beneath him, then, with a gasping groan that sent flocks of spectators scrambling for the outer air, he became still. He had escaped the hangman he dreaded, for the heavy link had cut through into his brain.

In the uproar that followed, Spillman and Fellows leaped upon their prisoner, handcuffed him and hastened him down the winding stairs back of the judge's chambers. Shugrue neither offered them resistance nor showed the least concern over the angry roar of the crowd that, its members seething with rage, poured down the front stairs of the Federal Building and overflowed onto the lawn. A mob bent upon handing out swift justice to him.

Deputy marshals and jail guards, stationed in the vicinity, formed a threatening barrier between the mob and the prisoner, and Spillman and Fellows hurried across the street toward the county jail, Shugrue walking calmly between them. What happened then fully explained his nervy exhibition of unconcern.

A touring car, powerfully engined, moved at a moderate rate down the street, the four men it contained giving no sign that they had more than passing interest in the scene being enacted before their eyes. The car moved more slowly still as it drew near the deputies and their prisoner, and came to a sudden stop directly across their way. Not a word was spoken, but those within hearing heard blasting revolver fire, followed directly by shouts and cries, and the eyewitnesses saw Spillman and Fellows fall dead in their tracks.

Two men leaped from the tonneau of the touring car. One took a bunch of keys from the dead Spillman's pocket and freed the prisoner, while the other menaced the frightened crowd with a pair of sixguns. Freed, Shugrue leaped into the car, and the two men on the ground followed. The engine roared, gears clashed—and the rescue car leaped forward like an arrow shot from a giant bow.

Bart Shugrue, nicknamed "Snake," had been securely caged for three long months, but was caged no longer. With a daring that left every law-abiding man in the country astounded, he had wriggled out!

HENRY WEBBER, United States Marshal for the Eastern District of Arkansas, a section embracing the vast and turbulent L'Anguile Bayou Swamp, threw open the door of his office and, stricken with grief, red-eyed with rage, had nearly reached his desk before he realized that, during his brief absence, someone had entered the room. That someone, a tall, lithe man in hunting togs and boots, was now sitting in a chair tilted against the wall, and puffing contentedly at a nicotine-blackened pipe.

"Leach!!" the marshal exclaimed, his face clearing a bit. "If ever I was glad to see a man, you're the man—and this is the time! When did you arrive?"

Don Leach, former secret-service agent, now at the head of his own detective bureau in St. Louis, was a tall, raw-boned, weather-tanned man of thirty. He had been a government agent at a time when the swamp lands of Arkansas and Louisiana were infested with gangs of counterfeiters that gave the Treasury Department years of intense activity before they were crushed out. As a wilderness man-hunter he had gained undying fame.

"Just got in," he replied, his gray

eyes glinting humorously through a thick screen of pipe smoke. "On a short vacation. I don't know what has happened to put you in such a stew, Hank—but if you haven't got something cooked up for me it will be the first time in three years that you've failed to spoil my vacation. Let's have it. What's doing?"

"Art Spillman and Jess Fellows, both known to you, were shot down in the street about fifteen minutes ago!" Webber exclaimed bitterly. "Four strangers in a motor car rescued Snake Shugrue, just sentenced to death—and the most desperate outlaw in the state is again free and on the prod!"

Leach's lean face hardened a trifle. "Shugrue," he said reflectively, "is the murderer from Moccasin Swamp, I recall."

"Yes," Webber told him. "It was Shugrue and a pal that dynamited the government levee at L'Anguille Point six months ago, when a family of settlers were killed. You've heard about the letter he sent to us right afterward?"

Leach showed his white, even teeth in a reminiscent grin, nodding his head slowly. "It ran something like this, as the papers reported it: 'Moccasin Swamp air full of snakes that air plumb pizenous to gove'mint men, an' I'm th' biggest an' pizenoust one of 'em all.' Hence the nickname—Snake."

Webber turned his chair about abruptly, leaned forward and looked Leach levelly in the eyes, while his face went grim and hard.

"Don," he said earnestly, "the Moccasin Swampers have grown too strong. If they're not stopped they'll get too powerful for us to handle. I want you, as a favor to me and your former associates, to go in after Snake Shugrue. All of my own men are known there. With that scoundrel out of the way for good, maybe we'll have peace in that section. You know the swamp, but it's been a long time since you were there, and it's ten to one nobody will know you now. What do you say, Don? Willing to go?"

"A helluva fine way to spend a vacation," Leach said with a sigh of regret. "But I'll go, of course—provided I'm allowed to work in my own way."

"Work as you wish!" Webber said heartily. "Shugrue now has vastly aggravated reasons for dying in gunsmoke, though, and it's only fair to warn you. He killed Cash Hatley, condemned with him for the levee murders, right there in the court room. Two government men were slain to effect his escape. If he could, by whatever hook or crook, have evaded the noose before, he knows it to be utterly impossible now. He'll be desperate, just as he always has been, only now he will die rather than submit to arrest. You'll need all your cunning, Don, to take him."

"Snake killed his pal, eh?" Leach said, raising his brows in surprise. "What was his idea?"

Webber's face was puzzled. "Something of a mystery there," he said. "Some think it was because Hatley weakened at the last, and Shugrue killed him out of sheer disgust. I don't think so. Hatley, as he was being handcuffed, broke away and cried out to the judge that he would tell him the name of the man who really ought to be hung, if the judge wouldn't let 'em hang him. Meaning himself, of course. Before he could say any more, Snake struck him down."

"The name of the man who should hang," Leach mused aloud. "Sounds as though there is somebody mixed up in the matter who hasn't appeared, eh? Any idea whom he could have meant?"

"Not the least," Webber replied.

"But I think as you do. All along, Don, I have been convinced that Shugrue did not blow up that levee because of the fact that it was built to reclaim a section of the swamp for settlement. I know the swampers are hell on homesteaders, but not to that desperate extent. Shugrue must have had a more obscure motive. I've scented a mysterious influence at work all along, but who or what it is baffles me."

"Maybe something will develop along that line, too," Leach commented. "What has been done about pursuing the bandits?"

"Deputies Brent, Carroll and Staten took up the trail in a fast car," Webber replied. "But there is so little likelihood of the fugitives being overtaken that I have no hopes in that direction. They'll reach the swamp, Don, and there the pursuit will end."

Leach smiled. "Even so, Hank," he said, "snakes leave trails. In the swamp or out of it, wherever one crawls it leaves signs."

"This snake will be hard to capture, though, no matter how easy trailing him may be," Webber declared. "Moccasin Swamp, where he was born and reared, is absolutely baffling to all except those who have learned their way about. You are one of the few outsiders who do know it thoroughly. Even so, Moccasin is thick with his friends and relatives, and an officer of the law is regarded there as fair game for anybody's gun. It's a tough assignment, Don, and your only pay will be my deep appreciation, and that of your old friends."

"That's plenty," Leach said shortly. "I'm going in alone, Hank," he went on, "but will call on you for help if I need it. So keep at least one ear open."

"And where will you try first for the trail, Don?" Webber asked eagerly.

"In Moccasin Swamp, Hank, of course," Leach replied. "That's where Snake will go, and he won't tarry any on the way. So long. I'll see you on the boat."

CHAPTER TWO

The Trail of The Snake

AT one o'clock the following morning, at a point on the river well above Helena, Leach launched a dugout from the lower deck of the Red Bird, a Mississippi River patrol boat, and shoved away through the darkness for the mouth of Moccasin Slough. The Red Bird resumed her journey northward.

At daybreak, he crossed Moccasin Lake and entered Little Moccasin Slough a crooked, lonely stream which runs a course through virgin forest and is the only feasible entrance to Moccasin Swamp. Five miles due south the swamp begins. It is heavily timbered, grown up with rank, water-loving brush, grass and flags, and dotted here and there with mud-banks upon which the cabins of native trappers and hunters stand. It was, at that time, a section shunned by peaceable, law-observing people.

Leach poled his craft down the slough, his objective being Bundy's Settlement, which was located on a bit of high ground at the very door of the vast, bowl-like depression in which the dismal swamp lay. Bundy's was a tough establishment, frequented by the men from Moccasin, as well as by such trappers and hunters as chanced that way. In the native garb he wore, Leach would not arouse suspicion there.

After he had put three miles of slough behind him and was just entering the upper reach of a straight bit of water, he abruptly held his paddle suspended, listened intently for a moment, then shot his boat under cover of a huge growth of water-flags which masked the shore on the left. Making certain that no part of his shell was visible from the stream, he steadied himself by grasping a clump of flags in one hand, and with the other parted the foliage to obtain a view of the slough.

The stroke of a paddle against the gunwale of a boat was what had driven Leach to cover, and presently the boat itself, traveling in the same direction the officer had been going, nosed into view. It was manned by a lank native, and in the bow sat a man in a curiously cramped position. As the boat came abreast Leach saw that the man in the bow was bound with rope, and that a blood-stained cloth bandaged his head.

"Carroll!" he exclaimed under his breath.

He had recognized the wounded man as one of the deputies who had set out from Helena on the trail of the escaped bandit, when a second bateau came into view behind the first. The second boat was manned by a gigantic native whose straight black hair was worn long and shaggy, and whose swarthy, sullen face had a look of ferocity that gave him a curiously animal-like appearance. A ragged scar began at the hair line above his left temple, and ended below the long, prognathous jawbone. It was a face that Leach instantly recognized.

The face of Snake Shugrue, outlaw and murderer.

Directly behind Shugrue another boat trailed. In the bow of the third was another bound man. Leach recognized Cal Brent, a deputy. The man poling the boat was short, heavy-set, and unknown to the officer.

The boats slipped by in silence, leaving Leach with a sense of helplessness abour mon to him. All his plans were

It was He had expected to play a

waiting game there in the swamp, but that was unthinkable now.

"They must have ambushed Staten's car," he told himself, still sitting in his boat among the flags. "There was a fight. Carroll and Brent were captured, and Staten—well, Staten isn't with them. So he's probably dead. So will Carroll and Brent be dead—if I don't move promptly."

But there was the trouble. What could be done for the two officers in Shugrue's power? The situation demanded careful planning and expert execution; for the least slip would spell death for all concerned.

Why, he wondered, had Shugrue taken the deputies prisoners? As bloodthirsty as he was known to be, it seemed odd that he had not shot them to death at once. Was he thinking to play some game in which the two men might prove of assistance?

Leach realized that speculation was useless. He waited until the three boats had had ample time to get far ahead of him, then he set out behind them, using the utmost caution not to betray his presence. A mile farther along he came to where the slough forked. The left prong he knew was a short cut into the very heart of Moccasin Swamp, while the right or main prong would take him to Bundy's Settlement. He elected to take the right fork, feeling certain that Snake Shugrue and his men had gone down the other. For the present it was important that he have no contact with the outlaw.

A MILE down the right fork of the slough brought him to a huddle of log cabins, all built on pilings although the location topped a ridge at a point which was dry except in times of extreme high water. In the approximate center of the huddled group of cabins stood a long, rambling building with a wide veranda clear across the front. There was no sign of any sort displayed but Leach knew the place to be Jake Bundy's general store and saloon. He made his boat fast at a wooden pier, climbed a path up the ridge and slouched into the store.

A tall, red-headed man of middle age sat in a splint-bottom chair beside a square box filled with ashes. He look-up at Leach's entrance, nodded, spat into the box, and greeted him.

"Howdy stranger!" he bellowed genially. "Whut with th' musketeers, th' buffler-gnats, th' pesky flies an' th' heat, we're all lucky to be alive, huh? Ain't I right? You bet I'm right! Yessiree! Right as rain—an' a good rain would be fine right now, I'm tellin' yuh! Th' dang swamp stinks like hell, it does. Fulla th' stagnaciousest water I've ever knowed in these here parts, an' I been here a long time! You wishful to buy somethin', mebbe?"

The big man, Jake Bundy in person, shot forth his remarks like bullets from a double-action revolver. Leach supported his lazy, sagging frame against a bar which ran almost the full length of the building on the left. From time to time while Bundy talked he nodded agreement, sympathy, his wide mouth stretched in a grin.

"Yeah," he drawled in answer to the proprietor's question, "I'm cravin' me a drink of likker. Seems like th' dang water a feller gits hereabouts don't squinch his thirst none whatever. I been chillin' a heap lately, too, an' you knows plumb well that this here water ain't good a-tall fur chills—"

"Two or three jolts of my bes' likker will knock out th' hoary-headest ol' settler of a chill that ever torminted sufferin' human flesh, stranger!" Bundy interrupted braggingly. "A quart of it will kill ever'thing in yuh—save an' except a hankerin' fur more. Try it out, stranger, an' see if I'm lyin'. Yuh air mebbe huntin' a place to locate, or jes' passin' through th' country?"

"A little bit of both," Leach answered, pouring a stiff jolt out of a black bottle. "I'm a timber worker, an' kinder foot loose right now. Some fellers up at L'Anguile P'int war a-tellin' me that thar's right smaht of timber-cuttin' goin' on in this here section, so I jest mozied erlong down here. Reckin them fellers wa'n't lyin'?"

Bundy let his little, fat-encased eyes rove over the long frame of the new-comer, then brought them to rest on his face. What he saw there evidently satisfied him, for he answered: "Thar's always timber-cuttin' goin' on here-abouts," he said, winking broadly. "Else how would th' fine trees ever git sawed up into good timber? Uncle Sam, which owns 'em, won't cut 'em hisself ner allow anybody else to cut 'em—if he knows it. But I hear tell that they gits cut, jest th' same. Ever cut any kind of them trees, stranger?"

"Barnes is my name—Gabe Barnes," Leach offered, his grin of understanding revealing tobacco-stained teeth. "An' I ain't none pertic'lar who owns th' trees I cut—jest as long as I draws my footage ever' Saturday night. Who does I see, an' whut's th' pay?"

"Take another snort, Gabe," Bundy invited. "An' yuh jest stick eround here ontil knockin' off work time tonight, an' I'll see yuh git fixed up with a job. Good timber men that will cut whichever trees th' boss says cut, an' don't ask no questions, don't have to beg fur work in these here parts."

Leach downed another shot which nearly took the lining out of his stomach the moment it hit bottom, wiped his mouth with the back of his hand, and said: "I'll fetch my tools up frum th' river, an' my blanket an' grub. Danged if I don't like y'this paddle friend, an' whut more kin a feller want than a job wharat thar's plenty good likker right handy? What more, I ask yuh?"

"Not nothin' more, Gabe!" Jake declared heartily. "Fetch up yore plunder, an' make yoreself plumb at home!"

WAS Bundy being a bit too cordial? Leach asked himself the question as he plodded back to the store with his outfit. He dismissed the idea as unlikely, because he felt certain that the storekeeper had not even heard of the escape of Shugrue. Certainly he would have no reason to suspect the true identity of Gabe Barnes, timber worker who had no inhibitions concerning whose timber he cut. Bundy was himself back of the timber-stealing operations, most likely, and really needed men. Leach chose to look at the situation in that light, at any rate.

He deposited his "plunder" on the floor back of a counter, had another drink, then proceeded to make himself at home. Business picked up in the store as the afternoon advanced, and when dusk came it brought swampers in boats from all directions. That Bundy's was a meeting-place for virtually the whole section soon became apparent. Two native bartenders were kept on the jump serving drinks, while Bundy stimulated trade on the customer's side of the bar. Everybody seemed happy. Everybody had money. Wages for cutting government timber were evidently high.

Leach, sitting back of a big stove and remaining as much out of the crowd as possible, listened intently but heard no mention of the escape of Shugrue, or the killing of Hatley. If the news had seeped into the swamp, the swampers evidently knew better than to talk about it.

It was nearing nine o'clock when Leach observed a thin, stooped native detach himself from the bar and stroll back toward where Bundy was drawing a jug of whiskey from a racked barrel. The saloonkeeper was alone at the time, and there was a stack of sacked flour between him and Leach. The native approached Bundy, made a remark concerning the need of rain, then added in lower tones—but not so low as to escape the officer's ear: "Turkey Islan', down Cattermount Creek. Any news?"

"Nuthin'. Stranger cum in this mawnin', but he ain't nobody but a nit-wit timber worker. I'm givin' him a job—an' keepin' cases on him. Tell Bart I'll not let nuthin' git by me—nuthin' a-tall!"

The stooped native shuffled back to the bar, and when Bundy came by the stove with the jug he saw that Gabe Barnes had gone sound asleep in his chair.

But Gabe didn't sleep long. As Bundy was delivering the jug to his customer, a broad, stocky figure loomed up in the doorway—and Leach's eyes suddenly narrowed to slits. In spite of the fact that the newcomer wore the regulation native garb, recognition in the officer's mind was instantaneous and complete.

The broad, stocky man in the doorway was Oscar Cowan, a deputy jailer from Helena.

Trouble was afoot. Leach knew that at once. Oscar Cowan would not be there at the door of Moccasin Swamp unless something urgent had sent him. Several natives greeted him as he walked into the store, and he answered the greetings shortly.

"Jake," said Cowan, while his narrowly set black eyes flashed searching glances about the crowded room, "I've got sum bizness with yuh."

Bundy turned and started toward

the back of the store, Cowan accompanying him. Leach did not wait. He had a hunch—and he played it. Before the pair got as far back as the stove, the officer had slipped around behind the stack of sacked flour and was making his way swiftly toward a door in the rear. The door proved to be unlocked, and he passed through, finding himself in a small room stored with whiskey barrels and cases of merchandise. He had just time to crouch down back of a barrel and near an open window before the door opened to admit Bundy and Cowan.

COWAN lost no time in opening up the business that had brought him at top speed into the swamp country.

"I didn't find it out ontel late in th' mawnin'," he said almost before the door was closed, "but Don Leach, frum St. Louis, war in town yes'day. He war seed goin' into Webber's office, an' he cum outta thar right soon afterwards. He wa'n't seed no more by th' feller that told me erbout him—but th' Red Bird, th' dang patterole boat that usually lays up at Helena, taken out a right short while atterwards. An' she headed up th' river, Jake. Thar ain't no question in my mind that that thar bloodhoun', Leach, war aboard of her—an' that he's somewhar in th' swamp right now."

"Th' hell yuh say!" Bundy exclaimed, startled.

"Yeah. That's whut I'm sayin'. It happened that I was due to take a vacashun tomorrer, so I got that ol' fool of a chief jailer, Spanner, to let me off right erway, an' here I am. I knows Leach by sight, an' I aim to find him——"

"Whut kinda lookin' feller is he?" Bundy demanded, interrupting.

"Tall—six foot two, or there erbouts. Sandy haired, gray eyes, talks native as good as you or me does, knows

th' swamp lands of Arkansas like he does th' lines in th' pa'm of his hand. Looks, acks an' talks like a borned an' raised river rat——"

"Hell!" Bundy ejaculated. "That takes off Gabe Barnes to a gnat's bristle—an' he jus' arriv' here at noon! But I war a-watchin' of him, Oss! He wouldn't of put nuthin' over on me! No sirree!"

"Whar at is this Barnes?" Cowan demanded, his voice brittle.

"He war asleep beside th' stove a few minnits ergo. C'mon le's see if he's thar now!"

"Bart an' th' boys ambushed that bunch of deppities," Cowan told Jake. "Kilt one, captured two. He lost Buck an' Jim, which war kilt too. Th' news cum in afore I got erway frum Helena. Wharever Bart air at, he's got them two deppities with him—an' Gawd only knows fur whut."

"Never min' whut!" Jake snapped. "We're losin' time. Le's go an' git Leach!"

The door closed behind Bundy and Cowan, and Leach, aware that exposure in his true character was imminent, glided softly to the open window. He paused, listened, heard the sound of rapid footsteps approaching the door and, delaying no longer, leaped through the window.

His body came in contact with something soft and yielding, and from the darkness beneath the window ascended a scream of fright. Leach righted himself, reached out and grasped a pair of shapely but strong arms in a grip from which there was no escape.

"Hush!" he whispered fiercely. "You'll raise the devil with that screeching! What are you doing here, anyhow?"

"Turn me loose!" came in subdued but insistent tones from the spy. "And run for it! Not toward the slough, but the timber! Follow me, quick, for Jake Bundy will kill us both if he finds us here!"

The next instant, led by a woman for whose presence beneath Jake Bundy's window he was wholly unable to account, Leach was running swiftly toward the timber on the west.

They had put two hundred yards between themselves and the store, and were almost within the friendly cover of the wilderness, when loud shouts came to their ears. Shouts of anger, stern command, as Jake Bundy unleashed his pack and set it to the chase.

From that moment on, Leach would be hunted like a predatory varmint. Before day dawned every swamp rat Jake and Cowan could muster would be running the sloughs and creeks, combing the donnicks and ridges, all with a common purpose. The swift capture and prompt killing of Don Leach.

CHAPTER THREE

"I Call Him The Masked Moccasin"

THEY plunged into the timber and the mysterious guide stopped.

"You are Don Leach, the man Oscar Cowan told Jake Bundy about," she said, in a voice that, now her fright had passed, was soft and musical. "You are lucky they didn't find you in that room."

"And you are lucky I didn't land directly on top of you when I jumped through the window," Leach came back promptly. "What were you hiding there for?"

"I wasn't hiding. I was there to listen. Jake Bundy uses that storeroom when he talks private business—and I suspected he'd have private business tonight. But this is no place for us to hold a conversation. Where were you

headed for when you left the storeroom so suddenly?"

The girl was not a swamper. Her words came in liquid tones, slurred, drawly. From some state to the south, he thought. So far, he had seen only a vague outline of her, and right then was a very good time to find out what she looked like. Abruptly, he shot the catch of his vest-pocket flash and directed the ray upon her. A low, amused laugh came from the girl. But what confounded the detective was this: the face of the girl was covered with a mask!

"Didn't they teach manners where you were raised?" she inquired rebukingly.

"I'm a detective, not a gallant," Leach said shortly. "And let me remind you that we are not in a ballroom, but surrounded by a hostile wilderness. If you've got a home near-by, I'll see that you reach it safely. As for me, I've got business to look after—and no time to waste."

The girl laughed again. The laugh was strangely irritating, under the existing conditions—but Leach had to admit to himself that it would, under different circumstances, be most alluring.

"But it happens that I have business with you, Mr. Leach," came the surprising statement. "Will you come with me—and try and forget that a mere woman almost scared you out of your wits tonight?"

Leach laughed amusedly at that and nodded agreement. "Lead on, Masked Lady," he said. "I'll try and find the courage to follow."

The girl, for that she was little more than that Leach felt sure, led off through the timber, bidding the detective stay close behind. Now and then they crossed small cleared spots, and the moonlight disclosed the girl more fully. She wore trousers, knee-boots.

a shirt of flannel and a soft hat of black felt. At a distance of only a few feet she would easily have been mistaken for a boy—unless she happened to start walking, when the natural grace of her carriage would have betrayed her.

Leach, despite the gravity of the situation in which he found himself, was frankly intrigued. Although not in the least degree romantically inclined, he must have been a man of wood not to have got a thrill out of being conducted through the trackless wilderness by a woman—and one whom he had already sensed was lovely—who chose to cover her face with a velvet mask! And Leach certainly was not made of wood.

With a directness arguing that she knew that section of the swamp thoroughly, the girl led the way for a distance of perhaps two miles, stopping finally at the edge of a clearing in which stood a low-roofed cabin of four rooms. Leach brought up beside her.

"You would not be welcome here, Mr. Leach," she informed him, "if the owner of the place were at home. He is not, however, and that accounts for me being able to masquerade in the timber as I did. For this evening it will provide a safe place for us to have a talk—and I am sure after we have had the talk, both of us will be benefitted. Come with me, and stay close, for there are dogs here. They won't bother you with me along."

LEACH followed the girl, his wonder growing with each step. What mystery was about to be disclosed? That there was a mystery, and a most intricate one, he was convinced.

A pair of gaunt hounds challenged their approach, but tucked their tails and retreated at the girl's command. She unlocked a door, passed into the cabin and lit a lamp. Leach followed, and found himself in a large sitting room. A room that would have caused him no surprise had he found it in more civilized surroundings, but which was so entirely foreign to the Moccasin Swamp country as to occasion him not only surprise but to elicit comment.

"These furnishings make me feel as though I had been transported on a magic rug and dumped right into the lap of luxury!" he exclaimed, his keen eyes taking in every detail of the room. "Surely, Masked Lady, this is not the home of a native!"

The colorful rug, comfortable lounge chairs, silken draperies, pictures—all the objects in the room, in short, were the belongings of a person of excellent taste. The brass andirons in the wide fireplace alone represented more outlay of money than would be required to furnish the entire house of a native. Leach's hunch that he had stumbled upon something more than ordinarily mysterious grew amid such surroundings.

"Sit down, please," the girl bade Leach, making no reply to his remarks. "You are wondering where I enter the maze you have come to untangle—all unknowingly. You left Helena with the idea that your job here was merely one of pursuit and capture. Pursuit of Snake Shugrue, and his capture if possible. Is that right, Mr. Leach?"

"Entirely so," Leach told her. "But I'd like to know how you got your information about me. I have been under the delusion that my coming to the Moccasin country was an absolute secret."

"Yet Oscar Cowan knew about it," she pointed out.

"Guessed at it, you should have said," Leach corrected. "But you appear to have had knowledge of it prior to overhearing Cowan's talk with Bundy. Will you explain that?"

"That will be easy. I knew, early in the evening, that Shugrue had escaped to the swamp, and I was certain that someone would come in after him. Cowan's statement that you had left Helena as you did was enough to tip me off to you. Does that explain?"

"Except that part about my being unaware that I am to have a maze of some sort to untangle, instead of a mere job of pursuit and capture," Leach returned.

The girl rested an elbow on the table beside her, nested her small, firm chin in the palm of her hand, and gazed steadily at Leach through the holes in her mask. At length, seeming satisfied that she could trust him, she spoke.

"You are here to return a reptile for punishment—Snake Shugrue," she said slowly. "That should be done, unquestionably. But you are going to find, unless your life ends too quickly, that Bart Shugrue lied when he wrote that famous letter which resulted in the nickname he bears—and which pleases him mightily. He boasted that he was 'the biggest an' th' p'izenoust snake' in the Moccasin country. He is big and deadly poisonous, no doubt—but there is another infinitely larger and more deadly than he. More deadly, even, than a hundred such snakes as Shugrue: For want of a better title, I have called him the Masked Moccasin."

"Rather fanciful," Leach commented, deeply interested. "And just why give such a title to this mysterious person?"

"Because," was the answer, "he stays in hiding, never revealing himself. Shugrue, for instance, is a mask for him. I suspect there are others, and it was my desire to find out whether a certain man I know was also one of his

masks that caused me to listen at that window tonight."

"Have you anything definite to offer in support of your belief that there is such a man as you describe?"

"I have. It is this: Bart Shugrue, although the best of tools, is not of the caliber necessary for real leadership. He is unlettered, superstitious, lacking in mental sharpness. Just a fierce and willing tool. Yet there can be no doubt that something is going on here in the swamp that could not function without a large and efficient organization back of it. That is where the Masked Moccasin comes in."

"Any idea as to what is going on?"

"No. But I do know that it is something that can't bear the light. I know that there are guards stationed in various places in Moccasin whose duty it is to stop suspicious strangers from entering—and to kill known officers at sight. Does that not indicate an organization?"

"It does," Leach acknowledged. "And now, please—who owns this cabin?"

"My uncle. He built and furnished it, at my wish, when I came to live here in the swamp a year ago."

"And your uncle—what is his name?"

"His name," the girl said slowly, "is Jake Bundy."

Leach had been in the act of lighting his pipe—but he held the match suspended until the flames scorched his fingers!

THE silence in the room was shattered by an uproar from without. The two hounds, disturbed by the approach of something, man or varmint, began barking savagely. The girl rose suddenly, listening.

"Go into the kitchen!" she exclaimed,

pointing to a door at the back. "Stay there until I come, or call you!"

She darted into an adjoining room, and Leach entered the kitchen, made certain that the sixgun he wore in a shoulder holster was in readiness for a quick draw, and waited. The dogs had evidently got the disturbing scent from quite a distance, for nothing to indicate the presence of anybody came to his ears.

Five minutes passed and the kitchen door opened. The girl stood there in the light of the lamp—but what a change! The male garb had vanished, and her slender person was now clad in a nightdress with a silken robe over it. Her short, brown hair had been touseled as though she had just raised her head from the pillow—and, above all, the mask was gone.

Leach was staring into a face of surpassing loveliness. The hint he had had of what the mask concealed had been more than fulfilled. He was about to speak when the girl placed a finger on her lips enjoining silence. She listened for a moment, then came closer to him.

"The hounds quit barking with suggestive abruptness," she whispered. "Someone is coming whom they know. It may be uncle. You had best go out the back way and I will pretend I haven't even been away. Come back tomorrow morning at nine o'clock. I will be alone then. Go quickly and remember that the swamp is alive with your enemies!"

She thrust him out the door and closed it behind him. Leach hesitated for an instant, then started off toward the timber at the rear. Given his own way, he would not have left the cabin until he had drawn from its surprising occupant every bit of information that might be hers to give. But there was nothing to be done about that now until morning.

Hopeful of finding an empty cabin in which to spend the rest of the night, he struck off on a course which he figured would bring him to Little Moccasin Slough at a point above the setlement. He did not go far, but stopped in his tracks at the edge of the timber.

Was it a cry he had heard?

The next moment he was certain of it. Shrilly, appealingly, came a cry for help. It was from the direction of the cabin he had just left—and was unmistakably from the lips of the girl!

Leach wheeled and ran. What a fool he had been to leave her! He might have known that she, as well as he, was in danger! Well, he'd make up for it now! The damned scoundrels—

He had all but reached the back door when a man emerged from it, whipped up an arm and fired. A bullet sang by, and Leach fired the next instant. The light, however, was not good, and he missed. The man darted for cover around a corner of the cabin, Leach's lead clipping splinters from the logs in his wake.

"Help! Help! They are taking me to—"

The voice was suddenly smothered, and Leach, swearing under his breath, ran straight for the door—to be greeted by a flash of flame from the kitchen window, and a slug of lead that dropped him in his tracks!

THE next thing of which the detective became conscious was a searing pain in his lungs, and a roaring sound in his ears. Then he felt smothered, as though something suffocating had been placed over his head. An instant later he realized that he was deep under water —all but drowned, in fact.

Beating back the almost overwhelming desire to breathe and relieve the pain in his lungs, Leach fought his way to the surface, gasped his fill of life-giving air, tried his arms and found that he could use them, then struck out for the vaguely visible tree-line which marked the nearer bank. Pulling himself out of the water, he lay nearly exhausted on the ground, his head, where a bullet had plowed the scalp, feeling like somebody had been using it for an anvil.

Then, with a rush, came the memory of the girl's cry for help, his attempted response, and that flash of flame from the back window. What had happened thereafter he could only guess. Doubtless the men at the cabin had thought him dead, and had dumped him in the slough as a convenient means of disposing of the body.

If that were the case, then he must be somewhere near the cabin. He came to his feet instantly. The girl had cried out that they were taking her somewhere. And, no matter how careful her abductors had been, there would be a trail. His eyes, long accustomed to searching for such things, could not fail him now. He thrust a hand beneath his left arm— and felt only an empty holster.

An oath sizzled on his lips, but oaths could not remedy the situation. There might be a remedy, though, and he set out to seek it. Surely there would be a weapon of some kind in the cabin, and, should it not be occupied, he would arm himself again. Laying a course by the moon, he struck off northward, and it was not long before the noisy barking of dogs advised him that he was near the cabin. A few minutes later, armed with a stout club with which to beat off the hounds, he was racing across the clearing.

The dogs, seeing the club in his hands, kept at a safe distance, nor was he challenged from the house. He entered it, glanced around at the over-turned furniture and torn draperies which told of the fierce resistance the girl had made, then hastily searched the place. There was no one present— nor was there a weapon to be found.

Leach, bitterly disappointed over having to tackle so dangerous a job without any better arm than a club, was about to set out to search for the trail of the men who had carried the girl away, when the dogs gave tongue again. He glanced across the moonlit clearing and saw two men coming rapidly toward the cabin. The dogs, spoken to sharply by one, immediately ceased to bark. They were evidently known.

It was too late for the officer to leave by way of the back door, since the moonlight would betray him, and seeking a place to hide, his glance rested upon the rungs of a wall ladder which ended at a man-hole in the ceiling of the sitting room. He had extinguished the light when the hounds first gave tongue, and with a bound he reached the ladder and climbed swiftly upward. A moment, and he was safe in the loft, the cover back on the opening.

The door opened and the two men came in. The lamp was lighted. Leach found a crack between the boards of the ceiling and looked down. Both men were visible, but he recognized neither of them. One, a squat, pock-marked native, spoke.

"Th' gove'mint shore do have hard luck with its of'cers when it sends 'em to Moc'sin, Abe!" he said, grinning with deep satisfaction. "How long you reckin it will take fur th' feeshes and turtles to pick th' bones of th' one we dumped into Little Moc'sin tonight?"

"Not long, 'Bud'," Abe, a lank man of thirty, answered as he rummaged in a wall cupboard and brought out a bottle and glasses. "Not much longer than it'll take you an' me to spen' th' jack we done taken outten his clothes, huh?"

The squat man started to raise a glass of whiskey to his lips, stopped before it touched them, then sat it down with a hand that trembled slightly.

"Abe," he said, almost in a whisper, "thar's been somebody hyar since we left!"

"How do you know that?" Abe demanded, setting his glass down too.

Bud pointed toward the rug. "See whar at water done dripped on th' floor?" he asked. "See them thar wet spots?"

Abe looked, and a slight pallor settled on his features. "You—you don't figger th' feller we kilt have cum back?" he asked, his voice rattling dryly in his throat. "You don't reckin he could, do you?"

"No—you fool!" Bud snapped. "Dead men don't cum back! Look thar!"

HIS eyes had followed the spots of dampness across the floor—and had raised unerringly to the trap in the ceiling above.

He moved with alacrity then. With his back against the front door, a gun in his hand, he motioned to Abe to move out of range of the trap. He was instantly obeyed.

"Cum down frum thar!" he called sharply. "You kain't git erway frum us, now we done knows you air up thar! Cum down, damn you—else we'll set fire to this shack an' smoke you out!"

Leach, never doubting that the natives would carry out the threat if necessary, thought quickly. He was in a desperate situation from which there seemed to be no escape. Only one chance to save himself that he could see—and he determined to try it.

"Air you cumin', er ain't you?" Bud called angrily. "Want to be smoked out like a varmint?"

Leach fumbled at the cover to the trap, slid it aside and thrust his pale, bloodstained face down in sight. "I—I'm about dead!" he exclaimed, his voice wheezing in his throat. "Give—me time—and I'll climb—down. Don't shoot—because there ain't—any danger from—me. I'm unarmed!"

"Whut you war armed with, air starin' you in th' face right now, feller!" Bud chuckled, indicating the six-gun with which he was covering Leach. "Thank you fur sich a fine weepin'!"

"Frum th' looks of him," Abe contributed, "he ain't never goin' to need no gun ag'in, huh, Bud?"

"You said it, Abe," Bud agreed. "Cum on down, feller—an' then if you air goin' to die, like you looks like, we'll take it kindly if you'll do it closter to th' slough. Save us frum luggin' you thar. Why'n hell didn't you stay thar, anyhow?"

Abe laughed uproariously and Leach began descending the ladder. He came down slowly, and it was evident to the men below that he was hardly able to support himself on the rungs.

Bud advanced into the room, his gun ready for action, and called: "Why'n't you jist turn loose an' drap? You needn't mind a few bruises, feller, seein' they wouldn't pain you fur long!"

"I—think I—can make it—all right," Leach gasped, as he turned his back against the rungs and clung to the outer edge of the man-hole with his shaking fingers. "I'll just—swing off and drop!"

He swung—but did not drop. Instead, with an outward thrust of his feet against the ladder, Leach released his hold on the man-hole and catapulted through space—to land feet first upon the squat body of the man with the gun.

There was a sickening sound of something snapping, and Bud, struck under the chin by a heavy boot, went down in a struggling heap beneath Leach's body.

Abe cried out in surprise, then went for his gun. But Leach had calculated his chances nicely, and before the native could draw and fire he had snatched the weapon from the floor and, shooting by instinct alone, sent a bullet through his heart.

Leach lost no time. Both the natives were dead, Bud's neck having been broken by the kick of the boot, and no information useful to him had been let drop. From there on he must move by guess work alone. But would it be guess work?

"On Turkey Island, down Cattamount Creek!" he exclaimed, suddenly recalling what he had overheard in Bundy's store. "That's where Snake Shugrue is holed up, sure as shootin'! And where he is Carroll and Brent will be!"

Armed with a pair of sixguns now, his pockets filled with cartridges, Leach left the cabin and struck out for Little Moccasin at a steady, distance-eating trot.

CHAPTER FOUR

"Yuh Ain't Out Of The Swamp!"

LEACH reached Little Moccasin well above Bundy's store, and after a search of a few minutes found a boat tied against the shore. He stepped into the stern, caught up the paddle and pushed off.

Straight up the slough he shot the craft, and when he came to where the stream forked he turned without hesitation down the smaller prong—the prong down which he now was certain Shugrue and his men had gone. Catamount Creek was still another arm of Little Moccasin, taking off from the

east fork three miles away. Turkey Island was a timbered knoll of some two acres in extent, lying four miles from the source of Catamount.

Leach knew the country perfectly, although he had not traveled it of late. Names of places in the swamp seldom are changed, however, and he knew his way about as well as any native there. Turkey Island was his present objective, but he had no intention of going there immediately. When he had covered the distance to Catamount Creek, meeting no one, he took his bearings, poled into the creek and shoved his boat under cover of some rankly growing river grass just below the juncture of the two streams. If he was being followed, he would soon find it out.

The wait was not long. Fifteen minutes later a long dugout swung out of East Fork into Catamount. Leach, having maneuvered his boat so that the bow was toward the channel, picked up his long paddle and planted the blade firmly against the shore. The other boat came on, paddled swiftly by a lone boatman. It came at length abreast of Leach.

With all his weight bearing on the staff of the paddle, Leach thrust against the shore. His dugout flashed from cover as though it had been shot from a huge gun, bow directed straight toward the mid-section of the oncoming craft. The paddler yelled hoarsely and sought to avoid what looked like certain disaster.

Leach, however, did not intend that the two boats should collide. With a deft flirt of his paddle at the stern, he turned the bow of the dugout up stream and brought it easily alongside. With his left hand he grasped a gunwale of the strange boat—and with his right hand thrust the muzzle of a sixgun under the paddler's nose.

"Go high, Cowan!" he ordered tersely. "You're all through for tonight!"

For the man in the boat was Oscar Cowan, whose appearance at Bundy's had knocked the officer's plans into a heap.

Leach's sudden maneuver had worked perfectly. Cowan had been too surprised, too concerned for the safety of his boat, to think of a weapon—and when he recognized the danger for what it was, it was too late to draw. He dropped the paddle and shot his hands up.

"Yuh can't git erway with nuthin' in this swamp!" he snarled at Leach.

Leach laughed. "I seem to have gotten away with one little bit of business, at any rate," he jibed, relieving Cowan of his gun. "Now," he ordered, "pass me the painter of your boat."

The officer towed the captured boat to shore, and ordered Cowan out.

"You're not so important to me, Cowan," he said as he cut the painters off both boats. "I had to take you, though, in order to keep you from warning Bart Shugrue, down on Turkey Island, that I was prowling the swamp in search of something to devour. You're a little reptile, so I'm just going to scotch you and leave you here."

"Damn yuh!" Cowan snarled wrathfully. "Th' whip air in yore hand now—"

"Down on your belly!" Leach snapped, poising his sixgun barrel for a blow.

Cowan bit off his words, and promptly stretched out as told. Leach bound his hands and legs, then turned him on his back. A bandanna handkerchief served nicely for a gag.

"Take my advice, Cowan," he said as he prepared to leave, "and don't squirm too much. The ropes are so knotted that they will tighten up a bit every time you strain 'em. You'll be picked up later, if I have the luck to come back. If not—well, you deserve to die for playing spy down at Helena for the Snake and his crew. See you later—maybe."

LEACH set out down Catamount Creek. It was then nearing morning, and if anything was to be done for Carroll and Brent it must be done soon.

There was a faint moon, and presently Leach made out the bulk of Turkey Island ahead, perhaps a quarter of a mile off. He ran down in the shadow of the timbered shore for several hundred yards, then shoved the bow of his dugout up on the marshy bank. Leaving the boat, he scouted along shore until he came opposite where three boats were tied up on the south side of Turkey. Then he crouched down, brought out a small pair of night-glasses and focused them on the island.

The glasses revealed a man sitting on a stump right at the edge of the water. He was smoking, sitting very still, and Leach would have thought that he dozed, except for the fact that now and then his pipe glowed as he drew upon it.

Something moved on the face of the water, and the officer directed his glance toward it. A log, he observed as the object came nearer, floating lazily in the creek's slow current. He stared for a long moment at the drifting stick, then got up and retraced his way toward his boat.

Before reaching the boat, however, his glance searched out the thing he had suddenly found himself wanting. A saw-log. The one he discovered was perhaps two feet in circumference, and lay on the low bank almost in the water where it had stranded at some period of flood. Without losing any more time, he stripped his clothes off, and hung them on a bush. Then, with a holstered sixgun slung around his neck, he bent down, got a grip on the log and rolled it, slowly and cautiously, into the creek.

After the log was in the water he crouched there on the bank, holding the big stick with one hand, and looked off steadily toward where the guard kept vigil. Nothing stirred down there, and a moment later he was in the water, the log drifting down the stream—and Leach drifting with it, expertly guided its course in the desired direction.

The log, guided surely but imperceptibly by the officer's hand, drifted over toward Turkey Island, reached it, went meandering down along the shore. It moved slowly, and it's bulk completely concealed Leach from the view of anybody on shore. Nearer and nearer to the anchored boats it came, and Leach, his senses strained to catch the slightest sound, heard the guard clear his throat. He risked a look over the top of the log, and saw him standing at the water's edge, eyeing the floating stick.

Cautiously, Leach steered the forward end of the log toward one of the boats. The guard swore softly. The log drew abreast of him, and he thrust out a foot to push it off the threatened boat.

At that instant Leach let go of the log, reached up and grasped the guard by the ankle. A powerful jerk, a startled gasp—and the guard was in the water, the detective's powerful fingers around his throat.

The fall of the guard into the stream had made no more noise than a large fish would make in leaping above the surface, and there were many large fish doing that then. The officer kept his grip until he felt the guard's body go limp, then he arose, shouldered the body and went ashore.

The guard was out completely. No stalling on his part. Leach stripped his outer clothing off and donned it himself, then tied him up with painter ropes. After that was done he sat down and waited for consciousness to return to his captive.

AT the expiration of about five minutes, the guard stirred. Leach drew a wicked-looking knife from a pocket of the captured trousers, opened the large blade and placed the point against the base of the recumbent native's throat.

The native opened his eyes, started to cry out. Leach brought pressure to bear on the point of the knife. The cry stopped in the guard's throat.

"Who's in the cabin?" Leach asked.

"Shugrue an' Rollins."

"Where's Carroll and Brent?"

"They're in thar too."

"When are you to be relieved?"

"Whut time air it now?"

"Three o'clock."

"Rollins oughta be here in er few minutes. He takes th' next watch."

"That's all I want from you," Leach told the guard, and promptly gagged him with a handkerchief. Then he dragged him aside into cover, and took the guard's place on the stump, back toward the path to the cabin.

At the end of fifteen minutes he heard somebody coming.

"Ever'thing O. K.?"

Rollins was at Leach's elbow when he spoke—and the next instant the barral of the officer's sixgun stretched him out on the ground. He did not even so much as grunt when struck.

Leach worked swiftly, ripped up Rollins' shirt, gagged and bound him and let him lie where he fell. Pocketing the two guns he had taken from the men, he began a cautious approach on the cabin. When he reached the door he found the place in darkness, and the snores of tired men reached his ears.

He did not have a flashlight, and to locate the bunk in which Snake Shugrue lay was a problem. A problem that must not be delayed in solving, for daylight was not more than two hours off. Suddenly he decided upon a scheme, and stepped cautiously inside the room. Reaching a position against the front wall from which he could command all bunks, he called: "Hey, Bart! Git up. It air yore time to go on watch."

There was a sound of stirring on one of the bunks at his right. Then came a muttered oath.

"Hell! How come yuh to call me so dang early? Hey—Rollins! that you?"

Leach was creeping stealthily toward the speaker.

"Rollins! Damn it all—why don't yuh answer?"

Leach's left foot struck a chair the presence of which he had not anticipated. It went over with a clatter. Came a furious oath from the bunk—then a flash of flame and a thundrous report.

Leach's own weapon, ready drawn, flashed in answer. A heavy body crashed to the floor, and a stream of profanity from Shugrue's lips sizzled in the darkness.

The next instant Leach had found a lamp, and its sickly flare lit up the room.

Shugrue, shot through the right shoulder, was writhing on the floor, trying to reach his fallen gun with his left hand. Leach kicked the weapon into a corner.

"That was a lucky shot, Snake," he said, as he bound the outlaw with a piece of rope. "A little farther over, and you'd have cheated the gallows, you know."

"I'll cheat 'em anyhow, damn yuh!" Shugrue snarled. "Yuh ain't out of th' swamp yit! Don't git to braggin' so soon!"

Leach laughed, then turned his attention to Carroll and Brent. He released them and after a few minutes both were able to get up and move around.

"Snake and his bunch ambushed us, Don," Carrol explained, "and they got Staten. What's the next move?"

"For you and Brent to take your prisoners out of the swamp before daylight dawns," Leach answered. "After daybreak—well, you'd never get out. There's another one to be picked up on the way. Oscar Cowan, a double-crossing deputy jailer known to both of you. One of the Snake's pet spies. Two more tied up at the landing. How do you like that plot, Snake?"

"And what about the girl?" Carroll queried. "Did you know about her?"

Leach wheeled toward him, pulses hammering. "What girl?" he demanded.

"The one brought here a short time ago," was the answer.

"Where is she now?"

Carroll walked to a door in the back and threw it open.

"She was taken in there," he said, indicating the small lean-to. "They had her bound and a gag—"

Leach was past him like a flash—to reappear an instant later with the girl, bound and gagged but conscious, in his arms!

CHAPTER FIVE

Under The Red Mask

WHEN the girl was free of rope and gag, with the detective's arms supporting her, she raised her eyes to his. Eyes that expressed surprise, relief—and something deeper that Leach was almost afraid to plumb.

"They said they had killed you!" she exclaimed.

"They were a bit hasty in disposing of me," Leach told her. "And if you refer to Abe and Bud—well, they paid up a bit later. You have not been harmed?"

"No. I was brought here by two men, swampers whom I do not know, and delivered to—that!"

Her eyes blazing with scorn and hatred, she pointed toward Snake Shugrue.

"Sarah Benson, yuh belong to me—an' yuh ain't never goin' to belong to nobody else!"

The words crackled from Shugrue's lips with the cold tinkle of icicles falling on frozen earth. Leach whirled upon him.

"What do you mean by that?" he demanded.

"I means that Jake Bundy brung her into th' swamps to be my wife," Snake answered. "That's whut I means—"

"That is true," Sarah interrupted, shivering with repulsion. "I was left alone, after my mother died, and when Jake Bundy, mother's only brother, came for me I went with him willingly enough. Until lately he has always treated me with kindness—and then, a month ago, he informed me that Snake Shugrue wanted me for his wife. Snake, he pointed out, was a man of power and influence, and I would be lucky to get him. Think of it! Snake Shugrue—thief and killer!"

"Yuh'll remember eatin' them words!" Shugrue gritted menacingly. "Yuh thinks yuh're safe with yore damned cop, but yuh're due to find out diff'runt! Yuh ain't out of Moccasin yit—an' yuh ain't never goin' to git out! Leastways, not erlive!"

Sarah Benson ignored him.

"There is something big on foot," she said, turning to Leach. "I heard enough from the men who brought me here to tell me that. Enough to inform me that the most gigantic theft of government timber ever known is about to

be consummated. Enough to understand why Snake Shugrue dynamited the levee at L'Anguile Point—"

"Shet yore trap!" Shugrue bellowed, lunging toward the girl—only to be caught and thrust back against the wall by Leach.

"Another word from you," Leach told him coldly, "and I'll gag you. Go on, Miss Benson," he directed the girl. "Let's have it. The levee was dynamited because it cut off the waters of Big Moccasin—and Big Moccasin is the stream down which Shugrue meant to float the logs. Is that correct?"

"How did you know?"

"It was obvious, after I became convinced that Bundy and others were cleaning out the hardwood in Moccasin," he answered. "Learn anything else? Who the Masked Moccasin is?"

"Not that," she answered. "But I know that Jake Bundy is one of the leaders, and that he could name the man you want most of all. The man poor Hatley was about to name when Shugrue struck him down."

"An' a name yuh'll never hear!" Snake spat venomously. "He's covered up—an' nobody lives that kin oncover him!"

Leach turned to carry out his threat by gagging Shugrue, but the hurried entrance of Brent, who had been down to see after the bound men at the landing, stopped him.

"Boats coming down the creek!" he exclaimed. "Too dark yet to see that far, but by the sounds, and the wash of the waves, there must be a bunch of 'em!"

SHUGRUE'S derisive laughter interrupted, and Leach promptly thrust a bandanna into his mouth. Then he turned calmly to the situation in hand.

"Take those two rifles," he directed Carroll and Brent, pointing to where the outlaw's guns stood in a corner, "and go with Miss Benson to the opposite side of the island.   Stay there until I come."

"Where are you going?   What are you intending to do?" cried the girl.

"I'm going to try and trap a nest of snakes," Leach answered grimly, as he threw Shugrue to the floor and began tying his ankles with a rope.   "And maybe the big one, that Masked Moccasin of yours, will be among them. Hurry, and do as I have said."

She moved close to him, laid a trembling hand on his arm. "Please," she said softly, "come with us. We can escape across the branch to the forest—"

"And be hunted down like rats," Leach broke in. "Besides, I came here for a purpose—and I'm not forgetting it. Go quickly!"

Without another word, Sarah Benson followed Carroll and Brent.

Leach, leaving Shugrue tied and on the floor, slipped out of the front door and darted into the brush which, clothing the small island like a dry, brittle canopy, grew close to the neglected cabin. Day was just dawning and objects were beginning to take vague shape. From the creek came the sounds of approaching boats, and Brent had not been mistaken when he said there were numbers of them.   They were then drawing near to the landing, and Leach, thinking the lucky thought that had caused him to hide the two bound guards in the brush, worked his way down to the stream, reaching it at a point two hundred feet above where the oncoming boats would land.

Four bateaux, each carrying two men, traveling one behind another, showed abruptly in the clearing dawn, and Leach, crouching low, watched them put in to the shore.   In the first bateau was a tall man whose features the detective strained his eyes to make out, but could not.   When the boat he occupied came

to anchor, he found out why this was.

The face of the tall man in the first boat was completely covered by a mask of red cloth!

Leach felt his nerves tingle.   He watched the eight men go ashore, and saw the masked man assign one of the number to guard the boats.   Then the seven started for the cabin.

Well, they'd damned soon get a surprise!

Leach, treading as noiselessly as a panther, crept down to the landing, his sixgun clubbed.   Before the guard had an inkling that danger was near, Leach was out of cover and on him.   One blow of the gun-barrel, and he fell like a poled ox.

The detective left him where he fell, and gave his attention to the boats. One by one, he cut the painter ropes and set them adrift, keeping only two for his own use.   After that was done, he disappeared in a patch of brush— and shortly after he had departed from the island, paddling one boat and towing another, smoke began to boil up from the brush, and flames twinkled in half a dozen places.

Paddling swiftly, he had reached the upper end of the island when back of him the morning stillness was suddenly shattered by shouts and oaths.   Leach smiled grimly and shot his boat down the left-hand prong.   A few minutes later he had reached a point directly back of the cabin, where Carroll and Brent waited with the girl.

HE leaped ashore, assisted Sarah into one of the boats, then he and the two deputies scattered and set more fires. The dry brush and grass blazed up like tinder, and within five minutes was spreading with an ominous roar.

"Get into a boat," Leach ordered Carroll and Brent, "and go back to the other side.   They'll waste some time trying to find out where their boats are gone, then those who can swim will be leaping off this fiery hell like frogs off a log. There's two men who must not escape. Get as many as you can, of course—but be sure and get the man in the red mask and Snake Shugrue."

Carroll and Brent were off instantly, and Leach shoved the second boat across the stream and, with Sarah clinging to his arm, disappeared into the brush.

"What will happen now?" the girl asked. "You set their boats adrift—"

"And, I hope, panicked them with fire," Leach finished. "A swamper is absolutely helpless without his boat, as you should know by now. I'm counting heavily on sheer panic—"

Two hatless, wild-eyed natives broke cover directly across the stream, having run over a burned and smoking patch of ground. Without a pause, they leaped into the stream, swam across— and landed under the muzzle of Leach's gun.

From across the little island the sound of rapid firing came, followed by cries and curses. Leach, with his captives disarmed and lying face down on the ground, heard Carroll's bull-like voice shouting above it all. Then a man appeared across the stream who caused him to forget everybody else.

It was Snake Shugrue.

Leach watched the bandit as he dropped into the water and started swimming with powerful strokes toward the shore. Watched him reach the shore and draw himself up out of the water. Then he stepped out directly in front of him.

"Let's go, Snake," he said quietly. "Down at Helena they're noosing a rope for you."

For a split second the outlaw stared— then both hands streaked for his guns. Leach, expecting just that, went for his.

Two reports thundered through the dim forest, flame blended with the coming sunlight, smoke boiled upward—

And when the smoke cleared, Snake Shugrue was dying on the ground— and Don Leach was holding Sarah Benson in his arms.

"Were you hit?" the girl cried, clutching him with trembling hands, raising flooded eyes to his.

"Yes," Leach answered, a sudden smile lighting up his grim face. "By you—and right in the heart!"

A shout from down the stream, and Leach put Sarah gently aside. Carroll was coming up the creek in a boat, but put in to shore before he reached the spot where the officer stood. There was something in the deputy's manner of landing there that told Leach to go slow.

"Stay here, Sarah," he bade the girl, and went down to where Carroll waited.

In the bottom of the boat lay the tall, masked man. He was dead.

"I thought maybe you would want to keep it from the girl," the deputy said, as he lifted the mask from the face of the dead leader.

The face Carroll exposed was that of Jake Bundy. Bundy, who in life had been the real power back of the evil in Moccasin Swamp, the secret head of the most destructive gang of hardwood thieves that ever laid waste to the nations reserves.

Leach covered the face again, returned to where Sarah awaited him—waited with a look of inquiry in her eyes. He nodded soberly.

"I think I must have known he was the Masked Moccasisn all along," she said quietly. "After all, what does it matter? I have lost an unworthy uncle, and gained—"

"All that I can give you—forever," Leach broke in, as he took her in his arms.

And There Was Murder

A Cardigan Story

by

Frederick Nebel

Author of "Six Diamonds and
A Dick," etc.

*Squashing political plums wasn't Cardigan's job. He tried to tell the
graft-grabbers that but they wouldn't believe him—not until their own
fingers got burned on the hot spot they'd warmed up for the big dick.*

CHAPTER ONE

Four Beers and a Body

HIS hair looked shaggier; his meditative frown was deeper. His burry gray topcoat bulked at the shoulders and his shoulders were close up to his ears, his chin down and crushing his collar. Elbows leaned on the bar and a big-fingered hand moved a glass round and round and made beer sudsy, and white foam stuck to the sides. He slid the glass spinning across the wet bar.

"Roll you, Toddy."

The bartender took poker dice from the cash-register, warmed them in a black box, smacked the box down. Cardigan rolled out and the bartender rolled and beat him.

"I'll take rye," the bartender said.

The only other man in the bar drained his glass of beer. "Let me buy this round."

Cardigan didn't look up. He put seventy-five cents on the bar and caught his glass of beer as Toddy sent it skidding toward him. The man at the other end of the bar blinked uncertainly behind spectacles.

"Thanks, Akeley," Cardigan said,

Cardigan grabbed Bush while McClintock fell on the senator.

"but this is my last. And I never go back on the dice."

The bartender raised his rye. "Well, mud in your eye."

"*Skoal*," Cardigan said, and drained half of the glass.

Akeley looked at his fingers and found that he had plucked a cigarette to shreds. He brushed the bits off. He had a thin face with fragile cheekbones and a timid mouth. He needed a haircut. There were stains on his tie. He went down along the bar rubbing his hand on the wooden rail and stopped at Cardigan's elbow.

"Beer again, Toddy," he said. He jerked a furtive sidelong look at Cardigan, edged an inch nearer Cardigan's elbow.

Cardigan looked at him—bluntly—from beneath shaggy eyebrows.

Akeley took his fresh beer, threw back his shoulders, took a big swallow, put the glass down with assumed nonchalance.

"How about it, Cardigan?"

"Been working up to it, huh, Akeley?"

"The boss—"

"You tell your boss for me to take a nose dive."

Akeley's chest shrank and his eyes blinked. He scratched at his neck. "Aw, Cardigan, there's dough in it for you and me—"

"I don't squawk!" Cardigan growled with sudden heat; then addressed his glass in a low throaty rumble. "I take care of myself. To hell with your boss. To hell with you, Akeley. You're a nice enough guy—but to hell with you."

Akeley wore a pale, self-pitying look. "It'd mean a lot to me," he murmured. "I got a wife and a couple of kids and the paper's cut me ten bucks a week and times are hard and if I got a story like that I'd be on Easy Street—"

"What a swell son-of-a-so-and-so you are," Cardigan muttered. "Pulling the old hearts-and-flowers on me because I'm Irish. Dragging in the frau and the kids to make me feel like a cheap punk if I don't spring."

"Look at me—from worry. Look at my clothes." Akeley made his face look woebegone. "It means a lot to me, Cardigan. It really does!"

The phone behind the bar rang. Toddy left a toothpick sticking in his teeth and took down the receiver. "Yeah? . . . Yeah, he's here." He lifted the instrument across the bar, said: "For you, Cardigan."

Cardigan took it. "Hello . . . Hello—hello!" He listened. He threw at Toddy, "Who was it?"

"Dunno. Jane."

"Hello—hello!" Cardigan snapped into the mouthpiece. "Hey, operator. I'm not calling any number. I've been cut off. Someone called me . . . No, and I don't know the number."

He hung up.

"It was a jane all right," Toddy said.

Cardigan put his hat on. "I'm blowing, kid. If she calls again I'll be at my apartment."

"I've got to go too," Akeley said.

"I'll drop you at your paper," Cardigan said.

Cardigan pushed open a swing door; tramped down a dimly lighted corridor toward a heavier door beyond. Akeley half skipped to keep up with him. Cardigan stopped to light a cigarette and Akeley opened the heavier door and leaned against it while Cardigan rolled past him into the dark street.

The door swung to hard, jolting Akeley in the back and staggering him past Cardigan.

A brittle clatter of shots rang in the dark. A weak, pitiful "Oh God!" ached up out of the reporter's throat. Blood was suddenly on his face. He stood erect as if held up magically by an unseen hand, his arms rigid and his fingers splayed; almost on his toes he stood, with his mouth gaping. But only for a split instant. Life blew out of him abruptly like air from a burst balloon. His body wheeled toward Cardigan; stopped with a jolt against Cardigan's rooted bulk.

Shadows made a drumming sound of heels down the street. While Akeley's body slid down past Cardigan's stomach Cardigan held a gun at arm's length. Its muzzle spewed flame and echoes banged violently against the house walls. The narrow street shook under the hammerlike blow of another shot. But the shadows were far away. The drum of heels petered out in the wake of the last gun-shot echoes.

Akeley lay at Cardigan's feet.

The heavy door made a sound. A section of Toddy's face appeared there. "Cur-ripes!" he hissed.

"Yeah," muttered Cardigan.

His big brown chin was way down, his neck was a rigid column, the skin tight on the back. There was a bitter, hateful look in his eyes. Vagrant gusts of wind plucked at his burry topcoat, but Cardigan remained rooted, feet planted wide.

"Cur-ripes!" hissed Toddy again. "What in hell— Is—is that Akeley?"

"Yeah."

Heavy footfalls came on the run. Cardigan looked over his shoulder, up the street. He slid his gun into his overcoat pocket and made a half turn. The houses made a ragged skyline up and down the narrow street. A few windows grated open and the blur of faces appeared and remained silent.

A cop came dodging from pole to pole.

"O. K.," Cardigan called dully. "It's all over."

The cop came out into the open and slapped his heels smartly on the pavement. "What the hell happened? Who are you?"

"This guy here got the works."

"Who's he? Who's the guy? Who are you?"

"Akeley."

"You're Akeley, are you?"

"No. The stiff's Akeley."

"And who are·you?"

"Cardigan. Cosmos Agency."

"Oh, yeah? Cosmos Agency, eh? You're Cardigan, eh?"

Cardigan said: "You don't have to kill time. The guys lammed like a light."

"Don't get smart, you. Never mind now getting smart. Just answer questions: that's all you gotta do, guy. I ain't taking lip from you, see?"

"Haven't I answered 'em?"

"That's all right; just answer them and nemmine the lip."

Cardigan said, "Ah, nuts," in a low, contemptuous voice, and bent down beside Akeley.

INSPECTOR KNOBLOCK was a tall horse-faced man with soft, brown eyes and wide lips that undulated slowly when he spoke. He always kept his eyes wide open and bland and had a habit of buttoning and unbuttoning his vest absent-mindedly.

Cardigan said, "We left together. I was right behind Akeley when we went out the door. The shots came from down the street. Six of them. I think four got Akeley. One was in the cheek. He fell against me and I—and I had a time getting my gun out. I took two pot shots and missed. It was dark and there was no chance of getting the guys."

"How many were there?"

"Two—I think."

Knoblock moved a paper-weight across the desk, then moved it back, as if he were playing a game. "Did Akeley show any signs of being afraid when he was in the speakeasy?"

"I didn't notice."

"Was he drinking hard?"

"He was sober."

Knoblock looked across at Toddy. "What do you think, Toddy?"

"He on'y had four beers, and the kind o' beer we serve, no guy even with a weak stomick could get soused on ten. He was down the end o' the bar talkin' to Cardigan here and when Cardigan said he was breezin' Akeley said he'd breeze to. There was a phone call for Cardigan—"

"A phone call," Knoblock said, merely as a statement.

"Yeah," Toddy said. "I swung the phone over and I guess they got disconnected."

Knoblock said, "Know who it was, Cardigan?"

"No."

"It was on'y a jane," Toddy put in.

"What time?"

"Eleven," said Toddy. "I know because at eleven I was to take some lousy medicine for me liver and it was eleven."

Knoblock made a notation; put his gentle brown eyes on Cardigan. "Cardigan, is there any chance that Akeley was the victim of an accident?"

"I don't get you."

Knoblock smiled gently; ran his tongue along the inside of his nether lip. "I'll put it this way: Is there a possibility that the shots were intended for you?"

"Where do you get that idea?"

"I'm simply asking."

Cardigan shrugged. "There's always a possibility. I've had a finger in sending many a guy to the pen, so why shouldn't there be?"

"I mean—" Knoblock moved the paper-weight to the center of the desk "—any particular possibility?"

"Nothing I could lay a finger on—right now."

Knoblock hefted the paper-weight. "You know, Cardigan, I like you. There are a few fellows in the department don't. But I do. I've watched your work. I like your guts. I'm an older man than you, Cardigan, and I've found out through experience that it's good policy to be free with ideas—not to hold them cooped up."

"Thanks," said Cardigan, straight-faced.

"This is murder. Murder of a reporter who was attached to The Star-Dispatch. You knew him. It's likely that he might have told you he suspected he was in danger of his life."

"I didn't know Akeley that well."

Knoblock sighed; put the paper-weight down slowly. "Very well, Cardigan. Very well."

The door opened and Detective Sergeant Bush came in. He didn't look at Cardigan. He looked straight at Knoblock.

"It was four shots, inspector," he said. "One went in one cheek and out the other. One got him in the belly. One in the left side. And one smashed his chest. Three o' the slugs were 38's and one was a 45. We looked around the neighborhood for ejected shells but didn't find none. Sergeant Stultz notified the paper and sent Goehrig out to break it to Akeley's family."

Knoblock nodded and said: "We've got to break this case, sergeant. Murder of a reporter usually raises a hell of a row. Break it—we've got to. When a reporter is killed it signifies that he knew something that might implicate someone high up. I thought—" he looked gently at Cardigan "—I thought our friend Cardigan might know, might have been told—even a hint—even the slightest hint . . ." His voice trailed off.

Bush kept looking straight at Knoblock.

Cardigan kept looking at Bush's stubby, hard-jawed profile. The spectre of a smile moved lightly—once—from left to right on Cardigan's lips.

"Anything else, inspector?" Bush said.

"Not right now."

Bush turned and went out, closing the door softly.

Knoblock wrote something. "What do you think of Bush, Cardigan?" he asked.

"I don't think about Bush," Cardigan said flatly.

Knoblock held his pen poised. "I always did like your guts, Cardigan."

CHAPTER TWO

Mac of The Star Dispatch

WHEN Cardigan let himself into his apartment the lights were on. His first reaction was to reach for his gun. But he saw Pat Seaward sitting on the divan. She was snapping shut an octagon-shaped, red vanity case. She was small and rather thin and she looked trim and pretty in a quiet, certain way.

Cardigan growled: "So now I suppose because you work for this agency you think you can hang around here."

"B-r-r!"

"Yeah? How'd you get in?"

"Picked the lock."

He heaved his topcoat over a chair, went to a secretary and took a bottle of Three Aces, took a stiff jolt and recorked the bottle. He scowled good-naturedly at Pat. "Well, what do you want?"

She said: "For a guy that was on the spot tonight you're pretty cocky."

"How do you know?"

"Well, I'm just a weak woman. I've been tailing you around for the past week, unbeknownst to you, kind sir. You were tailed to that speak by two men, and after you went in they concealed themselves in areaways. I was in another one. I waited a while, intending to do some shooting if trouble started. But I weakened. I hate to use a gun. So I walked to a store two blocks away and telephoned you. Something went flooey with the phone. As I came out I heard shots. I started for the speak and got to the corner and saw you on your feet. So I slipped away and reasoned this the surest place to find you."

"So you've been tailing me around, huh?"

"Forgive me, my lord."

"Cut that crap." He ran his fingers through his shock of hair, said dully: "Akeley got it. A little guy from The Star-Dispatch. He tried to get me to come through about Senator Ackerman. Dragged in a sob story about his wife and kids. Cripes—" he bent his shaggy brows "— feel lousy about the wife and kids."

"Yes you do."

"O. K., call me a mug." He leaned on a window-sill and looked down on Lindell Boulevard. He said: "I never liked Akeley and yet the guy accidentally saves me. He was a whining sort of guy; that's why I never liked him. He'd take advantage of you like a woman—through pity and hurt looks. I can't stomach that in a guy. And yet—" he stood up straight, turned, spread palms "—here am I and Akeley is at the morgue."

"Who did it?"

"Mobsters."

"Give me a cigarette."

Without moving he tossed her a package and said: "They were after me all right. Even Knoblock made a pass at that. I told him ixnay."

Pat lit up. "You big dope, why do you insist on holding back? Why don't you tell the cops that Senator Ackerman, Phil Gould and all that crowd are running chills and fever because of what you know? Why don't you? But no—" she shrugged "—you think you're tougher than the whole mob put together and you think it's too effeminite to run to the police."

He said, jabbing a finger toward her: "I've been marking time, sister. It wouldn't give me any swell kick to bust loose with a political scandal. You know me better than that. I've got to get something out of it."

"What you'll get will be what Akeley got."

"Horseflies! And look: I've got to prove that Ackerman sent his mob after me. I'm sure as sure myself, but what proof have I? I know—but I've got to prove it—that Senator Ackerman is the silent partner in the county gambling casino. I saw him out there on a wild party with some chorines from *Mean and Lowdown*. You know as well as I do that when White got bumped off by those guns they thought it was me. But who were the guns? And we've got to prove that they were heels from Ackerman's and Gould's scatter. I should go down to headquarters and clown around with a lot of theories? In the sweet by and by I should!"

Pat polished the nails of her right hand on the heel of her left. "To me sometimes you're a greater mystery than which-was-first-the-egg-or-the-chicken. Either you're over my head or you're just plain ga-ga. That indemnity company hired you to recover stolen ice from White. You recovered it and during the waltz-around you got mixed up in that gambling casino and they

thought out there you were trying to get something on them. They try to knock you off and now you recite some bed-time fable. My, you should be cast in bronze!"

He said, patting down the air with his palm: "I just don't run to the cops because some guys take a pot-shot at me. I know what I'm doing. I—"

There was a knock at the door. Cardigan looked at the door; looked at Pat. He drew his gun, crossed the room, opened the door. A man walked into the gun.

"Don't do that, dammit!" the man rasped. "Me with a bum heart and by God I can't come here but that you play cops and robbers—"

"What do you want, McClintock?"

"I want to kiss you, darling. Well! Well! Is there a law against me coming in? . . . Come on, Cardigan, for noisy tears smile and show the world—"

"Get in, then," Cardigan said.

McClintock entered with gusto, said: "Greetings, Miss Seaward," went directly to the secretary and poured himself a drink.

"Hey," said Cardigan.

"Lousy rye," McClintock said.

He was a wiry, dynamic man, with a snarly mouth, sharp eyes. He wore a blue topcoat; a derby raked over one ear. His hair was pepper-colored around the ears and his nose was pointed like a knife. He sat on the arm of an easy chair and put his feet on the cushion.

"What's the straight dope on it, Cardigan?"

"Your reporter was shot and killed."

"No!" McClintock had a raucous laugh. "Listen, big fella. I was just over to headquarters and they tell me that you don't know a damned thing. As soon as I heard that I knew that you knew something. Now Akeley wasn't on any spot. I know that. These guys that did the shooting were lying on wait and Akeley got in the way. And whom were they waiting for? Ah, that is the mystery—a deep, shadowy mystery larded with many ramifications. An enigma. A startling, provocative, teeming, dirty, lousy mystery. Yeah—like hell!"

He bounded from the chair to the floor, snapped: "You know damned well, Cardigan, that those eggs were promoting your own demise! You know damned well that Akeley's croak was an accident. I don't blame you for holding out on the cops. Not at all." He dropped his voice to a hoarse, rusty mutter. "Why the good cripes should you tell the cops when we can pay you five thousand bucks for the lowdown? Why should you?"

"You wouldn't be trying to bribe me, would you?"

"Bribe you? Dammit, I'll bribe anybody! Sure I'm trying to bribe you!"

"You're screwy," Cardigan said.

"Oh, so I'm screwy. What a belly-laugh I get out of that. Listen, Cardigan. Akeley was after you to spring some dope about some monkeyshines that took place at Gould's casino and here in the city. The killing of White was a fluke. We got a whisper that State Senator Ackerman is sugar daddy to that casino and there's one guy can confirm it. You're the guy. We like to believe that Gould's mobsters are after you because you know too much about the casino and Ackerman. We're willing to pay good money to verify it."

Cardigan took the bottle of rye and locked it up. "The trouble with you, Mac, is that you're taking a hell of a lot for granted. Akeley's been bothering hell out of me for a couple of weeks. I told him nuts—and I'm telling you nuts."

"But listen to reason, man! Why chuck over five thousand berries? You can't kid me. I know those guys had the finger on you and mobbed out Akeley by mistake. This rag I work for has dough and power and we're out to smear anybody we can. One of our men was murdered. We've got to vindicate him. We've got to make a splurge. It'll jump up our circulation."

Cardigan said, "You think you know they had the finger on me. You don't know, Mac—you don't know a damned thing. You can't bust in here and talk that way to me. It don't go."

McClintock rolled a cigar back and forth between bared teeth. His eyes glinted. "Six thousand, Cardigan."

"Go 'way."

"Seven."

"To hell with you and your rag."

McClintock cackled unpleasantly. "Or maybe you figure you can shake down Gould and Ackerman for more?"

Cardigan looked sullen. "You better go back to the city desk, Mac."

"You never were dumb, shamus."

"A punch in the kisser might do you good."

McClintock rasped: "You can't scare me, big fella! I've taken many a punch in the kisser. Dammit, I'm talking business with you! Akeley was murdered and we're going to get to the bottom of it. You're the key, Cardigan, and you'll turn or be sorry as hell."

"What can you do?"

"I'll do anything to get what I go after. Anything. And I'm after the lowdown on this song and dance and I'm going to get it. Get it, Cardigan!" He shook his fist vibrantly.

Cardigan made a half turn on his heel, walked heavily to the door, opened it. He looked somber.

McClintock bit off: "You're making

an enemy of The Star Dispatch, kiddo."

"Yeah. I'm making an enemy of a cheap snot of a city editor. And for two cents I'd throw him down the elevator shaft."

McClintock went to the door, his eyes narrowed, his lips bared tightly over his teeth. "I can find a way to make you strike a bargain, Cardigan."

"Nice big frame, huh?"

"I've got ideas."

"You'll have a broken jaw if you stand there much longer making faces at me."

McClintock shifted his cigar, jammed his hands into his pockets, strode through the door.

Cardigan closed it slowly and looked at Pat. "Mac's a rat," he said.

Pat said: "He'll do you dirt, chief."

CHAPTER THREE

Bush Butts In

CARDIGAN walked into his office at nine next morning and Miss Gilligan, his pop-eyed secretary, said, "Oh, Mr. Cardigan, another terrible, terrible murder! What's the world coming to when people—"

"Any wires from New York?"

"N-no, sir . . . It says here that you missed being killed by a hair's breadth—"

"Little more than a hair. Two hairs."

"Oh, Mr. Cardigan, you joke so about death."

"Being alive, I can afford to . . . By the way, if that lousy pest Schanzen calls up again about his stolen cash-register, tell him I'm not in. Tell him anything. Only tell him I'm not in. You look swell this morning, Miss Gilligan."

"Oh, thank you, sir!"

Cardigan went into his private office wearing a secret little smile, for Miss Gilligan was far from good-looking and made matters worse by using the wrong kind of rouge, the wrong kind of lipstick.

His staff came out of the adjoining room. Blaine, Hennessy and Katz.

"Ah, the three horsemen," Cardigan said, dropping into his swivel chair, shuffling the morning's mail.

Blaine said: 'So it's bruited about that you've been mixed up in an exchange of lead again. *Tsk, tsk!*"

"Yeah," sighed Cardigan. "That poor little slob Akeley . . . Did you ever have a dead man fall against you? Did you ever see a guy alive one minute, and then thirty seconds later dead and on his feet and leaning against you? Leaning against you dead—and sliding down you dead with his face shot to hell."

Katz droned: "You talk like a hangover."

Cardigan tore up a letter. "You're new with us, Katz. Ever seen a dead man?"

"Not yet, but I have hopes."

"That's not being hard, Katz. That's just bravado. Once you look in a dead man's eyes you'll never forget it. There's a hell of a fierce concentration in a guy's eyes just as he dies. A lot of ham writers talk about a blank stare. They're nuts. There's nothing blank about a man's eyes when he kicks off. Just like the crap I read about an express bullet whistling as it brushes the down off a guy's ear. That close, there wouldn't be a whistle at all. There'd be a distinct *snick* which is the vacuum of air closing in the bullet's wake."

"What's this a treatise on?" Blaine asked.

Hennessy said: "Was this guy Akeley on the spot? Did a wiper have the cross on him?"

"The chief's morbid this ack emma," Katz said.

Cardigan said: "I think I was the guy on the spot."

"Oh-ho!" Blaine exclaimed softly, nodding his chiseled head. "Am I to infer that certain hired hands of a state senator through a gambling-house owner tried to snuff out our illustrious boss?"

"Anyhow," Cardigan said, "Akeley got it. I went out to see his heirs this morning. A wife and two kids. One kid—three and a half—just over a double-mastoid operation. The other kid—five—in need of treatment for his eyes. Akeley was getting forty-five a week and his family living like a lot of hunkies in a lousy flat on the south side. And the wife anaemic—a little mud-gutter blonde who still can't believe her husband's dead. I tell you, gang, it got me—me of all guys."

"You don't mean to tell us you're going soft," Katz droned.

Cardigan's fist struck the desk. "Damn it to hell, Katz, don't be a smart aleck! I've had a dead guy fall in my arms. I didn't particularly like him—but he was a harmless, no-account reporter! I saw his wife and kids this morning and— You know, this is a lousy business we're in. A guy sees too much that isn't pretty. We're all wise; we're all hard. Until something gets right up close against us. You'll find that out, Katz. Or maybe I'm just a sentimental Mick—hell knows." He shuffled papers. "Go on, you eggs. Scram!"

The trio looked at one another. Blaine wore a thoughtful stare. Katz smirked and arched his eyebrows. Hennessy stroked his jaw and made a whistling mouth but didn't whistle. They went back into the large, adjoining room.

Shaggy-haired, leather-faced, Cardi-gan went through his mail, a hard party at odds with himself.

Miss Gilligan opened the outer office door, said, with a slight apologetic bow, "Detective Sergeant Bush, sir."

Cardigan glared. "I'm busy!"

"Yes, sir."

The door closed.

Half a minute later it opened.

"How busy?" Bush said.

Cardigan threw down a pencil, leaned back, creaked his swivel chair, folded his big hands on his hard flat stomach. "There's a law," he said, "against throwing out a cop."

Bush's hard jaw jutted as he took slow, studied steps across the floor. Haas, his partner, followed, closing the door quietly and saying nothing in a blank-faced way.

"There's lots of law," Bush grated. "There's a law that's beginning to wonder just how Akeley was bumped off last night."

Cardigan said, "By means of guns in the hands of unknown assailants. What's so tricky about that?"

"There's a trick to every trade, Cardigan. Even yours."

Cardigan stopped rocking in his chair. Two hundred pounds of him remained motionless, and his eyes steadied on Bush. "Your move again, Bush."

Bush sat down. "Maybe yours."

"I'll make one, fat-head. You've got a nerve trying to crack wise with me when I know you're friendly to Ackerman and Gould and that whole crowd in the county; when just a month ago you stood aside while Ackerman tried to bribe me to keep my mouth shut."

"This is murder, though, Cardigan," Bush said, "and I woke up this morning with a bright idea."

"Like hell you did. Somebody gave it to you. A bright idea would give you cataracts, Bush."

Bush sneered. "Where's that Sea-ward dame?"

"Be here any minute. Why?"

Bush grinned unpleasantly. "We're wondering about that phone call last night. It was damned funny about that. You get a call and then you take Akeley outside and he gets bumped off. Ain't that funny as hell?"

"That call was cut off."

"So you say. Who's to check up on you?"

Cardigan darkened. "You dirty—"

"How?"

Hate burned in Cardigan's eyes. "You dirty louse, you can't afford to try that on me! I didn't take Akeley out!"

"Toddy says you offered to drop him at his paper."

"But after he said he was leaving too."

Bush shook his head. "Toddy didn't hear that."

Cardigan's "Oh" was half muttered. For a long minute his brown jaw hung motionless, his eyes stared vacantly at Bush. His lips moved. "Toddy forgot, eh?"

"I didn't say that."

"I know what you said."

Bush leaned forward. "You were the only one who saw two men running away after the shots were fired. The thing is, was there two men?"

Red color began to creep over Cardigan's face. "You mean to sit there and tell me—"

"I'm not telling you anything."

"No?" roared Cardigan. "You're telling me that I put Akeley on the spot—that's what you're telling me! Why, you lousy—"

"Enough o' that!" Bush barked.

Cardigan's face was contorted. It was dull red in color, and the look in his eyes was malignant. Cords bulged on his powerful neck and red

seemed to streak his eyeballs and the corners of his mouth bent downward.

Haas moved from one foot to the other and his hand strayed to his right hip and remained there. His face remained white, expressionless, doughy. Out of the corners of his eyes he watched Bush. And Bush watched Cardigan. A glassy shimmer was in Bush's eyes; his lips were pursed in a fixed, forced smile that had in it nothing of humor. His chunky neck had hard, tight rolls of fat on the nape.

Pat walked in saying, "Good-morning—" and stopped short. Then she said: "Something tells me I've walked in on a conference."

Bush looked at her. "No, lady. You're part of the conference."

Pat pursed neatly carmined lips. "How lovely!" But a wily look was in her eyes.

Cardigan rumbled: "Don't take these guys seriously, Pat."

"What we want to know," Bush said, "is about that phone call last night, Miss Seaward."

She said: "What about it, sergeant."

"Cardigan here got a call in that speak. Toddy Moore, the bartender there, said it was a woman. He gave the phone over to Cardigan and Cardigan said the party was cut off. We began to wonder about that. So we poked around the neighborhood and found a call was made at a few minutes to eleven from a cigar store a few blocks away. The guy in the store remembered a woman had made it and you were easy to describe."

Pat looked at Cardigan, then looked at Bush. "By which I am supposed to infer—what?"

"A couple of minutes after you phoned, Cardigan walked out with Akeley and Akeley was rubbed out.

The cops that came around didn't see you. You didn't show up at the scene of the murder, yet you made a phone call only a few blocks away."

He stopped talking, hunched his chunky shoulders up alongside his ears, locked his fingers in front of his chest and leaned hard with his elbows on the arms of the chair.

"We checked up," Bush went on. "The phone call was made from that cigar store to the speakeasy. Cardigan says he saw a couple of guys running away—but that's only what he says. Nobody can check up on him because nobody else was in the street. Why did you make that call?"

Pat said: "I wanted to have some words with him. I was cut off. I couldn't get the connection back."

"So you left the cigar store."

"Yes I left the cigar store and started walking toward the speakeasy when I heard shots. I got far enough to see the chief standing on his feet and another man lying on the sidewalk. It was no place for me so I about-faced and left. I walked over to the Hotel Andromeda, hung around in the lobby for half an hour and then left."

"Where'd you go then?"

"Out to the chief's apartment, to see him and see what happened. I got out there about midnight."

Bush nodded slowly and wore a mocking smile. "In other words, you had plenty of time to ditch a gun on the way."

"I would have, yes, if I'd had a gun I wanted to ditch."

Cardigan growled at Bush: "Two guns did it, lame-brain. A forty-five and a thirty-eight."

"She has two hands, hasn't she?"

Pat smiled. "Isn't this all jolly!"

"So now maybe Bush, you can tell me why we would have put Akeley on the spot," Cardigan said.

"It may take us some time to find that out, but what interests us now is the trick about the phone call and this woman leaving the scene of the murder. Cardigan fired two shots—he says at two guys—but he could have fired them as a stall. It was pretty shooting that did Akeley in, miss, and we mind the time you came down to the pistol range at headquarters and shot the eye right out o' the target."

Cardigan kicked his chair back and stood up. "You're all wet, Bush. You're nuts to try pulling a stunt like this. Akeley was small change to me."

Bush stood up. "We're taking the woman to headquarters."

"You'll want me too, then," Cardigan muttered.

"No." Bush shook his head. "We want the woman first. We'll get you when we want you."

Cardigan went around the desk and gripped Bush's arm. He scowled malignantly. "You get this, you cheap gumshoe: you try any rough stuff on her and I'll beat the living hell out of you!"

"We heard," Bush said, "that Akeley was trying to get something on you for this paper. Something crooked about the recovery of them diamonds from Burt White."

"Oh . . ." Cardigan's voice was a hoarse whisper. "Oh, I see. I get you, Bush. So McClintock's been putting ideas in your head. Oh . . . I see. Sure, I thought you were acting abnormally bright this morning. I knew it couldn't be original."

Bush colored; blurted: "You can't make a monkey out o' me, Cardigan!"

"Why the hell should I pick on monkeys?"

CHAPTER FOUR

Fancy Frame-Up

CARDIGAN crossed the ochre-colored tiles of the Roxbury Hotel and entered the elevator. It let him off at the eighth floor and he walked somberly down the corridor, put his hand on the doorknob of 808 and pushed the door open. He hovered in the doorway like a dark cloud that presages bad weather.

McClintock half reclined in bed, the coverlet littered with newspapers. He had on loud pajamas and the room was filled with a haze of cigar smoke. A bottle of gin and glasses stood on a small table.

"Well, as I live and breathe bad air— the old mastermind himself! Come in and try finding a chair. You'll find it stuffy in here but I was born in a stuffy room and it's said that first impressions linger. Take a drink—gin—bell-hop gin. Two drinks and bells ring in your ears and your corpuscles hop. What do you think of the Chinese situation?"

Cardigan took a slow backward kick at the door and slammed it shut. He caught hold of the back of a chair, dragged it across the room and thumped it down beside the bed. He sat down, parked his heels on the edge of the bed and thrust his hands into his topcoat pockets.

"So you go lousy on me, huh, Mac? It takes a Mick to double-cross a Mick every time."

McClintock got off a hearty, raucous laugh and tossed a paper half across the room with great gusto. "The Chinese situation is yellow with age, Cardigan. Ah! A *bon mot!* Ah—China! Land of romance! Temple bells! Do they have temples in China?"

"Lay off, Mac," Cardigan muttered. "Lay off. That was a sweet one you pulled when you put ideas in Bush's head. You want to be careful. Ideas hit Bush like bad liquor. He might even get concussion of the brain."

"Bush is a fine, upstanding policeman."

"Sure, to put over a deal like yours you'd have to pick the only rat in the department. You rats run together, don't you?"

"Language, Cardigan! Language!"

Cardigan's voice rushed out: "You can't get away with a trick like that, Mac! You can't hang that job on Pat Seaward and me!"

"But what a story!"

"You told Bush that Akeley was trying to get something on me. You know that's a stinking lie!"

McClintock sat up, squinted one bitter eye, hitched up one corner of his hard-lipped mouth. "I went to you last night, you dumb ox, and offered you seven-thousand bucks to come across with some info that would put us on the right track and give us a chance to use the biggest headlines in the plant. But no—you got up on your high horse. You were holding out in the hopes of getting a bigger slice from the guys that bumped Akeley off."

"That's a dirty lie!"

"So you pretend! I came out straight with what I was after. I tried to bribe you in a straightforward way, on the up-and-up and no ace from the bottom. And you gave me a verbal kick in the pants. All right. Now—" he shook his finger at Cardigan "—I go you one better. I'll get what I want. I'll get it for nothing! I won't pay a cent for it! I'll plaster you and the jane in the swellest frame you ever saw. I'll make you squawk to get you and the jane out—and there won't be any dough in it. I'll get a knock-out legal battery. I'll get this story and to do it I'll rake your hide over the coals till you yell 'Uncle'! I'll get the straight about the recovery of those diamonds. I'll get the straight about Ackerman and his affiliations with Gould and that gambling crowd. That's what I'll do, my dear sweet Mr. Cardigan——you bum!"

"You'll drag in Bush. He didn't buy that new Lincoln on a cop's salary."

"To hell with Bush. I'll use him till I squeeze him dry and then to hell with him. Bush means nothing to me. You mean nothing to me. The jane means nothing to me. The only thing that matters a damn is whether or not I get that story. And, big fella, I'll get it! So help me God, I'll get it!"

Cardigan dropped his heels from the bed, reached over and yanked sheets and blankets to the floor. McClintock twisted. His hand shot beneath the pillow, came out gripping a heavy automatic. His lips snarled over his teeth and he cackled raucously.

"No you don't!" he rasped. "Get back, big fella, or I'll blow you to hell!"

Cardigan hung poised over the bed, scowling. "I guess you would, Mac."

"Sure. Why not? You broke into my room. 'Famous city editor kills private detective in self-defense.' A big stick on the right and the good old name of McClintock prominent in every paragraph. To make it more dramatic I'll say you pulled a gun on me. What a story that would be! And I'd like to make it one, Cardigan——I'd like to make it one. Make a grab at this gun——and give me a break."

Cardigan straightened, his jaw red and heavy, dull hatred smouldering in his eyes. "I'd like to meet you in a dark alley some night, Mac."

"So would I. I'd plug you in the back and make a big story out of that too."

Cardigan went to the door, put his hand on the knob. "Be seeing you again, Mac."

"Swell!"

Cardigan walked heavily down the corridor. He cursed and kept cursing deep in his throat till the elevator doors opened.

He went across to police headquarters and found Pat downstairs in one of two detention rooms. The room was clean and bright. Down the corridor were the women's cell blocks. A matron left Cardigan at the door and Cardigan entered the room.

"Didn't you bring flowers, chief?"

"Hello, Pat." Cardigan sat down on a chair, put his big hands on his knees and looked at her. "Good kid," he murmured.

"So this is McClintock's doing."

Cardigan nodded his shaggy head. "The rat . . . . What happened, kid?"

"Nothing much. I took your advice and didn't take Bush seriously. I kidded the ears off him. He got all hot and bothered and now he's waiting for Inspector Knoblock to show up. What should I say?"

"Stick to your story till I look around. This guy McClintock burns me up and I'm going to hurt him. I've got to get these guys red-hot that bumped Akeley off. This is no time to spring names at random. After all I've only got suspicions——no facts. That bum McClintock will never get this story——never. He's framed us and I'll pay him back with interest. How do you feel?"

"Fine and dandy."

"You're a brick, Pat. You're the berries. Give me till tonight to crash this frame. You'll never spend the night here, kid."

She said: "Bush wasn't so dumb. He didn't want you because he knows you. He knows he wouldn't get a murmur out of you. But he thinks I'll weaken. And he knows that if they make this case seem bad enough for me——

you'll be Irish and bust down and—"

"That's correct up till there, Pat. But Bush really thinks he'll nail us for this job because that great brain McClintock talked him into believing it. Bush'll work his head off—what head he has. McClintock's the brains in this. Bush is just a babe in his hands. McClintock engineered this."

"Don't worry about me, chief. Only if I have to stay here you'll have to run over to my hotel and get me a nightie."

He stood up. "You won't stay here, kid."

He walked to his hotel, entered the writing room, sat down and wrote three pages of dark, crisp script. He addressed the envelope to himself at the agency office and took it down to the post office. He sent it by registered mail and slipped the receipt into his vest pocket.

MR. ULLRICH, Senator Ackerman's right-hand man, was a rolypoly fat man with cheeks like red apples and bubbling, twinkling eyes. He had a big-toothed grin in a small mouth and tried to minimize the impression of avoirdupois by bounding around on his toes. The impression one got, however, was that Mr. Ullrich was an over-animated elephant.

"Well, well, well, Mr. Cardigan! How do you do, how do you do, how——"

"How do you do," said Cardigan.

Ullrich's office was paneled in dark wood. The desk was a massive, carved piece out of some museum. Ullrich had bounced and bobbed from the desk and gripped Cardigan's hand. Cardigan shook it, but not with enthusiasm. He had a dark, steady eye on Ullrich and the set of his face was not pleasant.

"This is a lovely day, Mr. Cardigan! It's wonderful to be alive on a day like this, to see and feel the sun——"

"Akeley's family, for instance."

"I beg pardon?"

"I suppose Akeley's wife is just doing a dance and raving about the beauties of nature too."

"Akeley . . . Oh, yes! Oh, my yes! Oh, you mean that poor chap who was murdered last night. Horrible!"

"Any minute I suppose you'll bust out and cry."

Ullrich affected a hurt look. "My dear Mr. Cardigan——"

"My dear Mr. Cardigan my dear sweet aunt's eye! I didn't come here to have you pull a burlesque on me! You're Senator Ackerman's mouthpiece. You be his ears too. And listen." His voice dropped. "Listen, Mr. Ullrich."

"Yes?"

Cardigan's voice dropped another note. "You know as well as I do that I was the one who was supposed to have got bumped off last night. Me. I was tailed to that speakeasy. The rats didn't have the guts to come in after me. They waited out in the street, probably all hopped up, and when I came out—and when Akeley stumbled and got in the way—those guys' hands were so hot on their rods they had to let go. Me they wanted. Akeley they got—a skinny little no-account newshawk. You hear!"

Ullrich stepped back, putting his hand to his chest, looking shocked and innocent. "But my dear Mr Cardigan, my sympathy is all with the family of the deceased. It is, truly. But yet I cannot fathom out why you burst in here——"

"For the love of God," Cardigan's deep voice throbbed, "don't go in for the old run around! Don't!" He chopped his fist through the air. "You know me. I know you. Standing orders from my boss in New York are never to break a political scandal. Never Unless it's the last resort. Phil Gould —and you—and Ackerman—you're all in a dirty big puddle. I could make a fortune springing what I know about you. I've turned down a bribe already. I never went out of my way to find these things out about you guys. It just happened. Yet, by cripes, all of you have done your damnedest to silence me. First by bribery—which I turned down. Then guns. Then guns again — last night — and another blunder. I was willing to play the lone wolf. I never run to the cops crying for help. I was ready to snoop out these heels of yours and shoot it out with them. But it's off now. It's no go. Somebody has to take the rap for the murder of Akeley. Somebody—" his voice grated "—in your own back yard."

Ullrich pulled a silk handkerchief from his breast pocket, patted his forehead, his cheeks, raised his chin and patted his throat.

"I will say, Mr. Cardigan, that you gave me a start. Indeed, sir, you gave me a start. Indeed you did!"

"You can't laugh it off, Ullrich. I promise you, you can't laugh it off."

Ullrich folded his handkerchief carefully, slipped it into his breast pocket, patted the pocket. "Now, Mr. Cardigan—my dear Mr. Cardigan. You assume too great a public spirit—and the weight of it may one day bear you down—"

"It's not public spirit, Ullrich. It's just that some guys have gone into a huddle and come to the conclusion that my aid Miss Seaward gave Akeley the works."

"How atrocious!"

"To me, it's just lousy. And there's only one thing to do about it. The night, one month ago, when Burt White was murdered while in my car, it was forgotten quickly because White himself was a heel. I'd recovered stolen diamonds from him and he'd shot his girl friend, run out, jumped in my car. A murder car got him—thinking it was me. That was easy to forget. But this time a reporter was bumped off. That's bad. So there's only one thing to do. I want the guys that did Akeley in."

Ullrich put his head on one side. "I see you are in deadly earnest, Mr. Cardigan."

"It's got to be swan-song for somebody—and not for Miss Seaward or me."

"You are an uncommonly hard man to handle, Mr. Cardigan."

"You and your mob have tried like hell to get rid of me, Ullrich. I'm hard to get rid of. In the beginning I never knew one tenth as much about you as you thought I did. But now I know a lot. Ordinarily I'd shut up. But you guys forced this. Get started doing something. Miss Seaward's in the holdover and she's got to be out by night."

Ullrich tried to look cheerful through a sheen of perspiration that had formed on his face. "Sit down, Mr. Cardigan. Please sit down." He bobbed to the desk, rubbed his hands together, took a deep breath, reached for the telephone.

Cardigan said: "And no clowning."

CHAPTER FIVE

Scarehead Stuff

SENATOR ACKERMAN was a lantern-jawed tall man with steely eyes weakened by dark half-moons beneath them. He closed the heavy office door quietly, flexed his lips against his teeth and put fists into the pockets of his dark blue coat. He made his stare hard and straight on Cardigan.

Ullrich said, bounding from one foot to the other: "Mr. Cardigan has a grievance."

"I like how you put it," Cardigan chuckled harshly.

Ackerman's voice was blunt. "Now see here, Cardigan; I've had enough of your interference."

"I'm not interfering. I'm here to get the guys that bumped off Akeley. I've not been engaged by anybody to get them. But headquarters has got Miss Seaward in for questioning and there's influence that will hang the kill on us."

Ackerman scowled. "What makes you think we know anything about the murder?"

"It's not the first time your mobsters tried to get me, senator. But it's the last. Miss Seaward got onto the tail of two guys that were tailing me last night. When I went in that speak they waited outside. She tried to warn me by telephone but the connection was cut off. Akeley got in the way—and Akeley got killed instead of me. There's only one guy would want to see me silenced. And you're the guy. I'm banking on that."

"You cannot prove that, Cardigan."

"Does Miss Seaward stay in the holdover tonight? Am I going to be hauled in on a framed charge, cost myself and my agency a lot of money? Or are you going to turn over the guys that killed Akeley?"

Ackerman's eyes were frigid. "I—am—going—to—do—nothing, Cardigan."

"You've got the most guts of anybody in your scatter," Cardigan said, "but that's not enough. Your reputation's at stake. I see your point of view. You'll brazen it out." He shook his head. "But you'll never make it. I can give what I know to The Star-Dispatch, but for spite I haven't so far. I can, though. I

hate McClintock and his whole tribe but I can forget that. I want the guys that did the killing."

He strode to the desk, put his hand on the telephone.

"Who made the pinch of your aid?"

"Bush."

Ackerman cursed. "Give me that phone." He called headquarters, spoke with Bush tartly, told him to come over. "And right now!" he finished hotly.

When Bush arrived he was quite out of breath.

Ackerman said coldly: "Bush, Cardigan tells me that you pinched Miss Seaward on suspicion for the Akeley murder."

"Yes," Bush said, scowling at Cardigan, "and before night we're going to clamp on this guy too."

Ackerman's voice grew colder. "Why did you pick the woman up, Bush?"

"We had a right to. She was around the scene of the murder. She made a telephone call to Cardigan from a store a couple o' blocks away. Then Cardigan takes Akeley out. Then Akeley's bumped off and the woman never shows her mug."

Ackerman scowled. "Why the hell didn't you tell me something about this?"

"I wanted to surprise you. It's a red-hot, Senator. Akeley was trying for a couple o' weeks to get something on Cardigan about the recovery of that ice from Burt White—"

"Who told you that?"

Bush colored, swallowed. "A—a guy on The Star-Dispatch."

Cardigan growled: "McClintock put that bug in his brain."

"McClintock!" Ackerman got up, his face darkening. "You fathead, what right have you to go into cahoots with McClintock?"

Bush looked scared. "I ain't in cahoots. But it was hot—it was red-hot. He was sure the woman did it and he gave me lots of reason for it."

"I don't give a damn what he thought!" Ackerman bellowed. "You half-witted idiot! McClintock—of all men, McClintock!"

Bush gaped. "But why?"

"I'll tell you why," Cardigan said. "And it's a scream. Mac's one of your great enemies, senator. And he's one of mine. I hate him like nobody's business. And here he is playing us one against the other. The bum tried to pay me seven-thousand bucks to break him some dope about you and Gould's casino and some other things I'm supposed to know about you. I kicked him out. Because I hate his guts and because I never take a bribe. I'd always have to be living it down. So he comes back at me—through Bush. He gets Bush all steamed up about Miss Seaward and Bush falls for it. Why? Because Bush hates me like poison. Because he'd like to see me take a long rap. And because he's dumb—or wise, and if wise, he's taking a slice of graft from The Star-Dispatch."

Bush shook with rage. Spluttering made his lips wet. "That's all one of your dirty lies, Cardigan. It's—"

"Shut up," Ackerman cut in icily.

The room fell silent.

"Oh," ground out Ackerman, "you unmitigated fool! You idiot! You hopeless blockhead!"

"Good gracious!" breathed Ullrich.

Bush stuttered, "B-but—"

"Enough!" chopped off Ackerman. "I see it all. I see McClintock's line of thought. No, you wouldn't. But it's got to stop, Bush! McClintock will throw you to the wolves when he's used you. You've got to take water. You've got to let that woman go, that's all."

Bush went white. "Let her go!

By God, I can't. It's slated for the evening papers. Inspector Knoblock's working on the case too, now, and—God, I can't take water! I can't explain. If I let McClintock down—"

"Who's your friend, Bush," Ackerman said, "McClintock or me? Who's the man who put you where you are today?"

"But don't you see—"

"I see either one of two things. Either you're dumber than I ever thought you were, or you're double-crossing me."

Bush raised a shaking hand, shook his head violently. "No—no, I'm not double-crossing anybody—"

"Me, you're trying to," Cardigan said.

"You—you!" Bush bellowed. "You are always razzing me! Ever since you came here—"

"Quiet," Ackerman said. "This guy Cardigan is after us. You'll have to drop this case against him. You'll have to tell Knoblock and the chief anything you want—but this case must be dropped. We can't afford it."

Bush made a sound something like a moan. "I didn't mean wrong, senator. Honest to God, I didn't!"

Ackerman was cold. "You made the wrong move, Bush. You've got to straighten it out."

The words ached out of Bush's throat: "But I can't!"

"My dear senator," said Ullrich, fluttering, "let us pause to consider, to reason things out."

"There's nothing to reason out," snapped Ackerman.

Cardigan said: "I'll say there isn't," and stood up, a lowering look in his eyes. "The whole trouble here is that all of you guys are in the mud. You want to throw Bush for the fall-guy now. But that won't end things. I'm tightening down. I'm after material evidence—and the best material evidence will be the two guys that bumped off Akeley. And that's what I want."

Ackerman, his face livid now, crossed the room and faced Cardigan. "I warn you to damper down, Cardigan."

Cardigan reached out and laid his hand on the telephone. "I warn you, senator."

Bush began raving like a man gone mad. "I won't be no fall-guy! I got the jane and this guy to rights. I can hang this kill—"

"You rat," Cardigan muttered.

Bush held his hand out. "I'll take your gun, Cardigan."

"You will?" Cardigan showed his teeth. "I'll show you something you won't forget, gumshoe. I'll show—" He slipped his hand beneath the left lapel of his coat.

Ullrich, his eyes shimmering, moved on his heel. A gun leaped in his hand. Exploded.

Cardigan turned half around, looking at Ullrich with shocked eyes. Cardigan wheeled against the desk, bounced away from it, hit a chair and crashed down to the floor, taking the chair with him. His head banged against a radiator.

Ullrich wore a pop-eyed smile. His voice leaped from his lips. "This does it, my dear senator! He tried to draw a gun on a police officer! Assault with intent to kill!"

Bush spluttered, "He—he—"

"Shut up, Bush!" Ullrich cried. "You saw him! You, senator—you saw him! It's the only way out—it's the only out! Indeed—indeed it is!"

Ackerman stood rigid, rooted to his feet, his eyes staring at Ullrich. "By George!" he whispered hoarsely. "You've hit upon it! I always knew you could be relied upon—in a pinch!"

Cardigan lay panting, half propped

against the radiator, his hands spread-fingered on the floor.

Ullrich took two bobbing steps, moistened his lips, gripped his gun hard. He looked at Ackerman.

He whispered, showing his teeth in a queer smile, "It would be doubly certain if he were exterminated completely. We hang suspended by a single cord." His wide, bubbling eyes turned on Cardigan. His gun came up.

Cardigan's voice rushed out. "Do it and weep, Ullrich! I'm no fool! Not all fool! Before I came here I wrote out the highlights in the dirt against you. I sent it to myself—registered mail—care of my office. It's in the mails now—where you can't get it, where, by God, you can't bargain with me to get it! Pull that rod, you wiper—pull it!"

Ullrich almost stumbled. His fat hand began to shake. His eyes did not bubble. His fat face became contorted and his lower lip popped out with a slight sound, hung loose and shining.

Bush put a hand to his eyes, moaned. Veins stood out on Ackerman's temples.

Outside the door, suddenly, there were sounds of a scuffle, a hoarse cry. The door whipped open violently and McClintock, his derby smashed in, his tie half undone, barged in, slammed the door shut, locked it.

"This is the lousiest, damnedest place to get into I ever saw!" he rasped.

THROATY, rattle-voiced, Ackerman said: "There has been a little unpleasantness here."

"Now isn't that news! By cripes, I've been parked half an hour on my pants downstairs trying to get up here. The longest I've ever waited for anybody—two presidents and a bootlegger included. So I heard the boom-boom . . . and was it a close race to the door with your secretary? Boy, did I sock him?" He became suddenly sly-eyed. "Well, senator?"

Ackerman nodded to Cardigan. "This fellow came in here. You know him, I believe. Detective Sergeant Bush came here after him—to take him to headquarters for questioning. He resented by attempting to draw a gun."

Ullrich nodded politely, saying: "I did my best to protect an officer of the law."

Cardigan got up slowly and leaned against the radiator. He took off his topcoat, suit coat and vest; took a handful of his shirt and ripped it off; ripped off his undershirt. He twisted his neck and looked down at his right side, where blood flowed slowly. He made a face.

"This is going to be a story," McClintock said. "A lalapaloosa! Did you shoot him from behind, Ullrich, or was he looking at you? How'd he do it Cardigan, you big bum?"

Ullrich said: "Cardigan went for his gun. He shoved his hand inside his lapel—"

"Oh, yeah?" Cardigan said. "When my gun is—" he drew it from his hippocket "—here!"

Ullrich stared. "You said—"

"I said I was going to show Bush something he'd never forget." He took from his upper left-hand pocket of his vest a small slip of paper. "This. The receipt for that registered letter. The letter that's in the mails now!"

Bush swung on McClintock. "You said you were sure Cardigan and the woman had a deal in that Akeley kill. Tell him! When I tried to pinch—when I asked him in a nice way for his gun—"

"You damned liar!" Cardigan roared. "You're all liars! I had you all tied up. Only Ullrich saw a way out—when you went meshuga and

asked me for my gun. Only Ullrich—and the fat slob yanked his gun and let me have it. Let me have it—because he had two witnesses to say I pulled a rod! *Pulled it from an armpit holster!* When you see—now—and even McClintock sees that it was on my hip. And I've got you all tied up now."

He lunged to the desk, grabbed up the phone. Ackerman jumped and got him from behind, around the neck. Yanked him away and sent him spinning against the wall. The phone banged to the desk. Drops of blood flew from Cardigan's wound.

"Let me at that phone!" Cardigan bellowed.

Ackerman said: "Listen—a minute," and got in Cardigan's path.

Cardigan hit him on the jaw and sent him against Ullrich, and Ullrich fell down. But Ackerman stayed up and flung himself between Cardigan and the desk.

"Let me—get Knoblock!" Cardigan snarled.

McClintock grabbed up the phone and snapped into it: "Get me The Star-Dispatch!"

Ullrich knocked him down and McClintock, hanging on grimly, tore the telephone wires from the box.

Ullrich panted: "Please, sir—"

"Please me—will you!" McClintock cried, scrambling to his feet.

He hurled the instrument at Ullrich.

Bush, looking horrified, turned and fled. Fled to the door. Got his hand on the knob and was turning the key when Cardigan came plowing across the room, grabbed him by the neck, swung him around and hurled him across the room. Bush recovered and tried again.

"Let me out of here!" he cried. "I ain't done nothing! I want to get—"

"Stay back!" muttered Cardigan savagely. "You heel, you're a disgrace to the shield you wear!"

But Bush was crazed. "So help me Cardigan——" His gun was in his hand.

Cardigan crowded him, grabbed Bush's gun hand. The gun boomed. A gash appeared in the dark wood of the wall and Cardigan, dripping blood and sweat, twisted Bush to the floor. twisted the gun from his hand, left Bush moaning and grovelling.

Ullrich fell into a chair, a glazed stare in his eyes.

Ackerman took two steps, ripped the gun from Ullrich's hand, turned it on himself. McClintock fell on him——but as the gun exploded. Ackerman went down to his knees, fell forward on his face.

The room was a shambles when a dozen men broke down the door and rushed in.

"Listen, Cardigan," McClintock barked. "What the hell's the use of bleeding to death? Why don't you let me bind you up?"

"You sure think the world of me, don't you?"

"Yeah——a world of dirty names. But I like your style, big fella. And—— say——what a story!"

THE room was still a shambles ten minutes later. It was filled with blue-coated policemen. There were an ambulance doctor, another doctor. Knoblock was there.

Ackerman lay on a stretcher. "We all went mad," he murmured. "Things happened so fast. There was no time —to talk—explain. I was in—deep. I knew I was in deep. Cardigan was after us. There was no shaking him off—no bargaining with him."

"You fool," Knoblock said, sadly.

"I know. And it was—pretty bad —knowing he knew something—and not knowing just how much he knew. I took the chance. I sent two men after him. To end—the suspense. They bungled. And then—there was nothing to do—but bargain—and he wouldn't—he wouldn't listen—to anything. Give Ullrich—and Bush—a break."

His head fell to one side and one of the doctors said: "That's all. That's the end."

Knoblock turned a clouded face toward Ullrich. "There'll be two men we want. He said—two."

Ullrich did not smile. His voice was like a ghost's. "Yes, my dear inspector. I can give you the names."

Downstairs, Cardigan was sitting in an ambulance, smoking a cigarette.

"Should you ask me," McClintock said, "I wouldn't hang around here."

Cardigan said: "That's an idea," and climbed out.

McClintock hailed a cab, handed Cardigan in and followed.

"Listen," Cardigan said, "I don't need you for a nurse. Go on. Beat it."

"Say—I'll get you a nurse that'll knock your eye out. Not because I like you, Irish. But because I like your style. You're the first real, honest-to-cripes opposition I've had in years. You're a pick-me-up after about a ten-year hangover."

"Baloney!"

McClintock laughed raucously. "And how I slice it!"

Next Month!!!

Another great *Cardigan* story by Frederick Nebel

Horror House

by

J. Allan Dunn

Author of "The Phantom of the Porthole," etc.

It was a place of splendor—this palatial Vista Del Mar—with its great gardens and sweeping lawns. Yet mystery lurked among the rare blooms which girt its grounds and triple murder dwelled within its spacious halls.

CHAPTER ONE

The Face At The Window

MURDER! A curious topic of conversation for such a time, place and company. It was midsummer. The scene, the spacious Spanish *hacienda* of Elizabeth Putnam, spinster millionairess.

The perfume of choice roses mingled with the fragrance of other blooms, with the salty tang of the sea in the breeze that gently ruffled the trees and shrubbery of Vista del Mar, built on an outstanding promontory of Long Island, a piece of property of almost fabulous value.

Four of the wealthy but eccentric spinster's week-end guests were in the spacious lounging room on the ground floor. Outside was a paved terrace. The long windows were open. The prime intention of the four had been to play contract bridge but the talk had turned to murder.

Other guests were entertaining themselves after their own fashion. There were launches, yachts, a hydroplane and a private bathing beach, besides a swimming pool and tennis courts. Two were following the fixed example of their hostess in taking an afternoon siesta. One more, an important one—no less than Miss Putnam's confidential adviser and legal counsellor, James Quincy Lubbock—was to arrive later in the day. His visit might well be one of pleasure but it would probably be combined with business.

Vista del Mar was Liberty Hall during the day. Only with dinner did its menage become formal and the hostess assume her benign but definite role.

Beside the table set for bridge there was a wheel-buffet that held refreshments; ice, limes, charged waters, excellent liquor—for Elizabeth Putnam mocked at prohibition.

She possessed several traits that were masculine rather than feminine, including a very definite idea of what she wanted to do. She was apt to be arbitrary though generous. She delighted to surround herself with celebrities, or with those who might become celebrities. She was the born patroness.

Her nephew, Lawrence Lawson, generally and genially known as Lorry—clubman, dilettante of many arts, master of none, a person of perfect manners, of leisure that was filled with entertainment—acted as a sort of superior majordomo to his aunt. He helped to entertain, to stimulate conversation, to exert his undoubted charms upon the guests. For this his aunt provided him with an income to which he jestingly referred as his salary for being a lion-tamer.

"I put 'em through their paces," he would remark. "Lions, and likewise, lionesses. You'd be surprised how shy some of 'em are—until they get started."

Lorry was supposed to be Elizabeth Putnam's chief heir. Undoubtedly she would endow foundations and hospitals but, if Lorry behaved himself—or was not caught in too flagrant an affair, he might inherit a fortune.

Now he lounged in a bamboo chair, smoking his special brand of Russian cigarettes through a long tube of amber tipped with ivory, sampling from the tall glass that held ice, seltzer and Scotch.

It was a seemingly chance word of his that had set Denton Quigley—Professor Quigley of the Chair of Psychology at Manhattan University—astride his hobby, while the bridge game waited.

To Quigley's own amazement, his book, The Psychosis of Crime, intended as a treatise, possibly as a textbook, had achieved a popularity far beyond the expectations of either author or editors. Coming on the crest of the crime wave, the book possessed the thrill of a detective novel, the vogue of a best seller.

Quigley was a man of forty odd, tall and lean. His body was still vigorous; it was a body that might have been that of an athlete, if his brain had not dominated. He was bald, save for a tonsure of grizzled, straggling hair. His eyes were piercing.

There was Mary Minturn Dodd, M.D., specialist in the glandular correction of children, third member of the mixed quartette in the lounging room, sipping a highball, smoking almost con-tinuously as the ashtray beside her testified. She was thin but not meager. Alert, neurotic, with vitality manifiest in her face, her skin was like a flower petal, giving out a faint odor of jasmine; her jet black hair cut short and brushed slick as a seal's back; full eyebrows almost meeting above a delicately chiseled Roman nose.

She had made no secret of her hope that she could get Elizabeth Putnam to endow a Dodd Foundation. She seemed to regard Quigley as a dreamer, rather than a fellow scientist. You could dissect and analyze gland tissue, know how it functioned, but psychology was an uncertain field, indefinite, not far removed, in her frankly stated opinion, from spiritualism. There was a certain antagonism, politely restrained, between her and the professor.

THE fourth of the loungers was of vastly different type.

This was Countess Romeska, who looked like a butterfly but gathered honey as diligently as any bee. She wore the mask of a romantic refugee and owned a studio as an interior decorator. Clever and forceful she contrived to appear preeminently feminine and appealing.

"Tell us about murder, Professor Quigley," she murmured. "It's so primitive, so fascinating."

Quigley took the bait. "Not always primitive," he said emphatically. "There is the coldly calculating murderer, using scientific methods, figuring out everything beforehand. It is generally considered a prime factor in the discovery of a murderer to find the motive and so choose the killer. Show me the type of murder and I will point out the motive and the individual. I will set my finger upon him, unerringly."

"Him, or her? Women seem as likely to murder as men, these days," suggested Lawson.

"They are more emotional, therefore more murderous," replied the professor

"All murderers are disorganised," Mary Minturn Dodd asserted. "The perfectly normal person, healthy, well balanced, with glands functioning normally, cannot be a criminal. A criminal is a physical pervert, not a psychological one. Correct their glandular irregularities and you—"

The countess gave a slight scream, started from her seat and fell back with a hand to her heart. "A man! A man just looked in the window!" she cried, her hand shaking. "He climbed down from above."

Lawson reassured her. "They're trimming the vines," he said. "Cheeky beggar though, to look in like that. I hope he didn't disturb my aunt; she is taking her nap right over us. But she would have her blinds drawn," he concluded.

"It wasn't that," said the countess vaguely. "The thing that really startled me was that for just a moment I almost thought it was Miss Putnam herself. The face, of course. The likeness is amazing. It was a man in overalls. Though I didn't see much of him except his head and shoulders," she added. "He must have looked in from a ladder, I suppose."

Lawson made no more comment on the incident. He changed the subject. "How about that game of contract we were going to play?" he asked. "That is, if you are all through with glandular secretions, murder and what-not."

Professor Quigley watched Lawson as the latter got up, set chairs about the bridge table, arranged score pads, shuffled a deck of cards, set them, backs up, for choice of partners.

The two women drew together.

"Contract has nothing to do with sex," declared the countess. "We shall probably bankrupt you men. What are we playing for?"

"Name your stakes," said Lawson carelessly.

He was a born gambler. The professor made no objection to the two cents the countess suggested.

On the first hand, which went to five no trump, the countess overlooked a finesse and she and her partner were set a trick.

She apologized. "That man distracted me," she said. "He looked so much like Miss Putnam. I'm sorry, partner. I won't let you down again."

Lawson dealt dexterously, the cards falling swiftly in place from his supple fingers, the digits of an artist, slender and brown and strong. Their tips were slightly spatulate; they interested the professor.

Lawson played brilliantly and while the professor was an excellent player himself, he had to be content to be dummy for the most part while Lawson performed.

Several times the two women bid well but high in an attempt to retrieve their losses, and got penalized, after they had become vulnerable with one clever victory. The points above the line were mounting into money.

SUDDENLY there was a thump on the ceiling. A few flakes of plaster filtered down in the sunlight. The dome of the indirect-lighting lamps quivered and shook.

It seemed as if some heavy body had fallen on the floor of the room above, the room where Elizabeth Putnam was, supposedly, taking the nap that should last for at least another hour.

The countess screamed, knocking over her glass.

They all rose hastily. The card table tipped, spilled cards and pencils and score sheets.

Mary Dodd's face suddenly became alert, hawklike.

Quigley stood looking upward.

As Lawson started for the door the countess clutched at her heart and fainted. Quigley caught her before she fell and carried her to a chaise longue.

As he set her down Dr. Dodd motioned him away, feeling the other woman's pulse. "Ice!" she said brusquely. "Get some ice, you fool!"

Then the door opened, just before Lawson reached it. The butler stood there, agitated, his ruddy face putty color.

"Miss Putnam is dead, sir," he gasped. "And Mrs. Trimble is in a swoon, sir."

"Dead! You say my aunt is dead!" Lawson's voice was pitched high in excitement.

"Yes, sir. I think she's been murdered, sir."

"Good God!" cried Lawson. "Doctor—"

"I can't come now," said Mary Dodd. "The housekeeper's a healthy woman. She'll come out of her faint all right. I can do nothing for Miss Putnam if she's dead. The countess is not dead, but she's not too far from it. Braddock."

"Yes, ma'am."

"Get me my small black bag from my room. Hurry. Fortunately I never travel without stimulants."

Countess Romeska lay as pale of cheek beneath her rouge, as if she had been drained of blood. Her eyes were closed, she did not appear to breathe.

Braddock, the butler, left the room wringing his hands and shaking his hanging head. He was an elderly man who had been with Miss Putnam for over a quarter of a century.

Lawson passed the man as he went up the stairs on his errand, slowly. Quigley was close behind. Lawson turned toward Miss Putnam's chamber while Braddock headed for Dr. Dodd's room. Quigley paused, checked him at the head of the stairs.

"Just a moment, Braddock," he said mildly. "How did you happen to discover this?"

The butler hesitated for a moment as if he resented the questioning of a stranger, looking toward Lawson.

"I wanted to see Mrs. Trimble, sir," he said at last. "I saw her go in—"

Lawson broke in authoritatively. "This is no time to question him, professor, even to practice your detective acumen. That belongs to the police. Quigley, my aunt is lying dead in there, with a woman who has swooned. She may be able to tell you more if you still feel like inquisition. The police will sift any evidence you may have, Braddock. You're upset. Get yourself together. Go into your pantry and take a drink."

"Yes, sir. I wouldn't want to make any mistake, sir. I could use the drink but I must get the doctor's bag first, sir."

He passed on and Lawson opened the door to the death chamber.

CHAPTER TWO

Hat-pin and Carver

ALL the blinds were drawn but one, and that was up to its limit, as if it had been sharply released. Sunshine rayed in through the gap. The plump form of the housekeeper, Mrs. Trimble, lay in the full light, on a crumpled rug.

She was coming to, half conscious, muttering, repeating the same words over and over.

"Oh, my God! Oh, my God!"

Elizabeth Putnam lay on the bed

clad in a dressing gown of dark green brocade. Its folds were undisturbed. The body lay on one side, extended, as if in placid sleep.

Something projected from her right ear, something that glittered. It looked like the head of an old-fashioned hat-pin, made of faceted jet, or its imitation.

"It's been thrust into her brain," said Lawson, in a stifled voice, straightening up from where he had bent over the bed. "While she slept."

Quigley's nostrils dilated, his eyes widened, glittering, as he looked out the window. "Cigar smoke," he said. "Notice it, Lawson?"

He did not wait for an answer but stepped to the windows, tried the casements which opened in tall, vertical halves. They were locked. There was a small balcony of wrought iron beyond them. He could see the top of the ladder that rested against the side of the window, close to but not touching the balcony.

Lawson helped the housekeeper to her feet. The woman still seemed confused.

"What are you doing in my aunt's room at this time in the afternoon?" he demanded sternly. "You know she always sleeps until three."

The housekeeper looked at him, passing her hand over her eyes. But, before she did so, she flashed Lawson a glance of hatred.

"Miss Putnam had headaches," she said. "Sometimes she woke up during her nap. She would not take medicines because her heart was bad and she was afraid of them. So she always kept a bottle of lavender smelling-salts. The one she was using had got weak and she told me to bring her a fresh one. I always keep a supply in the drug cabinet. That is in my closet at the end of the hall where we keep such things.

with other bathroom needs. I was busy, attending the guests. We are short a maid. I forgot it. I knew Miss Putnam might wake up and need it. She would be vexed if she found only the old bottle. So I brought the fresh one. It's there on the table, beside her bed. I hoped she would be asleep. She seemed to be. I had just placed the new bottle on the table when I saw a shadow on the blind. A man's head and shoulders. It startled me. I went to the blind to look through and I must have stirred the spring. The blind shot up. I saw the man, Rawlings, the new assistant gardener, on the ladder with pruning-shears in his hand, climbing down.

"I tried to reach the blind but the tassel had got twisted in the cord. It was out of my reach. I fussed around for a time, afraid the light would waken Miss Putnam. Then I looked— I looked—toward the bed and—I saw—"

She had been speaking composedly, lucidly, but now she swayed again. Quigley caught her by the arm.

"Steady now," he said. "Steady! you saw—what—"

"She saw my aunt lying there with her own hat-pin thrust into her skull," said Lawson. "Look at her hair, Quigley. You claim to know about crime. She's the only one with long hair in the house, in the neighborhood, probably. And she wears old-fashioned hats. She uses hat-pins—she alone. You won't deny this is your hat-pin, Trimble?"

AGAIN the housekeeper sent Lawson a look of venom. But she did not answer the direct question. "There's others might benefit, might be glad to see her dead," she flared.

"You noticed she wore hat-pins, Lawson?" asked Quigley mildly.

"Of course. We all did, joked about it and her hats. That isn't all. She wanted to quit. Wanted to marry a man who's aiming to buy an inn up in Maine. My aunt told her if she'd stay she'd leave her twenty-thousand dollars. She stayed. That's what she means by benefits. Twenty thousand—the inn—a marriage, at her age. It's good bait. Plenty of motive. And there's the hat-pin."

"It seems obvious," said Quigley. "Too obvious. I can't see why she'd leave it there. And I'm not so keen on motives. To whom did you refer by 'others,' Mrs. Trimble?"

"Plenty," she said sullenly. "They're always after her money. You might ask him."

"I suppose you're a beneficiary, Lawson?" asked the professor. "You knew your aunt's intentions?"

"She was the only one who knew them," returned Lawson. "Lubbock might. She drew a new will once a month. He might be coming here tonight for that."

"It will be a good idea to ask him, if he chooses to answer. In the meantime—"

"We'd better send for the police. This woman must be detained, Quigley. After all, you're only an amateur. You make deductions."

"Only when suggested by facts, Lawson. Not jumps in the dark. But I agree with you about the police. Also about my amateur standing. The body must not be touched. But this woman did not kill your aunt."

"No? I don't believe her cock-and-bull story. She is a vindictive old cat. As for the gardener who is supposed to look like my aunt by the Countess Romeska; I've noticed him. I'm going to see he doesn't leave the place."

"I'm not trying to leave," said the housekeeper, stolidly. "But I don't want to stay in this room."

Lawson left them.

"You don't have to," said Quigley. "We'll leave everything here just as it is. Lock the room. I'll hold the key. Is there a telephone in your quarters, Mrs. Trimble?"

"Yes, sir." The housekeeper was weeping, trying to wipe her eyes without a handkerchief. Quigley gave her this. "That looks like one of my hatpins, but I never would do such a dreadful thing. It may have my fingerprints on it, but—"

"There would not be anything definite on a surface like that," said Quigley. "Too broken up. And all crimes don't depend on fingerprints. You've got to brace up. Let's get to that telephone."

She went with him. Quigley locked the door, put the key in his pocket. The housekeeper suddenly faced him.

"What did *you* want of her?" she asked, almost fiercely.

"I? Nothing. I was invited here because of a book I had written. I am only a professor but I happen to be well enough off. Do I look like a murderer, Mrs. Trimble?"

She sized him up with welling eyes, shook her head and sprinkled tears. "No, you don't," she admitted. But neither do the others. I—I—loved her. She needed someone to love her. She didn't have to bribe me with twenty-thousand dollars to stay. I'd have done it for nothing. I told Talcott so—the man who wants me to marry him and run the inn in Maine."

"I don't doubt it," soothed Quigley. "But let's telephone for the police. Get yourself together."

"I will," she answered. "The quicker the police come, the better. They all were after her money. Mr. Lorry, he—"

"Be careful, Mrs. Trimble," warned Quigley.

"I will. But it's true. That female doctor, Dodd, she got half a million promised her this morning. I was a witness to a paper. And that Russian countess, making eyes at Mr. Lorry; him at her. Miss Putnam thought they might settle down, the two of 'em. But they'd make ducks and drakes of her millions. Then there's that slick secretary, Editha Stendall. She's a smooth one. Miss Putnam thought the world of her but she's a minx. Mr. Lorry tried to get solid with her, because she was close to Miss Putnam, but—"

"You are not being careful," Quigley said. He put in his call. "You have got to help us sift things out. Where is this Miss Stendall?"

"She went into Blueport in her own car. Miss Putnam spoiled her. I guess she was efficient enough but she's the sort would line their own nests. And then I'm accused. It's enough to—"

The call came through. Quigley talked briefly, gave his name, hung up.

A KNOCK came on the door of the housekeeper's room. It was Dr. Dodd. "The countess is better," she said. "She's a nervous type and she's got a rotten heart. Do you want me to see Miss Putnam?"

The professor shook his head. "As you said yourself, doctor," he answered, "it is better to look after the living than the dead. Nothing can do Miss Putnam any good, unless it is to find out who killed her. It was murder. I have sent for the police and the medical examiner. Have you seen anything of Braddock?'

"I saw him talking to Lawson, on the lawn for a few moments, some time ago, when I lowered the blinds for the countess. I think he came into the house. I am not sure of that, but I saw Lawson hurrying down through the gardens."

The two regarded each other a trifle antagonistically. They did not like each other. She thought him a meddler and somewhat of a fake and she was not a type he thought a woman should be.

"Lawson," he said, "seems to suspect this gardener who frightened the countess. But there is the matter of a hatpin—several matters. I should like to find out how long Miss Putnam has been dead but I think it would be better to leave all that to the authorities."

"I agree with you," she half snapped at him. "I have no desire to interfere in a professional, or an amateur capacity, Professor Quigley."

It was the second time the charge of amateur nosiness had been made but Quigley merely smiled. They went into the darkened room where the countess lay. Quigley picked up the upset table, the pencil, the score sheets and the cards. He tore up the scores.

"We'll not finish this game," he said.

"We were playing for money," said Dr. Dodd. "We owe you two men. It is a debt."

"I'm sorry," said Quigley. "I've destroyed the record. He had set the bits of paper in an ash receptacle and lighted them. Methodically he decked the cards. Dr. Dodd muttered something that sounded like 'old meddler.'

There came a shrill scream, and then another. The countess moaned and Dr. Dodd sternly admonished her to stay where she was while she herself followed Quigley.

They found two maids huddled in a passage with a man who wore a valet's waistcoat trying to quiet them.

"What's all this?" demanded Quigley. Dr. Dodd looked at him. The bald-headed professor seemed to have acquired a sudden and very sufficient authority.

"There, there!" cried one of the maids. "Look at it, under the door. It's still moving. It's blood! Oh—oh—oh!"

She went into violent hysterics. Dr. Dodd spoke harshly to her, led her away with the other girl.

"I'll be back in a moment," she called to Quigley.

"Who are you?" he asked the valet. He did not like the look of the man He was at once cringing and crafty, fawning and bold. "What do you know about this?"

"Me, sir? I'm Mr. Lawson's man. The nayme's Walker, sir. I don't know so much. Only that is Braddock's pantry. And 'e was a bit downcast over the 'orrible 'appening."

"Come with me," said Quigley and pushed open the swinging door to Braddock's own little domain.

HE saw a ghastly sight. The butler's body sprawled in a chair, his head on one side. There was blood on his clothes, blood still dripping on the linoleum and adding to the stream that had flowed into the passage. There was a screened window beside the chair, another door back of it. Quigley opened the latter and saw another hallway—empty.

He saw also an empty glass on the shelf of a silver sideboard. It smelled of brandy. There was a half-smoked cigar on an ash tray and it had not gone stale. On the floor was the lethal weapon, a small carver, keen, used for steaks or small game. It was streaked with crimson.

Braddock's throat was deeply cut. Quigley did not touch the body, nor anything else. But it was plain that the death wound had been inflicted by a strong and desperate hand. Windpipe and gullet were both severed.

The professor turned on the British-accented valet. "What do you mean by his being downcast?"

"Just w'ot I said, sir. 'E was in the family for years, sir. And much attached. The old lady, meanin' no disrespect to the dead, sir, was a reg'lar Queen Elizabeth but she'd be fair, after she blew orf a bit. And Braddock fair worshipped 'er. She 'ad 'im down in 'er will for a tidy sum. Told 'im so. More than she ever did for me. Though I 'old 'er no grudge for that. But I talked with Braddock a while back an 'e was like a man orf 'is 'ead. Crazy, you might s'y. 'I carn't stand it,' 'e says. 'I carn't stand it.' I told 'im it wasn't gettin' 'im anything to act like that but 'e only shakes his 'ead and leaves me. Then Esther came along, with Lucy, and I was talkin' with them about the 'ideous occurrence when Esther screams. She saw the blood, like we all did."

"I see," said Quigley. "Do you smoke cigars, Walker?"

The man looked at him cunningly, shook his head. "Not me, sir. Braddock did. No one else in the 'ouses, that I know of, sir, though Mr. Lawson always 'as some for guests. That was Braddock's smoke. I suppose 'e thought 'e'd soothe 'is nerves a bit. I ain't been in there all day; yesterday either, for that matter. 'E was touchy about anyone goin' in, unless they were invited. A rum cove, in some wy's. Must 'ave been a bit barmy to cut 'is throat like that."

Dr. Dodd came hurrying back. Quigley told her briefly what had happened.

"I trust the police will get here soon," he said. "The butler is dead. Beyond question. You can look at him if you want to. But the place must not be touched."

"Fingerprints, mister?" suggested Walker slyly.

Quigley ignored him. He was quite sure that the valet had lied to him in one or two details, if not in many. He was the type that cannot tell the truth in moments of stress.

"You had better get back to your master and your duties," the professor admonished.

CHAPTER THREE

"By The Same Mind"

QUIGLEY had summoned state troopers, as well as notified the local police. There were three of the former, besides the town chief, an important but phlegmatic sort of individual. The lieutenant in charge of the state force took hold. This was an important case.

He and another officer came to the house with Lorry Lawson and another man, who was handcuffed. The third officer had been left at the gates of the estate.

Quigley was interested in the face of the handcuffed man. Here was the gardener who had frightened the countess, and the resemblance between him and the dead face of Elizabeth Putnam was startling. He was no longer in overalls. Lawson had a general family resemblance to his aunt but this young Rawlings, new assistant gardener, might have been the murdered woman's younger brother. But for the discrepancy in age, he might almost have been her twin. The likeness was little short of amazing.

He seemed defiant, rather than sullen. Lawson was disheveled. His clothes were disarranged and he had a cut on the side of his head.

"I understand there's a doctor here," said the lieutenant, "Mr. Lawson, you'd better get patched up. Saunders, take care of this bird."

He looked at the little crowd of guests and servants. Two of the former who had been sleeping had learned the news. The other house guests were in a motor launch, it now appeared, making a picnic luncheon. They would not return for some time.

Quigley introduced himself. Lawson added details.

"Professor Quigley of Manhattan University, lieutenant," he said. "Wrote the book, The Psychosis of Crime."

The lieutenant grunted. "I've heard of it," he said non-committally. "Like to talk with you, Mr. Quigley. We've got to wait until the examiner shows up. He's on his way. You get that head fixed up, Mr. Lawson. Mr. Lawson says he suspected this man and caught him trying to make a getaway. He put up a fight and struck Mr. Lawson with the gun he flashed when Lawson—Mr. Lawson—tried to hold him."

"That's a lie!" said the prisoner. "He had the gun. I took it away from him. He meant to kill me."

"I'm warning you not to talk," said the lieutenant. "It don't look too good for you."

"That's a good idea," said Rawlings. "I won't talk, yet. But what I said was the truth." His hands were slightly calloused but his voice was that of an educated person.

"Another is dead," said Quigley. "Braddock, the butler."

"Braddock? Killed?" cried Lawson.

"I didn't say so," answered Quigley. "He might have committed suicide. His throat was cut."

The guests shuddered. Dr. Dodd supported the countess who seemed close to swooning once again.

"We'll look into it," said the lieutenant. He appeared efficient and he was deferential toward Quigley.

"You get that cut fixed, sir," he said to Lawson. "Where's that lady doctor?"

"I don't need a doctor," said Lawson. "I can handle it myself. I suppose I do look a bit ghastly. But I'll go to my rooms and fix it up. Change my clothes. Walker, come with me," he added to his valet.

The two went upstairs together. The trooper took charge of Rawlings.

"I'd like to see this butler," the lieutenant said to Quigley. "Will you come with me, sir?" They went into the pantry and the officer surveyed the scene with narrowed eyes. "It don't look much like suicide to me, Mr. Quigley," he said. "What do you think of it? We've heard of you, sir. That book of yours is a bit deep in spots but it's in all the post libraries and there's real stuff in it."

"I'm not a surgeon," said Quigley, "but, if Braddock killed himself, you'll find his fingerprints on that knife handle. If you don't, it wasn't suicide. I don't believe you'll find prints of any kind. I may be wrong."

THE lieutenant looked at him shrewdly. "Do you mind telling me what you've figured out, so far?" he asked. "I understand you don't like to appear publicly in this sort of thing."

Quigley nodded. "It might disturb my investigations, destroy their usefulness," he said. "You'll find Miss Putnam upstairs with a hat-pin in her brain. The housekeeper, Mrs. Trimble, found her and we found the housekeeper, in a faint. It was her hat-pin, presumably. She was the only one who uses one apparently. She acknowledged its probable identity. Braddock here, seemed inclined to talk but he was upset and Lawson warned him to reserve his evidence. Lawson practically accused the housekeeper, although he went after the gardener you hold. I suppose he told you about the man having been at work, frightening the countess, throwing his shadow on the blind for the housekeeper to see?"

"I got that," answered the officer. "It looks pretty mixed."

"Mrs. Trimble was promised a legacy, also Braddock." Quigley went on.

"Mr. Lawson told me that," said the lieutenant. "Said that he, this woman doctor, the countess and you, were playing cards when the housekeeper fainted on the floor above."

Quigley put a hand into his side pocket of his coat, as if absent-mindedly. "Yes," he agreed. "We were. But we don't know yet how long Miss Putnam had been dead when we found her."

"The M. E. should be here right away," replied the other. "Mr. Lawson went over most of the ground with me though of course he didn't know about the butler. But he said this housekeeper wanted to marry some man in Maine. They were going to start an inn. She was to get twenty thousand if she stayed with Miss Putnam until she died. Might not have got the inn they wanted, then. That's an angle."

"That's an angle," admitted Quigley. "There may be others. For instance, Braddock might have been jealous of that man, might have wanted to marry the housekeeper. And, of course, Lawson didn't know about Braddock. Then there's a mysterious secretary who appears to have been here in a confidential capacity to Miss Putnam. She's away but she'll be back soon. And Lubbock, who is Miss Putnam's attorney, is also expected."

"James Quincy Lubbock?" inquired the officer, with something of awe in his tones.

"That is the name, I believe," said Quigley. "He may tell us something about the will. Also, it seems that Dr. Mary Dodd was promised half a million dollars for her Gland Foundation, or whatever she calls it. There's an interesting woman, lieutenant. Altogether, it's an interesting problem. It should bring a lot of kudos to the man who gets the credit for solving it. A lot of people profiting by the death of a wealthy patroness. And this man Rawlings has a most remarkable resemblance to Miss Putnam. That is why he frightened the countess."

The lieutenant's face was slightly sour. "Looks to me as if you were getting a big kick out of this, Professor Quigley," he said. "I wonder how much you're holding out on me?"

"My dear chap," said Quigley. "I'm not down in her will. I'm lucky enough not to need it. But watch those who are. And I'm not holding out. I think I've a few cards and I reserve the right to play them as I see the game going. You may win it without me."

A CAR drove up. It was the medical examiner, fussy and annoyed at the interruption to his private practise, yet pompous.

Lawson suddenly appeared at the head of the stairs. He wore a dressing gown and his head was bandaged with adhesive over a wad of cotton.

"Come up here, quickly," he called.

Quigley bounded up. The lieutenant joined him at the head of the stairs.

Lawson led them to his suite.

They entered his sitting room, bachelor-furnished, luxurious. There were fine pictures of the exotic school, a heavy Elizabethan buffet and table, deep chairs and a club lounge, deep-piled rugs. His aunt had been liberal.

On the largest rug, with hooked fingers clutching at its nap, his body twist-ed, his face stiffened in a convulsion, foam on his lips, was the valet, Walker.

There was a bottle on the buffet. A siphon, cracked ice in a bowl of silver. Two glasses on the table, one filled.

"It was just by the grace of God," said Lawson, "that I didn't get it too. I fixed the cut, got off my clothes and Walker, poor devil, drew me a bath. He was going to lay out fresh things for me. He looked rotten and said he had been talking with Braddock just before he was murdered. It had upset him, he said. I told him he looked it, that I felt the same way myself. I told him to take a drink for himself and bring me a highball in the bathroom. He thanked me and said he thought he'd take it neat.

"The water was running and I didn't hear anything, but I wondered why he didn't come in with my drink. So, before I got in the tub, I came out and found this. Someone has poisoned him. Someone who meant to poison me, and came damn near doing it."

He shuddered.

"Plenty of work for the coroner," said the lieutenant grimly. "We'll analyze that bottle and the stuff you didn't drink. He's dead, all right but we'd better have the doc look at him first, though I don't think he's got a chance."

The coroner, summoned from his examination of Miss Putnam confirmed this. He took one look at the dead valet, sniffed at his mouth, regarded his set eyes.

"Hydrocyanic acid," he announced. "Death instantaneous. Two deaths within twenty minutes of one another. As for Miss Putnam—" He paused and regarded the three men, holding back his words for effect. "I left Dr. Dodd with the body of Miss Putnam," he said impresisvely. "Dr. Dodd is an excellent woman. I know her professionally. She agrees with me but it will take an autopsy to definitely establish our opinion."

"And that is?" asked the lieutenant as the coroner again deliberately checked his speech.

"That Miss Putnam was not murdered."

"Not murdered?"

LAWSON'S voice shook slightly, high-pitched with surprise, incredulity and excitement. Quigley, kneeling by the body of Walker, looked up from his examination of the valet's person, gripped with astonishment at the astounding announcement.

"There was an attempt at murder which would have been successful," went on the medical examiner, if the victim had not been already dead. We find no slightest trace of external hemorrhage, I do not believe that any internal or cerebral hemorrhage will be found. She died of heart failure. It is probable that she passed away peacefully, in her sleep. The person who thrust the hat-pin into her brain undoubtedly considered her alive, took no time to make any close observations. He, or she, committed the crime and fled. The dead woman went to her room at the usual hour for her nap, directly after luncheon, within a minute or two of one o'clock. She was found at three fifteen. And she had been dead for almost two hours when discovered. She must have died soon after she lay down. At what moment the murder was attempted is difficult to determine. It was well after her heart ceased to function and her blood to flow."

Lawson suddenly broke down, burying his face in his hands, unnerved, his shoulders shaking. The coroner went back of his chair and spoke to him. He made an effort to recover but his features were drawn and twitching, his eyes looked as if they had seen some fearful vision.

"This is a house of horror!" he said slowly and dramatically. "A house of horror! First my aunt, then poor Braddock and now Walker. For God's sake, gentlemen, let us get busy and determine what fiend is responsible for all this!"

A scared maid rapped on the door. "Mr. Lubbock is here," she announced. "He just drove up in his car. He saw the policeman with Rawlings and he wants to know if he can come up to see you."

"We'll come down," said the lieutenant. "Doctor, you don't have to stay any longer, if you don't want to. There will be an inquest later that you will preside over, of course. The chief and myself can conduct the examination, with Mr. Quigley. We'll hold it in the room under Miss Putnam's where they were playing cards."

"That suits me," said the doctor. "I have several visits to make. I shall be in touch with you later."

"I'll meet Lubbock," said Lawson and followed the doctor out.

The lieutenant turned to Quigley. "Well?" he asked.

"The first attempt at murder was unnecessary," said Quigley. "The would-be killer would have attained his or her end, without assassination. Yet I hold that the belief in such murder having been committed led to the horrible death of Braddock, to the poisoning of Walker."

"By the same hand?"

"By the same mind," said Quigley.

The lieutenant nodded. "Rawlings could not have killed Braddock," he commented. "He was with Lawson at the time, which lets Lawson out. Who tried to poison Lawson and did kill Walker? That hat-pin makes it look bad for the housekeeper. Well, we had better go down and check up. There were other guests. Some of them have been out since the middle of the morning, won't get back until late afternoon. We'll overhaul the rest."

CHAPTER FOUR

Death Ends It All

LUBBOCK was there, eminently the counsellor of degree, grave, somewhat portly, judicial. He greeted the lieutenant without remarking on the tragedy, shook hands with Quigley.

"Heard of you, professor," he said. "Read your book with great interest. A bit academical, but sound. Glad you are here."

The local chief of police from Blueport came in, with a town constable.

They were soon assembled in the lounging room. Rawlings was there, handcuffed, in custody. The celebrated lawyer looked at him with keen interest. The two guests who had been sleeping turned out to be one Arturo Simonetti, a popular portrait painter, who had been hoping to get a commission from Miss Putnam, extremely shocked at the news; and Eleanor Mayall, a widow, a distant relative of Miss Putnam, an unassertive dependent, who seemed utterly crushed at the catastrophe.

The household was checked up. Only the secretary, Edith Stendall, was still absent. Mrs. Trimble explained that the secretary's trip to Blueport was probably connected with errands for her employer. She was clearly not in favor of the secretary and sniffed audibly when asked if Miss Stendall was a confidential employee.

"She thinks so," she answered.

The lieutenant produced the hat-pin, brought now into evidence, with the pantry knife and the poisoned liquor.

He was conducting the inquiry well, Quigley considered, a competent man who would go carefully and thoroughly.

"I don't know that it's mine," said the housekeeper. "It looks like it might be. I've others of the same sort. I use hat-pins. But I loaned one like that to Miss Stendall the other day when she was going riding, horseback. She has a tricorne hat and she thought it might blow off. And there's one pin missing from my set."

"She didn't return it?"

"No, sir, she did not."

"That will do for now, Mrs. Trimble. Please do not leave the house."

The chief of Blueport police spoke up for the first time.

"I saw Miss Stendall in Blueport," he reported. "She was going into the bank. How about seeing if that hatpin is in her room, lieutenant, while she's away?"

The lieutenant accepted the suggestion. A maid showed them to the secretary's quarters.

Downstairs there was silence. No one even whispered. The local policeman and the subordinate state trooper kept quiet and watchful charge. The chief and the lieutenant were away for perhaps ten minutes. When they came down the latter beckoned Quigley into a corner, introduced him to the chief of Blueport.

"I want to show you what we found upstairs, in the secretary's room," said the lieutenant. "The chief discovered it. I was looking through a checkbook, Miss Putnam's. It was not unusual, I suppose, for Miss Stendall to keep it in her office, but there was a check drawn this morning that the stub shows was marked 'personal account,' for ten thousand dollars. The chief saw her going into the bank. I presume the signature was authentic. I am wondering if Miss

Stendall is coming back here. She left in her own car. The maid thinks she took no clothes, but ten thousand dollars might offset that. I have set things in motion to have her brought back, in any event."

It was plain that there had been ample opportunity after lunch for almost everybody present to thrust the hat-pin into the dead woman's ear while she lay asleep. Luncheon had been at noon. The bridge players had not gathered until somewhere between one-thirty and two, the time unmarked definitely and therefore uncertain. They had all gone to their rooms after luncheon for various reasons. Miss Stendall had left somewhere round two.

SOME of the outside servants were quickly eliminated. The head gardener testified that Rawlings had been trimming the vines since half-past twelve. He had not kept him in constant sight. He stated that Rawlings was a good, steady man who had only been at Vista del Mar for seven weeks but had proven quite satisfactory. He had applied personally to Miss Putnam for the job, with a letter, and she had sent him to the head gardener with a request to take him on if possible.

"Did you notice any resemblance between Rawlings and Miss Putnam?" the lieutenant asked him.

"None that I would care to be set down a mentionin'," said the witness.

The Blueport constable on duty outside came in, saluted. "Miss Stendall's outside, sir."

"Send her in," said the lieutenant.

The secretary entered. She was good-looking, comparatively young, though not a girl—well-dressed, grave, composed, discreet. Quigley bowed to her and she bent her head, taking the chair he placed for her.

"Miss Stendall, secretary to Miss Putnam?" queried the lieutenant.

"Yes."

She took off her hat, close-shaped to her head. Her hair was brown, gathered at the neck, emerging from a bob. She could gather it in a knot on top of her head, Quigley reflected, wear it that way under a tricorne felt, but need a hat-pin, perhaps, to help keep on the hat in a gallop. And she was the type that would gallop, he fancied, scattering the cares of a job that was good, but might be trying, on the wind.

"Miss Putnam was found dead with a hat-pin thrust into her ear," he said brusquely, concealing the fact of previous death, if it was a fact. "Mrs. Trimble states that she loaned you a similar hat-pin and that you have failed to return it. We did not find it in your room, Miss Stendall, or in your apartments, which we felt justified in searching; but we find a check stub for ten thousand dollars, marked 'personal account' and the chief of police at Blueport saw you entering the bank upon which it was drawn, today. Did you cash that check?"

"I did," she answered calmly. "I have the money with me. It was drawn for a special purpose which I have been, so far, unable to fulfil. That inability had delayed my return, from failure to meet a certain party. But Mrs. Trimble is mistaken about the hat-pin. Her memory is not accurate."

"Do you care to tell us whom you expected to meet, to whom, if anybody, the ten thousand dollars was to be paid? You hold the option of not answering, at this present inquiry."

The lieutenant's warning was patent. The atmosphere was charged with suspense. But the girl was not upset. "I do not care to do so," she answered.

Then the lieutenant ruthlessly played what might be a trump, what might indeed, prove another kind of trump; a trump of doom. He thrust a sheet of paper under the eyes of the secretary. It was the find of the Blueport chief of police.

"Will you acknowledge having written, or printed this?" he asked.

"Certainly," she replied and Quigley, watching her, admiring her aplomb, saw the faint flicker of a smile pass over her lips. A clever young woman, he decided—well poised.

The lieutenant read out loud the sentence pencilled on the paper.

"DEATH ENDS IT ALL"

THERE was a pregnant silence. Even Lubbock looked grim. Coupled with the hat-pin, the ten-thousand dollars and the denial of willingness to tell of its destination, the situation looked sinister to the ordinary onlooker or hearer. But, to the astonishment of them all, Quigley emitted a dry chuckle and then looked almost ashamed of it. It was not a loud sound but it had sounded like an explosion.

"Mind spelling your name, Miss Stendall, both names; with your permission, lieutenant?" he queried and caught a glance of reserved amusement but not so remote comprehension in her eyes. Lustrous eyes of brown, they were, under delicately penciled brows. Quigley took a notebook and pencil from his pocket.

The secretary spelled out her name and Quigley set it down.

"When did you write this?" he asked.

"Last night. It was rather a silly thing to do but I was tired, not ready to sleep and disinclined to read. If there had been a crossword puzzle handy I might have done that instead."

Quigley nodded understandingly.

"Some people, even learned ones," he said, "do crossword puzzles for relaxation. Others juggle with anagrams. 'Name' anagrams. The idea is popular. You attempt to produce an intelligent sentence from the letters of your own name. Not using any twice except when so present, nor eliminating any. The sentence is supposed to reveal your character. I have tried my own hand at it. My name is not favorable for that sort of thing but Miss Stendall's offers several variants. One of these is the striking sentence, especially at a time like this, that reads 'Death Ends It All.' But it has nothing to do with murder."

He exhibited what he had written, with letters crossed out, carried down. They made up the sentence the lieutenant had read with such emphasis, and the secretary's name.

Editha Stendall—Death Ends It All

" 'Death' is in the Christian name," explained Quigley, "leaving 'I' over. The first, third, fourth and fifth letters of the surname produce the word 'ends'. The 'I' left over and the second letter 'T' make 'it', leaving the last three letters 'all'. 'Death ends it all.' A most succinct phrase, but it does not cover the findings of this triple murder. I say triple murder because, whoever set that hat-pin in its fatal and horrible position, was intent upon murder. The fact that Miss Putnam was dead when it occurred might be twisted by a clever defence attorney to change the accusation from first degree, but it does not shift the original endeavour."

"Thank you, Professor Quigley," said Miss Stendall. "You have stated what might have seemed foolish, coming from me alone. I did try to anagram my name, for amusement. The result was a trifle disconcerting but I did not take it seriously."

CHAPTER FIVE

Heir To Murder

THE tension was broken. Lubbock polished his glasses. The Blueport chief of police looked foolish. The lieutenant shrugged his shoulders.

"Thank you, Mr. Quigley," he said. "That will do, Miss Stendall, unless you would like to volunteer some more information?"

"I do not choose," she answered.

"I would like to ask you one more question. Were you, to your knowledge, a beneficiary under Miss Putnam's will?"

"I was not. The matter was broached. Miss Putnam had heart trouble. She had a definite belief that she might pass out in her sleep. She mentioned the matter of a bequest because she stated that she did not wish to change her intimate contacts. I declined because I did not care to be under any obligation other than that of my own inclination."

"That's all."

"Good girl. Stands on her own," Quigley told himself.

The lieutenant consulted a few notes he had made and recalled the housekeeper.

"There was a smell of cigar smoke noticed in Miss Putnam's room," he said. "Braddock seems to have smoked cigars. Did any other member of the household present, guest or servant, do so, to your knowledge, Mrs. Trimble?"

She closed obstinate lips and shook her head. "None that I know of," she said.

"You noticed the cigar odor, Mr. Quigley? Do you care to ask any questions?" said the officer.

The housekeeper looked as communicative as a stuffed turtle but Quigley's first query startled her.

"Mrs. Trimble, did Miss Putnam ever smoke? Anything stronger than cigarettes. Small cigars, for instance?"

"I won't answer such questions."

"You must, sooner or later," warned the lieutenant. "Or be in contempt of court."

"Mrs. Trimble," Quigley went on, "we want you to help us find out who tried to kill Miss Putnam. Please answer. I think your reply will settle this one matter—and eliminate it from any future record."

Mrs. Trimble looked at him, despairingly, and his gaze gripped her own, stripped it of resistance.

"She did smoke," the housekeeper admitted. "The doctor told her not to, but she did. They were Cuban cigarros. They soothed her, though they might have been bad for her heart. I told her so. But what was the harm, outside of that?"

"None," said Quigley soothingly. "I appreciate your attitude, Mrs. Trimble. You were protecting her but also protecting her enemies. When you entered the room, did you remove the end of the cigarro, the short, slim cigar she had smoked?"

"I did. I always did. I got rid of it in the bathroom."

"One more question. Did you ever think about the remarkable resemblance of the gardener, Rawlings, to Miss Putnam?"

"I'd noticed it. That's all."

"That's all, Mrs. Trimble. Thank you."

The lieutenant looked at his notes, consulted with Quigley, including the somewhat crestfallen Blueport official, from motives of courtesy.

"We'll try to narrow down this investigation," he said. "I want the following to remain. Mrs. Trimble, Miss Stendall, Mr. Lawson—" he whispered again to Quigley. "How about the countess?"

He flung the cards full in Quigley's face slugging Lubbock on his way to the door.

"I think we can leave her out of it," said Quigley.

"And the prisoner, Rawlings," concluded the officer. "Mr. Lubbock, we should be glad to have you with us. Have you any suggestions?"

"You might take the handcuffs off Rawlings," said Lubbock drily. "I will be responsible for him. And you might also ask Mrs. Mayall to remain."

Quigley nodded acquiescence.

"The rest of you may leave," announced the lieutenant. "But do not leave the premises, or try to," he added drily.

THEY left, most of them obviously relieved. Dr. Dodd was close to the countess, who seemed perturbed.

"Do you care to make any statement, Mr. Lubbock?" asked the state officer. "As to whether your visit here was purely a social one, or perhaps in connection with a new will for Miss Putnam?"

"It is as well to clear matters as speedily as possible in the ends of justice," said the eminent attorney. "Miss Putnam was desirous of making a new will. She felt that her lease of life was uncertain and she wished to settle her affairs up to the last moment. I understood that she favorably entertained a proposition to help finance the Dodd Foundation, which she had previously considered. I had a communication through Miss Stendall concerning that tentative codicil, to be decided after a talk with Dr. Dodd. I may say here that Miss Stendall is a beneficiary under Miss Putnam's will, despite her own declination. Miss Putnam valued her highly as a discreet and valuable aid.

"The most vital change was a bequest in favor of John Rawlings, provided he showed himself still worthy after certain tests. He is, like Mr. Lawrence Lawson, a nephew of the deceased. The whole truth is spoken on these occasions. He was the son of her sister Ruth, long dead. Not a nephew by process of law but one by blood, one by love mating. I unearthed the facts for Miss Putnam. Rawlings' father died in an accident before he could marry Ruth Putnam. She did not tell her sister of her circumstances. That was unfortunate. But the child, after the death of Ruth Putnam, was cared for by Mrs. Mayall. He wanted to be a landscape gardener. Mrs. Mayall brought him to the notice of Miss Putnam, who was struck, as I was, by his outstanding family likeness to her and the family. Miss Putnam questioned Mrs. Mayall, also a relation, and then turned the matter over to me. She had certain Victorian reservations about legitimacy but she was willing to have the lad tried out. He made good. I understood, through Miss Stendall, that she was willing to advance him the money to go into partnership with a grower on Long Island. Ten thousand dollars. If he continued to advance, he would become an ultimate heir to a large part of her estate."

"That was the ten thousand dollars you drew today, Miss Stendall?"

"Yes," said the secretary. "I was to meet John Rawlings at Blueport. He said he had a job of vine-trimming he wanted to complete, because the vine was infected and needed pruning carefully. He had studied such matters. He kept quiet about his relationship, grateful for Miss Putnam's help and, I think, unnecessarily sensitive about the question of his legitimacy. Miss Putnam was, in some ways, Victorian, but she always believed that blood and breeding told."

"He was discreet," put in Lubbock. "As you have been, Miss Stendall." Quigley silently endorsed the attorney's judgment. Rawlings, his handcuffs taken off, sat silent. He was a thorough Putnam.

"All this," broke in Lawson vehemently, "doesn't clear up these murders. Who thrust the hat-pin belonging to Mrs. Trimble in my aunt's ear? Who slit Braddock's throat, who tried to poison me, and did poison Walker?"

"How does Mr. Lawson stand, under the will, or the will-to-be, Mr. Lubbock?" asked Quigley.

"Miss Putnam approved of the Countess Romeska," said Lubbock. "She trusted that she might prove a curb upon Lawrence Lawson's flightiness by uniting him with worth while connections. If he married the countess he was to receive, at the end of a year without scandal of any sort, a million dollars. If he was definitely engaged to the countess at any time before the consummation of the marriage, during which period Miss Putnam might die, he would fall heir to half that amount. That," Lubbock ended definitely, "is all I have to say at present."

"Mrs. Mayall?" asked the lieutenant.

"It's all true," she said. "I took care of the lad. A fine boy. Ruth was afraid Elizabeth would have nothing to do with her but Elizabeth was fine. She talked the Ten Commandments but she had her own ideas. She was fine to me."

"That's all, Mrs. Mayall. You may go. You may too, Miss Stendall. Mr. Lubbock, it's your option. Rawlings, you have your liberty."

The gardner stood up. "Thank you," he said. "I'll stay around for a while—outside. I—I didn't know my aunt was such a thoroughbred."

There were five of them left. The lieutenant, Lubbock, Lawson, Mrs. Trimble and Quigley.

"How about it, Mr. Quigley?" asked the state policeman. "I think you may have something up your sleeve, or in your pockets," he added.

"I have," said Quigley, gravely. "Mrs. Trimble, you respected Miss Putnam?"

THE housekeeper looked at her inquisitor. She folded her hands to steady them. She was badly shaken, still inclined to be hostile.

"I loved her," she said. "I wouldn't have stayed here if I hadn't."

"Good!" said Quigley. "Now, Mrs. Trimble, we want to prove her attempted murder, as dastardly an act as an actual killing. But it must be proven. You haven't been too good a witness. You have given your opinions rather than facts. You have exhibited prejudice. Undoubtedly you were unnerved, on the defensive, startled at the discovery of your hat-pin. I want to clear you if you are innocent, as much as you do yourself. But I want the truth from you, the whole truth, and nothing but the truth.

"This is murder. You said things against Miss Stendall that were without foundation. I am quite sure you knew more about Rawlings than you admitted. You were vague about 'others' who were after Miss Putnam's money. You maligned Dr. Dodd, a most reputable physician with a worthy project that Miss Putnam was glad to further. You are not in too nice a situation, Mrs. Trimble. Now, what have you got against Mr. Lawson. We'll clear that up, first."

Lawson rose to his feet, indignant. "Are you going to listen to this old fool?" he asked. "She ought to be examined by a lunacy commission. She has no memory. Miss Stendall showed that. She is a meddling old mischief maker, and always was."

"You augment suspicion when you object to our examination. Sit down, please. Now, Mrs. Trimble, go ahead, and be brief."

"I will," she said as Lawson subsided. She had steadied. She was vindictive now toward the man she looked at steadily as she spoke.

"Miss Putnam stood for a lot from him," she said. "She thought he was her only close flesh and blood, until she heard of Rawlings. She was always paying gambling debts for him. Miss Stendall could tell you that, if she wasn't so confidential and close-mouthed. Then he fell in love with the countess. He was always falling in love, as he'd call it," she sneered. "There were two maids left on account of him and now there's another in trouble. I caught him with her the very night his engagement to the countess was given out. Miss Putnam thought that marriage might steady him down. But I told him he'd do the right thing by the maid, countess or no countess. Or I'd tell Miss Putnam and the countess, too. I didn't have to do that, I reckon. She had found out he wasn't the grand gentleman he posed to be. I thought he'd have choked me then and there. But he didn't."

Her voice rose shrilling. She pointed a finger at Lawson. "He murdered Miss Elizabeth, instead. He got one of my hat-pins and tried——"

Lawson was on his feet again. "I've had enough of this," he cried. "Lubbock, are you going to stand for this sort of thing?"

"I was your aunt's attorney, I am not yours," returned Lubbock.

"Then I'm damned if I am going to listen to such ridiculous charges. If they had any substantiation——"

"They have, Lawson," said Quigley. "Sit down. Mrs. Trimble, you are excused. Now, Lawson," he went on as the housekeeper left the room. "We'll start at the beginning. We were playing cards when we heard Mrs. Trimble fall on the floor overhead. I was your partner. You were a good player and perhaps you were lucky. But you are the spendthrift type. That is not deduction or theory, it is precise analysis. Therefore I suspected your good luck."

He laid on the table the deck of cards he had retrieved from the floor.

"These are cleverly cut," he said. 'Shaved', is the technical term. The average player cuts the short way of the pack. You did not. Walker laid out these cards, I find. He was an accomplice of yours in that deal. He is an ex-convict. He walks with what they call in England the 'lag's limp.' That can be checked up.

"You cut off Braddock when he tried to talk, perplexed, upset, wanting to do the thing right, not to believe that you could be guilty. And then, before he could be questioned officially, you had him killed while you tried to implicate Rawlings in the crime. You used too many red herrings, Lawson. And you were not consistent. You shut off Braddock to wait for the authorities to conduct the case, but you were lavish with your denunciation of Mrs. Trimble.

"Braddock was killed because he knew too much. Walker killed him. There was half a million dollars at stake. You could have had a million if you had married but you were involved with this maid, threatened with exposure that would ruin that marriage, leave you an outcast. Miss Putnam had another heir who had made good. The countess had lost her interest in whatever false glamor might have surrounded you. So you got Walker to kill Braddock——"

"You'll prove that," cried Lawson. "Braddock committed suicide."

"I can prove he did not. Walker cut his throat from behind. He left by the door that leads to the passage from which he was able to come in an opposite direction and, seeing the maids, use them as an alibi. Braddock was not wearing gloves, as he sometimes did. There were no prints on the knife handle. But blood spurted from that wound and Walker wiped blood off his hands as he left. With a handkerchief. He put that in his pocket as he walked through the hallway. Later he got rid of it but he forgot one thing, that the blood on it would leave traces in the lining of his pocket. It did. I have seen them. It is extremely probable that you will also find blood beneath his nails. The maid, Lucy, testified that he was cleaning them when he first started to talk to her. But there should still be a corpuscle or so."

"What has that to do with me?" demanded Lawson.

"Establishes motive," said Quigley quietly. "Braddock knew too much and then Walker, after killing him, would also know too much and want too big a split. You, therefore, poisoned Walker. Logical and true. When we get his record—"

LAWSON, his features knitted, his brows drawn, sat with his hands in his trousers' pocket. Suddenly he lunched a kick that upset the table at which the lieutenant sat, the only armed man in the room. It baffled the officer as the table landed in his lap. Lawson had snatched at the deck of cards and he flung these full in Quigley's face, slugging Lubbock on his way to the door.

Quigley shouted and the door opened. Rawlings stood there. He did not need Quigley's cry to stop the man. He believed that Lawson had tried to kill him, to fasten the murder of Miss Putnam upon him and he tackled Lawson above the knees, bringing him down.

The lieutenant's gun was out but the two figures were too closely mingled. Lawson fought furiously. Quigley went to Rawlings' help as the latter called out: "I can handle him. I've got him."

Suddenly Lawson went limp. Rawlings got slowly off him as the lieutenant now covered his man. But Quigley made a dive for the man he had shown guilty. Lawson's hand crept up, twitching toward a top vest pocket, then shot into it and came out again with a tiny phial.

There was a scent of almonds in the room, distinct, a fragrance that spoke without denial, that did not need for corraboration the fragments of glass on Lawson's lips, where he had bitten through the little container in his eagerness to take the poison.

The room was full now with crowding and horror-struck people. The state police officer ordered it cleared.

"Beat the rap," he said to Quigley. "It was all up. He lost the money and queered the marriage and you had him tied up with Walker."

"He tied himself up with that," said Quigley. "He kept some hydrocyanic for himself. It's quicker than the chair."

"Yeah," said the lieutenant. "Saves the state a lot of trouble and money, at that."

"And there's still a good story in it, lieutenant. It can't be smothered, so I'll leave you to tell it, in your own way."

The officer nodded. His face expressed appreciation. "Where you going?" he asked.

"Not far," said Quigley. "The fact is that I need a good secretary. Miss Stendall is an heiress but she's out of a job and I rather fancy she doesn't like being idle. I want to talk it over with her."

In Our Own Corner

Just to prove that the best laid plans of mice and men—yes, and editors too —gang aft—How does it go?

Anyway we were all set to use these last two pages this month to let you readers know about the extra-special thrill fare that's in store for you in the coming issues of DIME DETECTIVE MAGAZINE. Our minds were being cudgeled for the proper phrases which would convey to you an inkling of the great line-up of action-mystery-adventure yarns that are on the way. We knew we had managed to get hold of a stack of stories worth talking about and we were all ready to talk—loud and long—when Edward Parrish Ware crashed through with a letter which was so interesting and appropriate, coming as it did on the heels of The Masked Moccasin, that we had to muzzle ourselves and let him take over.

Here it is and we don't mind saying that any time anyone has anything as interesting to talk about as Mr. Ware has, we're more than willing to go over in a corner and sit listening quietly. Even when we have something as exciting to bring up as Mr. Ware's own yarn, The Skull of Judgment, which you'll find in the March issue. It's as hair-raising as— Did we say something about a corner? Pardon—forgive. Mr. Ware has the floor!

Albuquerque, New Mexico
November 28th, 1931

Dear Mr.—

I have been absent from my desk because of an infected thumb, which accounts for my tardiness in supplying the information asked for in your recent letter. Here is some dope on the Sunken Lands.

Years ago, the government found it advisable to patrol the Sunken Land region in order to protect its timber against thieves, and this forest-patrol was made up entirely of deputy marshals under the supervision of a chief deputy. The natives of the swamp dubbed the patrolmen "rangers," and as such they became commonly known. In fictionizing this group I chose to call them rangers. While there were never any definite regulations regarding uniforms, most of the patrolmen wore trousers and blouses of brown duck, laced boots, and the round-brim, peaked-crown Stetson in use by the Mounties. When I describe the uniform in a story, which I do not always do, I picture it as above.

In later years, when the government decided to do some draining in parts of the swamp and to encourage homesteaders to locate there, another menace arose to be combatted. The natives, most of them born and reared in the swamp as were their fathers and even grandfathers, stubbornly opposed all efforts to transform their trapping and hunting paradise into an agricultural country. As rapidly as homesteads were filed on and cabins built, the natives removed the cabins by means of fire. They also intimidated the homesteaders to such an extent that homesteading fell off almost to the vanishing point. Then a patrol was established by the government for the protection of the homesteaders, and this body of men was composed also of deputy marshals. As a consequence, some parts of the Sunken Lands promise to become, in time, highly productive under the plow. Not yet, it is true, but there is promise. Fictionized, this later group is my St. Francis River Patrol. Kahki jackets and britches, laced knee-boots, and black, crushed-crown Stetsons were commonly worn by them, but whether that was regulation I do not know.

While these two groups of men were sent to the swamp primarily to protect the government's direct interests, they were frequently drawn into activity in offenses of other sorts. That was because they were often the only officers of the law to be found in the wilderness, and in those instances it became their duty to take hold of any offense brought to their notice. In my yarns about the Sunken Lands I have taken certain liberties with these groups, probably bestowing upon them broader powers than they actually had from the government, but I believe I have been warranted in so doing.

As a matter of fact, nothing I have ever offered as fiction could do justice to the actual state existing in the Sunken Lands even now. If there is a wilder, more lawless region within the boundaries of the United States I have never heard of it. Perhaps the most notorious outlaw who ever made of the great swamp a rendezvous for himself and his men was John A. Murrel. It was his custom to establish places in the swamp for his numerous followers to gather, by making a certain mark on trees at points along the St. Francis River. That is how Marked Tree, frequently mentioned in my yarns, came by its rather odd name. Another famous outlaw who made his home in the swamp was a character known to criminal history as The Swamp Angel. Another was a mysterious person known as The Black Prince. The James gang made good use of the swamp sanctuary while on its well-known jaunt into Arkansas, Tennessee, Kentucky and Illinois. That is naming only a few. Countless others have hung out there, and still do. Once inside the big waste, it is a hundred-to-one shot against a crook ever being brought out. It is now, always has been, a nearly perfect hide-out for men on the dodge.

I was reared within forty miles of the heart of the Sunken Lands, and spent many years running its countless rivers, creeks and sloughs, and there are yet remote sections to which I have never penetrated. I found in the swamp, and not so very long ago, old men and women who had never seen a railway train, never worn shoes other than crude gear of their own contriving. And while it may seem incredible to many people, I have talked with natives there who had only the vaguest notions in regard to the Bible, and to whom the word religion was meaningless. Until the Arkansas legislature, many years ago, passed a "blanket" law by which it automatically married to each other all men and women openly living together as man and wife, marriage in the remoter parts of the swamp was a very simple procedure indeed. But, to the credit of the swamp folk, it was never a loose alliance. Once married according to their simple customs, always married.

As for the physical appearance of the great wilderness, I am not artist enough to paint the picture. But I have always thought that Mrs. Stratton-Porter must surely have visited the Sunken Lands before she wrote her Limberlost into literary history.

I hope that what I have written will enable you to give the readers an idea of the swamp and its people. As a matter of fact, it's hard to stop me when I get going on the Sunken Lands, and I am now getting "that way" about the Ozarks. Both are wonderful, no matter what the season may be.

With best wishes,
Sincerely,
Edward Parrish Ware.

Who else wants to learn to play....

at home without a teacher, in ½ the usual time and ⅓ the usual cost?

Over 600,000 men and women have learned to play their favorite instruments the U. S. School of Music way!

That's a record of which we're mighty proud! A record that proves, better than any words, how *thorough*, how *easy*, how *modern* this famous method is.

Just think! You can quickly learn to play any instrument—directly from the notes—and at an average cost of only a few cents a day.

You study in your own home, practice as much or as little as you please. Yet almost before you realize it you are playing real tunes and melodies — not dull scales, as with old-fashioned methods.

Like Playing a Game

The lessons come to you by mail. They consist of complete printed instructions, diagrams, and all the music you need. You simply can't go wrong. First you are *told* what to do. Then a picture *shows* you how to do it. Then you do it yourself and *hear* it. No private teacher could make it any clearer.

As the lessons continue they become easier and easier. For instead of just scales you learn to play by *actual notes* the favorites that formerly you've *only listened* to. You can't imag-

ine what fun it is, until you've started!

Truly, the U. S. School method has removed all the difficulty, boredom, and extravagance from music lessons.

Fun — Popularity

You'll never know what real fun and good times are until you've learned to play some musical instrument. For music is a joy-building tonic —a sure cure for the "blues." If you can play, you are always in demand, sought after, sure of a good time. Many invitations come to you. Amateur orchestras offer you wonderful afternoons and evenings. And you meet the kind of people you have always wanted to know.

Never before have you had such a chance as this to become a musician— a really good player on your favorite instrument—without the deadly drudging and prohibitive expense that were such drawbacks before. At last you can start right in and *get somewhere*, quickly, cheaply, thoroughly.

Here's Proof!

"I am making excellent progress on the 'cello—*and owe it all to your easy lessons*," writes George C. Lauer of Belfast, Maine.

"I am now on my 13th lesson and can already play s i m p l e pieces," says Ethel Harnishfeger, Fort Wayne, Ind. "*I knew nothing about music when I started.*"

"I have completed only 20 lessons and *can play almost any kind of music I wish*. My friends are astonished," writes Turner B. Blake, of Harrisburg, Ill.

And C. C. Mittlestadt, of Mora, Minn., says, "I have been playing in the brass band for several months now. I learned to play from

your *easy lessons.*"

You, too, can learn to master the piano, violin, 'cello, saxophone—any instrument you prefer—this quick, easy way! For every single thing you need to know is explained in detail. And the explanation is always *practical*. Little theory—plenty of *accomplishment*. That's why students of the U. S. School course get ahead *twice as fast* as those who study by old-fashioned, plodding methods.

Booklet and Demonstration Lesson — FREE!

The whole interesting story about the U. S. School course cannot be told on this page. A booklet has been printed, "Music Lessons in Your Own Home," that explains this famous method in detail, and is yours free for the asking. With it will be sent a Free Demonstration Lesson, which *proves* how delightfully quick and easy—how *thorough*—this modern method is.

If you really want to learn to play at home—without a teacher—in one-half the usual time—and at one-third the usual cost—by all means send for the Free Booklet and Free Demonstration Lesson AT ONCE. No obligation. (Instruments supplied if desired—cash or credit.) U. S. SCHOOL OF MUSIC, 862 Brunswick Bldg., New York.

Thirty-Fourth Year (Estab. 1898)